The Man Next Door

A Novel

by

Erik Walter

BOOKS BY THIS AUTHOR

LOVING JOHNNY
THE MUSIC PROFESSOR
NO REGRETS
THE MAN NEXT DOOR
JUST MY LUCK
NEVER AGAIN
THE GALLERY
THE INHERITANCE
THE STORM
A HOME FOR STEWART
LOGAN AND BUDDY'S STORY
THE REUNION
TO SLAY A DRAGON
JOURNEY BACK TO GREEN GROVE
AN EXTRAORDINARY ORDINARY MAN

FOREWORD

I'd like to say a few words to the reader before you
begin this book. This is a purely fictional story,
filled with fictional characters and locations.
However, much of the spiritual journey experienced
by a few of the characters is actually very similar to
my own real life experience. Please understand that
I believe that every person on the planet has the
right to live their own spirituality, without judgment
or criticism, and that every person has their own
unique path to follow. Whether a person chooses a
religion, or a philosophy, or no beliefs at all, the
choice belongs to the individual. No one has the
right to force their beliefs on someone else, and no
one has the right to judge someone else because
they believe differently.
As a gay man, I've lived much of what you'll read
in the following pages. I've felt the pain, guilt,
shame, and eventual joy and peace of spiritual
fulfillment that my characters experience in this
book. It took many years, and though I'm still
learning and growing, I am becoming the person
that I longed to be as a young man.
So, while my characters have different beliefs and
ideals, I don't judge any of them, because I have
been where they are at one point or another in my
own life. And wherever you are on your spiritual
path, I wish you only happiness and contentment, as
I do the characters in this book.

CHAPTER ONE

Jacob Porter arrived at his new home in Green Grove, Illinois, just thirty minutes ahead of the moving van that was bringing all of his worldly belongings from the only home he had ever known, his parent's house. He got out of his rather bland light brown seven year old Chevy Impala and fumbled with the keys the friendly realtor had handed to him along with a folder of legal paperwork a few minutes earlier at his downtown office. Indianapolis and his family seemed very far away to him at this moment. He unlocked the front door of the two bedroom bungalow on Maple Street which his parents had bought for him. It was a quaint little house with its white siding and dark green shutters. He stopped on the front porch and turned to look around apprehensively. Not surprisingly, the old brick street was lined with beautiful tall, mature maple trees, as well as a few oaks, elms, and sycamores. Most of the houses in this block were fairly small, well maintained homes similar to his, while the larger and older homes lined the street as it gently curved closer to the center of town.

Town, he thought with a mournful sigh as he gazed at the immaculate lawns, neatly trimmed hedges, and colorful flower gardens. He supposed it qualified as a town, but it hardly compared to Chicago, Indianapolis, or even Rockford. There were no museums, no theater, no shopping malls, and barely anything that qualified as a restaurant, as far as he was concerned. He might as well be living in the middle of a desert, he thought glumly.

Green Grove was a picturesque town of approximately ten thousand people in north central Illinois, about an hour and a half west of Chicago. It consisted of a busy downtown, neighborhoods filled with lovely, well cared for old homes, several farm related businesses, and a small but very active hospital.

As pleasant as the town appeared, Jacob already missed home. This was the first time he had ever been away from his family, and the twenty-six year old felt more than a little frightened to be on his own, if he was to be honest with himself. He had prolonged his schooling as long as possible, but his parents had eventually put their foot down when he had finally received his Bachelor of Music Education Degree from a small Christian college in Indianapolis. They had nicely, but very firmly insisted that he act like an adult and get a job. In other words, he thought wryly, grow up and act like a man.

So here he was, accepting a job in another state as a music director at a church in a town he had never even heard of a few months ago. If that wasn't being an adult, what was?

Jacob had grown up in a very strict religious household, attending church three times or more every week. His parents, sister, brother, and he had centered their lives around their church for as long as he could remember. He didn't mind, because it had always been a safe haven for him, a sharp contrast to the pure hell that had been high school. He had accepted the teachings of Pastor Paul as infallible, even though some of the strictly conservative ideas taught from his pulpit were particularly damning to him personally. However, even though he was being told he was going to hell, church was still preferable to the rest of the cold, cruel world, which seemed even more threatening and dangerous to him. At least it was safe there, he thought; no one was going to beat him up in church. He could, and did, pray constantly for forgiveness for his evil desires, always hopeful that surely God would forgive him for being a…a… No, he couldn't even think the word in his own mind; it was too wicked.

As he grew older, it puzzled him that he had had these desires, been this way, for as long as he could remember. He hadn't chosen it, as Pastor Paul suggested, and no older man had 'converted' him. It was just the way he was, and had always been for his entire life. So how could God punish him for something that surely wasn't his fault? Was God really that cruel? He didn't like to think so, but he couldn't think of any other explanation. He had fought it so desperately his whole life, begging for forgiveness for having such impure thoughts, living with the shame and guilt of his despicable secret, and praying that no one would ever know.

The Man Next Door

Finally, in his late teens he reached the point where he had resigned himself to a life lived alone, without love. He knew he could never marry, as the whole idea of being with a woman seemed unnatural and distasteful to him. The church had convinced him that it would be a sin for him to be with a man, so what was left? He had come to the unhappy conclusion that a life of solitude and celibacy was the only option for him. It made him sad to think about it, so he resolved to keep that part of his life as far from his thoughts as possible. This wasn't easy, because everywhere he looked there were handsome men: younger, older, blond, brunette, bald, thin, heavyset, it didn't matter. He found himself attracted to practically every man he saw. But it's only because you can't have them, he reasoned. You always want what you can't have, and the church said you can't have them if you want to go to heaven.

Still, it seemed so unfair. He could go to heaven as long as he remained miserable and alone on earth. He knew that same-sex couples were now being allowed to marry in the United States, thanks in no small part to President Obama, and he was secretly thrilled with the whole idea. But Pastor Paul and the religious community that he knew personally held some decidedly un-Christian views on the matter, as far as he was concerned. They taught that God hated gay people, and they were far wiser and more spiritual then he was, so they must be right. As a result, he knew falling in love with another man would never be possible for him, not if he wanted to please God and go to heaven.

So here he was, making his career in the church, the very vehicle of his own condemnation, but at the same time his only source of comfort. And as long as he prayed hard enough, resisted temptation, and kept his secret hidden, the church and heaven would welcome him with open arms. And as afraid of the rest of the world as he was, he felt it was worth the secret shame he carried deep inside to be accepted by such a 'loving' community.

The three moving men had his meager belongings unloaded and in the house in a matter of an hour. His household furnishings consisted of a small maple dining table and four chairs, sofa, easy chair, bed, dresser, and television, most of which were second hand. His only possession of any value was his Yamaha Clavinova, an amazing instrument that resembled a spinet piano, but which could actually imitate quite accurately a wide number of string, wind, brass, and percussion instruments. Otherwise, he had only his clothes, laptop, and numerous kitchen items and other odds and ends his mother had purchased for him to unload from his car.

He thanked the movers as they left, and then looked around him at the jumble of mismatched furniture and stacks of boxes with a sigh. Thankfully, his parents had had the foresight to turn on his utilities, including his wifi, so he didn't have to worry about those things. Might as well get unpacked, he decided. Moving the furniture took less than an hour, although he finally gave up trying to force the queen size mattress and box spring through the back bedroom door. Perhaps he could convince somebody from the church to help him with it later. As he was unpacking the boxes labeled 'kitchen', he heard a knock on the front door. Apprehensively, he walked from the kitchen and through the small dining room. He paused and peered around the wide living room doorway, where he saw what appeared to be a large dark man standing on the other side of the screened storm door.

"Yes?" he called nervously from his partially hidden position, several feet away from the front door. "Can I help you?"

"I was going to ask you that," the man said with a chuckle. "It looked like you were all alone, so I thought you might need some help moving furniture or something. I'm your next door neighbor, by the way."

Jacob hesitated a moment before finally walking over to the door and unlocking the screen with a tentative smile.

"That's very nice of you," he said, pushing the door open.

He looked at his visitor as he stepped from the shady front porch into the living room. Tall, definitely over six feet, broad shoulders, thick black hair, with a neatly trimmed five-o'clcock shadow and a perfect smile. He was wearing a plain white tee shirt and cargo shorts, with just sandals covering his feet. The whole effect was very easy and casual, and made the smiling man seem friendly and welcoming. Wow, is he handsome, Jacob thought! Tall, dark, hairy, and masculine. Just my type! He frowned as he looked down at his own drab beige slacks, brown shirt, and brown sensible shoes.

"I'm Anthony Miller," the stranger said in a friendly voice, extending his right hand.

Jacob looked at the well-muscled arm and hand reaching out to him, and couldn't help feeling a little thrill at the sight of the dark hairs covering them. He reached out nervously and gripped the strong hand tightly.

"Hi, I'm Jacob Porter," he said as a tingly shiver traveled up and down his spine at the masculine touch.

"You're not from around here, are you?" Anthony said. "I know most people in town, but you don't look familiar."

"No, I'm new here," Jacob admitted. "I'm from Indianapolis."

"Indy, huh?" Anthony said, nodding thoughtfully. "What the hell brings you to a little town like Green Grove?"

"I'm the new music director at Grace Community Church, which I believe is somewhere on the north edge of town."

"Really?" Anthony blinked. "A church?"

"Yes," Jacob frowned a little defensively. "What's wrong with that?"

"Nothing, nothing," Anthony said hastily. "I'm just surprised that someone like you would be working in a church."

Jacob frowned at him.

"Someone like me? What does that mean?"

"Oh, nothing," Anthony said appeasingly. "I didn't mean anything by it. Just forget it. And sorry for saying hell."

He quickly changed the subject.

"So, is there anything I can do to help?" he asked, rubbing his hands together and looking around the room.

"Well," Jacob said, looking around as well. "I do need some help getting the mattress into the back bedroom, if you wouldn't mind giving me a hand."

"Bedrooms are where I do my best work," Anthony grinned mischievously.

Jacob smiled uncertainly and turned to the queen size mattress and box spring, leaning against the dining room wall. Anthony followed his gaze, and with what appeared to be very little effort, he picked up the mattress by the handles on the top edge and carried it into the adjoining room, where he leaned it against a wall next to the dresser. Jacob watched with awe as Anthony returned and picked up the box spring and toted it easily into the next room. He followed him into the bedroom and helped him set it on the bed frame, which he had already assembled. The mattress came next, and in a matter of minutes, his bed was set up and ready to sleep in.

"How did you carry that by yourself?" Jacob asked with an admiring smile.

"Muscles," Anthony chuckled lightly. He flexed his left arm, revealing more of his upper arm with its barbed wire tattoo running the circumference of his bicep.

Jacob's jaw dropped as he tried to discreetly admire his masculine beauty.

"I'll say!" he exclaimed, trying not to stare.

Anthony winked at him, and then looked around as they walked back to the dining room.

"What's this?" he asked curiously, pointing to the Clavinova.

"It's called a Clavinova," Jacob said with a hint of pride in his voice. "It's like a piano, but it can sound like just about any instrument."

"Really?" Anthony asked, intrigued. "Show me."

Jacob lifted the fallboard and pressed the power button. Within a few seconds, the instrument powered up and indicated it was ready to be played. He played a few bars of a Chopin Prelude that he was particularly fond of.

"Now, would you like to hear a pipe organ?" he asked with a grin.

After pushing a few buttons, Jacob pressed the keys and the rich, dramatic tones of a huge pipe organ filled the room.

"Oh, my god!" Anthony laughed with delight. "That's amazing. Do something else."

Jacob proceeded to show him how the instrument could sound like a harpsichord, violin, trumpet, and even a choir.

"Wow, you are really talented, Jacob," he said, placing a friendly hand on his shoulder.

Jacob trembled at the touch of this handsome man's hand. He stood up quickly and stumbled across the room awkwardly.

"I do okay, I guess," he said shyly.

"More than okay from what I just heard. So, what else can I do?" he asked.

"I just need to unpack my clothes and carry all the boxes down to the basement, I guess," Jacob said, looking around. "As you can tell, I don't have a lot of stuff."

"First time on your own, huh?" Anthony asked shrewdly.

"Yeah, I guess it's pretty obvious," Jacob acknowledged sheepishly.

"A little," Anthony nodded in a matter of fact way. "How old are you?"

"I'm twenty-six," Jacob said, a little reluctantly. "Guess I'm a late bloomer."

"Nothing wrong with that. I remember what it was like when I was your age."

"How old are you?" Jacob asked him. "You can't be much older than me."

"I'm thirty-four, but thanks for that," Anthony grinned at him. "Well, I guess I'll be going. But hey, if you need anything, I'm right next door. Come over anytime."

He said good-bye and headed out the front door.
Jacob followed him out the door and watched him
walk down the front steps and across the lawn to the
charming Cape Cod style house next door. Wow, he
thought, I'm going to have to avoid him if I don't
want to have a lot of impure thoughts. He is
incredibly beautiful!
Anthony stopped and turned to look back at Jacob,
who was still standing on the front porch staring at
him. Jacob blushed and dropped his eyes when he
realized he'd been caught.
"If you don't have any plans for supper tonight,
come over and we'll get a pizza or something,"
Anthony suggested. "Ciminello's has the best pizza
around."
"That'd be great," Jacob said immediately.
"Thanks!"

CHAPTER TWO

Oh my goodness, he thought as he went back inside, what did I just do? I just told myself I needed to avoid this gorgeous guy, and not two seconds later I'm accepting a dinner invitation from him. I'm an idiot! I'm supposed to be resisting temptation, not going over to its house at the first opportunity to eat pizza with it. Oh, well, surely I can control myself and my mind for one evening, for heaven's sake. I'll just have to pray really hard and concentrate on something else when I'm around him!

Anthony walked back down the wide paved driveway and in through his back door. He grinned as he thought about the young man next door. He was such a nice looking guy, with that tall, slim, athletic build, great smile, short brown hair, and those rimless glasses. But where the hell did he get those god-awful clothes? He looked like the bookish type, so Anthony wasn't surprised to find that he was a musician. He was flabbergasted, however, to learn that Jacob had taken a job at Grace church. What was a gay guy doing in a church, particularly that church? He had to be aware of the church's stand on gay people, didn't he? How can anyone be that naïve, he wondered? He shook his head. He didn't understand it at all. It would be interesting, though, to see what makes this guy tick. Maybe I'll have to get to know this unusual man a little better.

Jacob called Calvin Hanson, the pastor of Grace church, to let him know that he had arrived in Green Grove. Pastor Hanson welcomed him warmly to his town, and told him he was looking forward to meeting him. Pastor Paul and Pastor Hanson had been good friends since their college/seminary days, and it was for that reason alone that Jacob had been hired with just a quick phone interview. They agreed to meet the following morning at the church, and Jacob ended the call. He finished putting his clothes away, and then stepped out of his back door from the kitchen onto the small porch and surveyed his fenced backyard. He would need to buy a lawnmower, he thought. The lawn was small, but neat, with his two-car garage on the left side at the end of the driveway that ran alongside the house. Apparently he and Anthony shared the wide drive, he noted with surprise. Anthony's garage, nearly identical to his own, sat next to his. He looked over at the open garage door and saw Anthony sitting on a short stool next to a large motorcycle in the doorway.

"Hey," he called.

Anthony looked up at him and gave him a friendly smile. He beckoned to Jacob to come over, and then returned to the task at hand. Jacob walked through the chain-link gate and stood shyly beside him.

"Working on your motorcycle, huh?" he said awkwardly.

"One of them," Anthony replied. "Do you ride?"

"Oh, good heavens, no," Jacob answered with a distasteful look on his face. "Are you kidding?"

"You sound like you disapprove," Anthony said as he looked up at him with a frown. "What's wrong with riding a motorcycle?"

"Nothing," Jacob said hastily. "I'm sorry, that didn't come out right at all. I think motorcycles are...great, I've just never ridden on one. I'd be too afraid to try. I've never met anyone who rides motorcycles before."

Anthony relaxed and grinned at him.

"Seriously? Well, you want to go for a ride?" he asked, standing up and brushing himself off with his hands. "Come on, I'll take you."

Jacob looked at him with a deeply concerned expression on his face.

"No, no, no," he said quickly in a panicky voice. "I...I...I don't think I should."

"Why the hell not?" Anthony said. "Come on, I've got an extra helmet. Just let me put this back together, and we'll go."

He sat back down.

"Hand me that wrench, will you, Jake?"

Jacob looked down to where Anthony was pointing and handed him the requested item.

"Actually, it's Jacob," he said seriously. "Not Jake. Please call me Jacob."

"Oh, okay," Anthony said easily. "Jacob it is."

In a few moments, Anthony had everything replaced on the motorcycle. He quickly put his tools

17

away in the spotless and neatly organized garage. Jacob noticed a second reddish colored motorcycle sitting in the shadows at the back of the building next to the front of an enormous new royal blue Chevy 4x4 pickup. Anthony handed him a black helmet from a nearby shelf. He watched the younger man struggle with first his glasses, and then the chinstrap for a few seconds. Finally, suppressing a grin, he reached over and quickly adjusted it so that it was snug. Jacob studied the handsome face just inches from his own, and he tried desperately to keep the blood from rushing to his groin. Piercing blue eyes with long lashes, black stubble on his chin and cheeks. So rugged and masculine. He forced himself to look down as Anthony continued to work with the chinstrap. Anthony couldn't completely keep the grin from his face as he watched Jacob try to avoid looking at him. He actually considered ripping the helmet off and kissing the handsome young man, but he restrained himself. He chuckled at the thought of how Jacob would react to a kiss; he seemed like such a nervous young thing, he'd probably pass out or something. He deftly donned his own helmet and climbed aboard the huge black and chrome Harley Davidson Electra Glide. With the push of a button, the sleek, shiny machine came to life. Anthony held out a hand and looked at Jacob expectantly. With much trepidation, Jacob shakily accepted his hand and climbed aboard behind him. Quickly, the older man explained how to lean into the turns with him when the motorcycle tilted to the side. He gave him a few more tips as well before pushing the kickstand up with his foot.

"Now, put your arms around my waist," he added. "And for god's sake, try to relax and enjoy it."

Jacob swallowed nervously and nodded rapidly. With a chuckle, Anthony kicked the bike into gear and slowly released the clutch. The motorcycle glided smoothly forward and Anthony raised his feet onto the footrests as he pulled out onto the old brick paved street. He drove a few blocks to Perry Avenue, and then headed south for four blocks, past a newer subdivision of upscale ranch houses, toward the highway that bisected the town. He twisted his neck to look back at Jacob when they stopped at the intersection.

"Are you okay?" he asked in a loud voice over the noise of the engine.

"I think so," Jacob called back. "Just a little nervous."

"Hang on to me tight," Anthony told him. "You'll be fine, Jacob."

He revved the engine and released the clutch as Jacob tightened his grip around his waist. Once again, the streamlined machine glided forward effortlessly, and it leaned sharply to the left as Anthony pulled out onto the highway and guided them out of town. Once they had left the city limits, he shifted gears until the bike was rolling smoothly along at fifty miles per hour down the two-lane road.

Jacob held onto Anthony tightly and leaned against him slightly. He had to admit that it felt extremely exciting just to be this close to an attractive man. He hadn't had many opportunities to touch another man in his lifetime. After a few minutes on the highway, he allowed himself to relax just a bit and he looked around at the green and gold countryside drifting by. Oh, my god, he thought – oops, I took the Lord's name in vain! What I meant was oh, my goodness, this is incredible! He released his hold on Anthony for a moment, enjoying a feeling of freedom and recklessness that he had never before experienced. He felt exhilarated as he looked up at the clear blue June sky above them.

"Wahoo!" he yelled to the corn and bean fields as he dared to raise his hands high above his head. "Wahoo!"

The motorcycle skimmed over a bump and Jacob quickly wrapped his arms tightly around Anthony's middle once more. The roar of the engine as well as the wind that whistled around them drowned out Anthony's boisterous laugh. A few miles from town, Anthony slowed the bike and leaned to the right as he guided them to a stop in the enormous parking lot of his uncle's fertilizer plant. He waved at his cousin Mike who was working on an anhydrous ammonia tank with another man. Mike waved back cheerfully and continued his work. With a loud revving of the engine, Anthony carefully guided the big motorcycle back on to the highway heading toward town. He rapidly shifted gears with his foot until he had the bike up to speed once more. He slowed as they approached the city limits, but instead of turning on Perry, he stayed on the highway through town, past the hospital and the high school on their left until he reached Market Street, which led all the way through the downtown. After they crossed Main Street, Anthony drove on north to the edge of town where a large modern church building stood behind a broad paved parking lot on their right. He slowed and turned into the drive, pulling to a stop in front of the main entrance. "So this is where you're going to be working now?" Anthony said over his shoulder.

"Yeah, I guess so," Jacob said hesitantly as he looked around at the rather intimidating building.

"Hmm," Anthony shook his head in a perplexed manner. He murmured under his breath, "I hope it works out for you."

In a louder voice, he asked, "Do you want to ride some more, or would you rather head home?"

"I'd love to ride some more, but I guess we should go home. I'm getting hungry."

When they arrived back home, Jacob followed Anthony through his back door into the kitchen. While Jacob's kitchen was fairly modern, with nice oak cabinets and new black appliances, Anthony's kitchen took his breath away. Someone had spent no expense creating this state of the art culinary space. There were top of the line stainless steel appliances, granite countertops, and hickory cabinets, all very sleek and elegant. A bay window with a padded bench seat extended out toward the back yard and deck, with a round hickory wood table centered in it. Jacob looked around appreciatively.

"Wow, this is really nice!" he exclaimed. "Did you do this?"

Anthony smiled and looked around the room with a satisfied expression.

"Yes, I did," he said. "I'm proud of it."

"You should be," Jacob said with an awed voice. The rest of the house proved to be just as sleek and modern as the kitchen. Muted wall colors, gleaming hardwood floors, and recessed lighting were the norm throughout the home, with tasteful contemporary furnishings filling each room. The downstairs consisted of the kitchen, laundry room, dining room, living room and master suite. There were two more bedrooms and a bath upstairs, all filled with warm, inviting furniture.

"Who did your decorating for you?" Jacob asked curiously as he looked around admiringly. "This is really beautiful!"

"I did all of it myself," Anthony admitted modestly.

"Wow! I could never do this," Jacob said, shaking his head somewhat wistfully. "I wouldn't have a clue how to make a place look like this."

"Well, first you need a little more furniture than what you have," Anthony chuckled. "What style of furniture do you like?"

"I don't know," Jacob said thoughtfully. "I never thought about it before. I always thought furniture was furniture. But I love this. Your house is beautiful."

He admired the rest of the house as Anthony continued the tour.

"Do you have a basement?" Jacob asked him.

"Yes, but most of it is just my gym, and the rest…I don't think you're quite ready to see yet," Anthony said dryly.

Jacob looked at him curiously, but Anthony didn't elaborate, so he dropped the subject.

"How about we order that pizza?"

The two men chatted amiably over their food at the kitchen table. Anthony drank a Coors, while Jacob settled for a soft drink.

"You don't drink, huh?" Anthony said, setting a bottle of soda in front of him.

"No, there was never any alcohol in our house when I was growing up. I was taught it was a sin to drink."

"Well, before you condemn something you've never tried, I want you to drink a beer, at least," Anthony said with a grin, holding out his beer bottle to him. "Come on, at least taste it."

"No…er, no thanks," Jacob said hastily. "I couldn't."

"You couldn't imagine yourself on a motorcycle, either, and yet there you were today, flying down the highway on a Harley," Anthony reminded him.

"Who knows? Maybe you'll like beer, too. Nothing goes better with pizza than an ice-cold beer. Maybe you'll find it's not such a sin."

Jacob looked at him doubtfully for several seconds. Finally, with a frown, he hesitantly reached out and took the bottle from him. He raised it to his lips and, taking a deep breath, took a drink from the bottle. He frowned and looked at the bottle.

"That's not bad," he said in a surprised tone as he held the bottle out to give back to Anthony.

"You keep it," Anthony said with a grin. "I'll get another one."

They continued to eat, drink, and laugh together throughout the evening. They moved into the living room and sat down on the comfortable sofa. Jacob visibly relaxed as the alcohol took effect. Anthony asked him about his past, and he shyly told him what little there was to tell.

"I have a brother and a sister. We grew up in the church, and I have a degree in music," he summed up. "That's my life in a nutshell. Not very interesting, huh?"

"I think it is," Anthony told him solicitously.

"So what do you do, Anthony?" Jacob asked him curiously.

"I'm a nurse," Anthony told him. "And I'm a personal trainer."

Jacob burst out laughing.

"No, really," he said. "What do you do?"

"I'm a nurse and a personal trainer," Anthony said with a frown. "What's so funny about that?"

Jacob sobered immediately.

"Oh, I'm sorry!" he exclaimed. "It's just that you don't look like a nurse."

He hastened to explain.

"I mean, you're so big and strong and masculine. I can understand the personal trainer. But you're more the biker type, not the caregiver type. I mean…."

His voice trailed off helplessly.

"So, because I'm a big strong biker type, I can't be a nurse, too," Anthony said with annoyance. "Is that it?"

"I'm sorry, Anthony," Jacob said earnestly. "I really didn't mean anything by it. You just took me by surprise, is all. I've never met a male nurse before. Or a biker, for that matter."

"Let me guess," Anthony said dryly. "The only people you know are church people. They all work in offices and drive Buick's. Am I right?"

Jacob nodded as he took a large gulp of his beer. "Pretty much."

"Have you ever thought about expanding your circle of friends?" Anthony asked.

"I was raised in the church, Anthony, so why wouldn't I know mostly church people?"

"I'm not saying there's anything wrong with 'church people', Jacob. I just think it's healthier to know all kinds of people, not only the people who are just like you."

"It was the other kinds of people who beat me up and picked on me when I was growing up. That's why I stick close to the church," Jacob told him. "At least no one beats me up there."

"No, they just tell you that you're going to hell there!" Anthony exclaimed sarcastically.

"They're just teaching what the Bible says," Jacob said defensively.

Anthony shook his head.

"And you believe everything the Bible says?"

"Of course I do!" Jacob exclaimed. He looked at Anthony as if he was crazy. "Don't you?"

"No, I don't," Anthony said simply.

"But you go to church," Jacob said with a confused expression on his face.

"No, I don't," Anthony repeated with surprise. "What made you think I'm a church goer?"

"I just..." Jacob sputtered. He thought for a moment. "But you believe in God?"

"I believe there is order to the universe, that things happen for a reason, and that there is a force behind all of it. You can call it God, or the Great Spirit, or Divine Energy, or whatever works for you. But the god of the Bible? No way!"

Jacob stood up and looked down at him incredulously.

"I can't believe this!" he exclaimed. "Don't you know you're going to go to hell for not believing in God and Jesus?"

"I don't believe in hell," Anthony told him calmly.

"How can you say that?" Jacob said loudly, clearly outraged. "It's in the Bible!"

"And I don't believe in the Bible, either," Anthony said with a slight grin. He was starting to become amused at the other man's indignation.

Jacob's face turned red as he stared at the older man.

"Look, Jacob," Anthony said. "I don't believe in religion. Any religion. To me, they're all man made creations used to manipulate people into feeling guilty and ashamed, and I want no part of that."

"So you think I'm wrong, that I'm stupid for believing in the Bible?" Jacob said coldly.

"No, Jacob, not at all," Anthony said in a conciliatory tone. "I believe everyone has the right to believe whatever they want, as long as they don't push it off on everyone else. You should absolutely believe whatever works for you, but you don't get to judge me because I don't believe the same way. It's as simple as that."

Jacob shook his head vehemently.

"But you have to believe the Bible, or you won't go to heaven. There are no two ways about it!"

"Jacob, did you know that there are more than four thousand religions in the world?" Anthony asked him.

"No," Jacob frowned uncertainly.

"It's true," Anthony said. "So why do you believe that Christianity is right and all the others are wrong?"

"Because…because…that's what I was taught," Jacob said. "You have to accept it on faith. And you have to believe it or you won't go to heaven."

"According to your church, neither you or I are going to heaven anyway."

"Well, I know I am!" Jacob said emphatically.

"Really? I thought gay people didn't go to heaven. That's what your church teaches, isn't it?"

Jacob gaped at him in outrage.

"What did you say?"

Anthony smiled at him and shook his head silently.

Jacob stood up and gave him an angry glare.

"I am not…gay! Are you crazy?"

"Okay, you're not gay," Anthony said, continuing to smile at him. "Whatever you say. My mistake."

"It is a mistake! I'm…I'm straight!"

"Fine," Anthony said soothingly. "You're straight."

"Well, I am!" Jacob insisted.

"I believe you," Anthony said.

Jacob stared at him uncomfortably for a few seconds.

"I've got to go home," Jacob said abruptly. "Thanks for the pizza and the motorcycle ride."

"Jacob, chill out," Anthony chuckled. "Come on, sit down."

"No way am I going to sit here and be accused of being a homo…homosexual!" Jacob yelled at him. He stormed out the back door and ran across the driveway, through his back gate, and into the house, slamming the door behind him.

CHAPTER THREE

Anthony watched him hurry out of the house. He smiled to himself and shook his head. Wow, this guy is so deep in the closet, I wonder if he'll ever find his way out. He thought back to his own upbringing. He had grown up in a religious household, too. But in spite of being devout Christians, his parents were very open minded people, and they had taught him to never judge anyone based on their religion, skin color, sexual orientation, and so on. No one is any better than anyone else, his father used to tell him. That ideal had stuck with him all of his life. He smiled as he thought about his parents. Good, loving, down-to-earth people who never judged or spoke badly about anyone that he could ever remember. They would always be the standard for him as far as 'Christian' behavior went, and they were the main reason he had remained in Green Grove. By the time he was in his twenties, they were fairly advanced in years. He had looked after them as their health failed, paid their bills, mowed their lawn, and taken them to doctor appointments whenever he could. His brother, Thomas, who was twelve years older than him, had married and moved to Chicago after college, but he helped out whenever he could get away from his job. After his parents had passed away, Anthony had already settled into his small town life and was content to remain where he was. He reasoned confidently that the Universe would tell him if he needed to be somewhere else, so until something changed, he would live his life happily where he was.

One of the best memories he held dear was the time he had come out to his folks. He had struggled with being gay through his teen years because it conflicted drastically with what he was taught at church. Finally, his inner turmoil surfaced at the age of sixteen one night at the supper table. His mother had asked him what was wrong, and he had unleashed all of his anger, frustration, and self-doubt on his folks. After ranting for fifteen minutes, his father had placed his hand gently on his shoulder.

"Son, listen to me for a minute. I believe that God doesn't care who you love, or who you sleep with. He only cares about the kind of man you are. If you're honest and kind and good, that's all you have to worry about. So forget about what anyone tells you, because none of that even matters anymore. That nonsense in Leviticus was written for that specific culture, and it was written by narrow-minded men who wanted to impose their own ideals on everyone else. All you need to know is that God loves you and wants the best for you. Just like your mother and I do."

His mother nodded her agreement as she smiled at him tearfully.

"You are a wonderful boy, Anthony, and we love you very much. All we want is for you to be happy,

and the only way to be happy is to be honest with yourself. Just be who you are, sweetheart."
From that day on, Anthony learned to like the person he was becoming. He stopped listening to the angry, unloving voices around him and focused on only the positive influences in his life.

Jacob ran angrily into his own kitchen, wiping tears from his eyes. How could Anthony possibly know? What had given him away? He felt naked and exposed for the first time in his life, and the sensation was frightening! The idea of another person knowing his deepest, darkest secret seemed almost unbearable to him. The only thing to do was to avoid Anthony in the future at all costs. The man was a bad influence anyway, with his lack of faith, his motorcycles, and alcohol, not to mention the fact that he was apparently gay. He was definitely not the kind of person his parents and church would approve of at all.
Wouldn't you just know it, he thought, my first time living on my own and I'm living right next door to a gay guy who just happens to be the most gorgeous man I've ever seen! Thanks a lot, God! Talk about a cruel joke! Well, he decided finally, it must be a test, to see if he could resist temptation. From what he had learned in church, this was just the kind of thing God would do to determine his worthiness. Well, he would have nothing more to do with Anthony. As long as he didn't see him again, there would be no problem with temptation. He thought

about his motorcycle ride earlier, and the feeling of
his arms around the big handsome man.
Immediately he felt a tightening in his shorts, and
he desperately tried to think of something, anything,
else.
My first night in my own home, he thought with
trepidation. Here he was in a new house, a new
town, even a new state. It was all a little
overwhelming and, to be honest, a bit terrifying.
He'd never been more than a few hours from home,
and never away from his family. He thought back to
the time his parents had taken him and his siblings
to Chicago to see Phantom of the Opera at the
Cadillac Theater when he was a teenager. How he
had thrilled to the beautiful music, he remembered
with a smile. His expression grew grim as he also
remembered his parents' unkind remarks about an
obviously gay couple sitting in front of them, not
caring if the young men heard them or not. It had
seemed to him that his parents had regarded them as
nothing more than dumb animals whose feelings
were unimportant. He had cringed at the cruel
words they had spoken; it was as if those words
were said to him as well. And so they might have
been, if his parents knew that he was just like those
two nice young men, whose only crime was
wanting to enjoy a pleasurable evening out on the
town. He thought of his brother and sister, laughing
and agreeing with their parents' harsh words. A few
tears formed in the corners of his eyes as so many
memories flooded his mind. So many good times

with his family and the people from church; he had been shown friendliness and kindness from these good people. But what would his memories be like tonight if they had known he was gay? He was sure he would be remembering things very differently. That thought, and the picture of the handsome Anthony in his mind, suddenly made him feel very alone and sad as he settled into his bed and switched off the bedside lamp. But at least those were the feelings he was accustomed to, he thought with a sigh.

He awoke the next morning feeling exhausted from his restless night. Thoughts of Anthony, as well as worries about his new job filled his mind as he tried in vain to sleep. He had been here less than twenty-four hours and already someone had figured out he was gay. He turned pale as a new thought suddenly occurred to him. What if Anthony told someone about him? The whole town would know and he would lose his job, which would mean his family and the whole church back home would know, and he would be forced to return to Indianapolis in shame. The thought sent a feeling of sheer terror through his whole body until he was actually trembling.

After a while he calmed himself down, sighed, and decided to get up. He quickly showered and dressed, putting on the dark brown suit he had bought at a big-box store back home. It fit him fairly well, he thought as he studied his appearance in the full-length mirror on the bathroom door with a critical eye. Just an average guy, nothing special, he thought grimly. He looked like a nerd. He probably didn't need to worry about some guy falling in love with him because no guy in his right mind would want him anyway. He was so ordinary, so….blah. Brown hair, brown eyes, brown clothes. There was nothing interesting to see when he looked at his reflection.

He looked at his watch nervously. He was supposed to be at the church at eight o'clock, so he'd better get going. With a sigh, he climbed into his brown (of course), ordinary car and drove up Market Street to the church.

Pastor Calvin Hanson greeted him warmly as he walked through the front door of the vast building. He was a large, heavyset man with carefully groomed hair and a loud voice. He gave him a thorough tour, ending with Jacob's office, a small dark paneled room next to the large sanctuary. The pastor gave him a brief overview of his responsibilities as the new music director and introduced him to the church secretary, a plain, bespectacled young woman named Lisa. He also told him that a dinner was to be held in his honor that evening in the church annex. He would be able to meet the church board and members of the choir and worship teams.

He spent the afternoon looking over some of the choir music and the instruments used during worship services. With his music education degree, he was familiar with a wide variety of musical instruments, and the music he had found was much the same as his church back in Indianapolis. He sighed with relief as he leaned back in his desk chair. This would be very similar to what he was used to back home. He walked into the sanctuary and examined the instruments on the wide, low platform at the front of the large auditorium.

He sat down at the beautiful, shiny black grand piano and played a basic Bach Invention that he had memorized years ago, followed by some simple choruses that were popular back in Indy.

"Sounds good to me," a voice called from the back of the room.

Jacob jumped and looked around until he spotted an older couple smiling at him as they approached the stage.

"Thanks," Jacob said diffidently.

"We're Carl and Edna Johnson," the man said, reaching out to shake Jacob's hand eagerly.

He was a big man with white hair and a ruddy complexion. Edna was also tall with grayish-white hair, stylishly arranged, and she wore elegantly tasteful clothes and jewelry. Carl's clothes seemed particularly fashionable as well, Jacob noted vaguely.

"I'm Jacob," he said as he shook Carl's hand. "It's nice to meet you. Are you members of the church?"

"You're the new music director, aren't you?" Edna said extending her own hand toward him.

Jacob nodded as she continued.

"Yes, Carl here is an elder, and I teach Sunday School."

"We're also in the choir," Carl told him enthusiastically. "We're so glad you're here. Pastor Cal has said such good things about you, Jake."

"Has he?" Jacob said with a slight frown. "That's nice of him. And it's Jacob, not Jake."

"You play beautifully," Edna complimented him with a warm smile.

"Thank you very much," he said glibly.

"We'll be at the dinner tonight, so we can introduce you to everyone," Carl said with a sly wink. "We'll give you all the dirt on everyone."

He laughed heartily at his little joke.

"Now, Carl," his wife admonished, nudging him with her elbow. "Gossip is a sin. Of course, it isn't gossip if it's true, right?"

Now the two of them were laughing together. In spite of himself, Jacob couldn't help but laugh with them. There was something about these two, he thought, something that he liked immediately.

"I'll look forward to it," he said warmly.

"Good," Edna said as she looked him up and down. "Now, honey, tell me who picks out your clothes, 'cause we are going to have to have a serious talk. I mean, brown? Puleez!"

Jacob looked down at himself with a frown. His face turned red.

"I guess I don't have much fashion sense, I'm afraid," he said apologetically. "I've just started to notice that most of my clothes are brown."

"Well, we will have to fix you up with our son, Peter," Carl said eagerly. "Well, I don't mean 'fix you up' with him, of course. He works downtown at Larson's, the men's store. He can work wonders. That's why Edna and I look so good."

He put an arm around his wife, and the two of them struck a pose for a moment, before they burst out laughing again. Jacob couldn't resist laughing with them.

"You go see him right away," Edna told him. "And I do mean right away. There isn't a moment to lose, am I right? Sweetie, I mean, that suit is hideous!"

"I suppose it is," Jacob agreed.

"In fact, let me call him right now and we'll go with you," she said excitedly. "Oh, this will be such fun!"

She dug through her bag for her phone, and then turned away as she held it to her ear, ignoring Jacob's protestations.

"I really can't afford new clothes right now," he insisted. "You know, with the move and the new job and all…."

He stopped talking as he realized neither of them was listening to him.

"Fine, we'll be there in a minute, dear," she said into the phone before placing it back into her purse.

The next thing Jacob knew, he was being whisked away in a big white BMW 7-Series sedan the few blocks to the downtown. Peter was an attractive blond man of about thirty or so. He hugged his parents in a warm greeting and then paused to look Jacob up and down, tapping a finger to his lips repeatedly in a thoughtful manner as he walked around him.

"Well, thank god you got here when you did!" he exclaimed jokingly. "Sweetheart, where did you get that dreadful suit? No, please don't tell me; I don't even want to know that such stores exist."

He walked over to a wall lined with men's suits and began picking a few tasteful ones, along with some dress shirts, belts, shoes, slacks, jeans, socks, and even some smart underwear.

"Come along, darling, there's not a moment to lose. I can't wait to get you out of those clothes."

He winked at the three of them, and his parents laughed gaily at his little joke. Jacob tried not to laugh, but finally couldn't resist their contagious good humor.

After a few hours, the four of them had picked out a couple of elegant suits with all the accessories, a few sports coats, several dress shirts, stylish shoes, belts, and ties, plus a number of casual slacks, jeans, and shirts. Jacob protested, knowing full well he couldn't afford a whole new wardrobe, but the Johnson's steadfastly ignored him.

Peter stepped into the dressing room with him as he tried on yet another pair of slacks.

"Oh, girlfriend, that underwear has got to go. Have you been wearing those for the last twenty years or what? Because they look terribly sad. You'll never get laid wearing those. Take them off and put these on."

He handed Jacob a pair of form fitting white boxers.

"Um, do you mind?" Jacob said hesitantly.

"You're modest?" Peter chuckled. "Oh, honey, that is so cute! I could just eat you up!"

He stepped out of the dressing room while Jacob finished changing.

"He is too adorable!" Peter said to his parents.

"Isn't he, though?" Edna agreed. "If you were still single, I'd have fixed you two up immediately."

"Hush, you two!" Carl said. "You don't know for a fact that he's gay. He hasn't come right and told us, anyway."

"Oh, please, Dad," Peter said with a laugh. "He's just about as straight as I am!"

The three of them laughed together.

Jacob stood in the dressing room with a horrified expression on his face as he listened to this exchange. Did everyone in Green Grove know he was gay, for heaven's sake? Was he wearing a sign on his back that said "GAY" on it? He would lose his new job before he even got a chance to start it if word got out. Hesitantly, he pushed the curtain aside and stepped out in front of the three way mirrors.

"Oh, yes," Edna exclaimed, placing her hand on her chest. "Just look at how handsome you are!"

"Very nice," her husband agreed.

"Perfect!" Peter added.

"Peter, could I talk to you for a minute?" he asked tremulously.

"Sure, Jacob," Peter said, gesturing to the dressing room that Jacob had just vacated.

Once they had pulled the curtain once more, Jacob looked at Peter earnestly.

"Your parents know I'm gay?" he whispered anxiously.

"It wasn't too hard to figure out, sweetie," Peter said dryly, carefully adjusting Jacob's collar.

"Is it really that obvious?"

"It is to us," Peter told him honestly. "I suppose most people probably wouldn't know, but Mom and Dad are used to gay people so they could tell right away. And any gay person could tell, of course. You are a little obvious, you know."

"I'm obvious?" Jacob whispered loudly. "Oh, my god! I'll lose my job!"

"Come here," Peter said, taking him by the hand and pulling him out of the dressing room. "Mom, Dad, Jacob's gay."

Carl and Edna looked at the two of them, obviously confused.

"Yes, dear, we know that," Edna replied, as if she were talking to a small child. "I think we've already established that fact."

The Man Next Door

"He's afraid that everyone will know and he'll lose his job," Peter told them.

"Oh, son," Carl rushed to reassure Jacob. "You don't need to worry about that. This will be just between us. No one else needs to know, and we certainly aren't going to tell anyone."

"Jacob," Edna said. "Not everyone in the church is homophobic, dear. Some of us are actually enlightened. Of course, Carl and I have Peter to thank for that. He sat us down when he came out, and said 'Mom, Dad, I'm gay and it's fine, so get over it already. Forget what the church tells you, because it's not true.'"

She looked at her son adoringly.

"And he was right, of course," she added. "We educated ourselves right away, and we understand all about being born that way, and so on."

"You'll have to meet his husband, Neil," Carl added. "He's a terrific guy. An attorney. Maybe they can find a nice guy for you, too."

Jacob stared at the three of them in amazement. He was unsure how to react to the enormity of the fact that suddenly other people knew he was gay, and didn't care. That was something he had never before experienced in his entire life. Based on his church and family life, he had long ago accepted as fact that all Christians hated gay people, and would just as soon eradicate them all from the face of the earth, with violence, if necessary. That was why he had so desperately hidden who he really was his entire life. True, he had lived an extremely sheltered

41

life, carefully guided by his parents and his church, so perhaps his perceptions were a little skewed. But to have these people standing here in front of him, openly accepting who he was without judgment was a brand new, nearly unbelievable experience for him.

"Jacob, if you want my opinion, keep your sexuality to yourself if you want to work at Grace," Peter advised. "But don't forget to have a life, too. And promise me you will never, ever deny who you really are."

Carl and Edna nodded in agreement.

"There are a lot of ignorant people in this world, both in the church and out," Carl told him, clapping a fatherly hand on Jacob's shoulder. "That may never change, but you've always got us on your side."

After insisting again that he couldn't afford all of the new clothes they had picked out for him, Peter totaled everything up and handed the bill to his dad, who pulled out a wad of large bills from his pocket.

"Please, Carl, you can't do this!" Jacob exclaimed for the tenth time. "I can't let you pay for all of this!"

"Now, hush! You can, and you will," Edna scolded him. "We can't have our music director looking shabby. I won't stand for it! Besides, it's only money."

"We want to do this for you, Jacob," Carl added. "It's our welcome present to you."

"But you don't even know me yet," Jacob protested.
"Of course we do," Edna said, waving his words
away with her manicured, bejeweled hand.
"You might as well give it up, Jacob," Peter smiled
at him. "Once Carl and Edna have made up their
minds, you can't win. Just be glad they're on your
side."
He turned to his parents with a frown.
"But for the love of god, will you please stop
spending my inheritance!" he told them in a stern
voice. "I've got big plans for your money!"
His dad slapped him on the back as they all laughed
together. Peter hugged them all tightly as Jacob and
Carl and Edna prepared to drive back to the church.
"Thank you, Peter, I can't say that enough," Jacob
said sincerely. "I just don't know how to ever repay
you."
"There's nothing to repay, Jacob. I'm glad to help,"
Peter told him sincerely. "You're way too good
looking to go around wearing such hideous clothes.
Now, take everything in your closet at home and
burn it immediately!"
"I will," Jacob laughed.
"Stop laughing," Peter frowned. "I'm serious. Don't
sell it at a garage sale, and don't donate it to charity.
You won't be doing anyone a favor! Burn it all!"

CHAPTER FOUR

Jacob had so much to think about. For the first time in his entire life, other people knew he was gay. What's more, none of them seemed to have a problem with it. Of course, two of those people were gay themselves, but even a couple of older straight people, religious people, apparently thought nothing of it. How could this possibly be, he wondered? In his mind, being Christian automatically meant being anti-gay. At least, that's the way he had been raised to think. He knew of no one back home who approved of gay people; yet here, in this small town that he'd only been a part of for one day, he felt accepted for who he truly was. That was a new feeling, something he had never experienced before. Accepted for who he was, he thought wonderingly. These good people accepted something in him that he had struggled with and failed to understand all of his life. But what about God? Didn't God send gay people to hell? That's what he had always been taught. If that were true, why were these warm, caring people okay with it when God certainly wasn't? It didn't make any sense to him.

He sighed. It was too much to think about right now. He had to get ready for his dinner reception. Since his two new suits had been sent to the tailor's, he selected a pair of cream colored slacks, light blue shirt, navy blazer, and a pair of stylish brown loafers. He found a brown belt and a rather chic tie

to complete the outfit. When he was dressed, he
stepped in front of the full-length mirror and studied
his appearance with a critical eye.

Wow! Clothes really do make the man, he thought!
He looked good, maybe even almost attractive. He
felt a strange new self-confidence flicker to life
inside of him as he stared at his reflection, turning
this way and that. Why didn't I dress like this
before? Why on earth didn't somebody tell me how
bad I looked? Did they all care so little about me? I
never realized how awful my old clothes were, or
that I could look this nice. He smiled at his
reflection, hesitantly at first, then with more
assurance.

He locked the back door just before six o'clock and
walked down to the garage, carefully avoiding
looking over at his neighbor's house. Just as he got
to his car, parked in front of his garage, he heard a
loud wolf whistle. He looked around until he
spotted Anthony emerging from his own garage,
wearing only a baggy pair of shorts, wiping his
greasy hands on an old rag.

"Wow, look at you!" he whistled again. "You look
like a million bucks."

Jacob couldn't keep from staring at Anthony's
muscular build and beautifully hairy chest. Finally
he looked up at Anthony's handsome face and
smiled at the compliment in spite of himself.

"Thank you," he said curtly, quickly opening his car
door and jumping behind the wheel. "I'll see ya."

He closed the door and backed out of the drive onto the street.

He sat between Carl and Edna at the dinner, which was held in the large church annex. Pastor Cal introduced him to dozens of people, while the Johnson's whispered interesting tidbits about each one in his ear. He chuckled at the often humorous information he was learning about many of the parishioners, and was pleased to note that neither Carl nor Edna ever said anything unkind, but still managed to get their message across. It was an enjoyable enough evening for Jacob with them by his side, but he quickly grew weary correcting church members who insisted on calling him Jake. As the evening wore down, Jacob stepped into his office and leaned against the closed door behind him with a sigh of relief. So many people, he thought! It was a little overwhelming to meet such a large number of new people in one evening. As he moved to sit down behind his desk, a sudden knock came at the door. He carefully put a smile on his face and opened the door.

"Hi there, Jacob," an attractive blond man in his late thirties or so smiled back at him. "I'm Lance Martin. We met out there a while ago."

"Oh, yes," Jacob said. "You're married to…"

"Linda," Lance finished for him. "I know you met so many new people tonight, your head must be swimming."

"A little," Jacob agreed with a grin. "What can I do for you?"

"I just wanted to tell you how glad Linda and I are that you're here. If there's anything we can do to make you feel more welcome, I hope you'll let us know."

"I appreciate that, Lance," Jacob said sincerely, shaking his hand. "Everyone has been so nice already."

Lance continued to hold his hand as he looked directly at him.

"I want you to be happy here, Jacob," he said with an unexpected intensity to his voice.

"I'm sure I will be, once I get settled," Jacob said, pulling his hand back uncomfortably.

"You're over on Maple, aren't you?" Lance said as he reluctantly released his hand.

"Yes, I am."

"Well, my office is only a few blocks from you," Lance said with a grin. "Maybe I'll drop by sometime."

"That would be great, Lance."

Lance leaned in and gave him a hug.

"Welcome to Green Grove, Jacob."

Jacob pulled into his dark driveway and parked in front of the garage. Wearily he shut the car door and looked over at Anthony's house for a moment.

"Have a busy night?" Anthony called out.

Jacob looked around, startled, trying to find his neighbor in the low light.

"Anthony? Where are you?" he replied.

"Back here," Anthony said.

Curiously, Jacob passed in front of Anthony's garage and stopped at the chain link fence separating the driveway from his backyard. Strands of tiny white lights lit up the roof of the deck that ran the width of the back of the house. A comfortable looking grouping of patio furniture took up the far end of the deck, while a variety of potted plants filled its perimeter, adding a lush and colorful border along the railing. A hot tub sat in the middle of the deck against the back of the house, recessed deeply so that its cover appeared to rest on the floor.

Anthony, still wearing only his baggy shorts, walked over to the gate from the darkness next to the garage. He smiled warmly at Jacob.

"Come over and sit on the deck for a while. It's such a beautiful evening," he said, beckoning with his hand.

"Oh, er, thanks," Jacob hesitated, "but I really shouldn't."

"Why not?" Anthony asked with a frown.

"Well…"

"Is this because of what I said before? I didn't mean any disrespect toward you, Jacob."

"I know, it's just that I'm tired and should probably go to bed."

"At nine thirty?" Anthony said doubtfully. "Come on, have a beer with me. I promise we won't talk religion."

He turned back toward the deck. Jacob hesitated, looking longingly over his shoulder at his own house, and then opened the gate to Anthony's backyard.

He waited on the deck until Anthony returned with a couple of bottles of Miller Lite. He handed one to Jacob and gestured to the comfortable furniture. Jacob sat down primly on the edge of the settee while Anthony sat down heavily and sprawled back on the nearby chair. Jacob carefully avoided looking directly at Anthony because he knew it would only lead to the lustful thoughts he was desperately trying to avoid. The man was so incredibly beautiful that it almost hurt to look at him, knowing that he could never do anything more with him.

"So what did you have going on tonight?" Anthony asked him.

"It was a dinner at the church, so that the board members and elders and choir could meet me," Jacob replied, looking appreciatively around the deck. "This is really nice back here."

"Thanks," Anthony smiled as he gazed around the dimly lit area. "This is one of my favorite places, especially at night. It's very private and secluded, which I like for the hot tub. In the daylight you'll be able to see the garden I built last year."

"How long have you lived here?" Jacob asked curiously.

"Oh, I guess about six years," Anthony mused. "I've been working on it ever since."

"Well, it is really beautiful," Jacob complimented him. "Very comfortable and welcoming. I wish I knew how to decorate, but I'm not very creative."
"Well, you're a talented musician, so I'd say you're pretty creative."
Jacob took an awkward drink from his bottle as he looked away.
"Why won't you look at me?" Anthony asked him with a slight grin. He was pretty sure he already knew the answer, but he wanted to hear it from Jacob himself.
"I'm looking at you," Jacob said as he shifted his gaze from the garage to a nearby flowerpot.
"Well, you must think I'm a bunch of flowers, because that's what you're staring at. You've looked everywhere but right at me."
"That's crazy," Jacob said lightly.
"Look at me, Jacob," Anthony said firmly, sitting up straighter in his chair.
Jacob frowned and looked into the other man's eyes. Oh, my goodness, he is so beautiful, he thought! He wanted to do so much more than just look at him.
"See," he shuddered slightly. "I'm looking at you."
"That's the first time that you've actually looked at me tonight," Anthony said, smiling warmly at him. Jacob just wanted to leap into his arms and kiss him as he allowed himself to really appreciate just how beautiful he was.
"So, what were we talking about?" Anthony said, relaxing back into the soft cushions. "Oh, yeah. You

said you weren't good at decorating. I could help you there, if you like. There is a really good resale shop downtown with a lot of nice stuff. We ought to go over there sometime, and I could help you pick out some furniture and pictures to dress your place up a little. If you want to, that is."

"That would be really great, Anthony," Jacob said eagerly. His earlier nervousness seemed to disappear as they discussed a few interesting possibilities for decorating his house. When a lull in the conversation developed a little later, Jacob took a deep breath.

"I, uh, met Peter Johnson," he said abruptly.

"Really?" Anthony said slowly. "Okay…"

"He's like you, you know."

Anthony smiled to himself.

"You mean he's a nurse?" he asked, pretending to be confused.

"No," Jacob said hesitantly.

"Oh, he's a biker?"

"No. At least, I don't think so."

"Then what?" Anthony said seriously, trying not to laugh.

"He's….gay," Jacob whispered, looking around nervously.

"He's what? Gay?" Anthony said loudly. "Oh, my god! You're kidding!"

"No, I'm serious," Jacob said quietly.

Anthony couldn't hold back anymore. He laughed cheerfully at the expression on Jacob's face.

"I know he's gay. He and Neil are two of my best friends," he said as his laughter faded away.

Jacob frowned at him.

"Oh, so you're laughing at me?"

"No, Jacob," Anthony said, trying not to smile. "It's just that you take this whole gay thing so seriously. You ought to just relax and enjoy it, because it's no big deal. There are millions of gay people all over the world, you know."

"I have to take it seriously. I don't want to go to hell when I die."

"You really believe that, don't you? You think all gay people will go to hell? Millions of good, decent people?"

"Of course, I do," Jacob said. "It's in the Bible."

"Do you know what else is in the Bible? Murder, genocide, incest, and rape. And that's what the good guys are doing! How can Lot, who was supposed to be 'a righteous man', be considered a good guy when he slept with his own daughters and then pimped them out to visitors? How can eating bacon or wearing blended fabrics be a sin, Jacob? How can loving someone be a sin? If you can explain how all of that applies today without saying 'because God says so', we might be able to have an intelligent discussion about being gay and going to hell!"

"You know what," Jacob shouted, standing up and striding over to the steps leading down to the gate, "there is no talking to you about this. You won't listen to reason."

The Man Next Door

"Reason?" Anthony said heatedly. "You believe that words written thousands of years ago for a very specific, tiny culture thousands of miles from here still apply, and you accuse me of not listening to reason? I'm trying to help you, Jacob!"
Without another word, Jacob banged the gate closed behind him and ran to his back door, where he fumbled in the dark for the right key for a few awkward minutes. Finally he opened the door and slammed it shut behind him.

Oh, my god, Anthony thought, this kid is in really bad shape. He can't stand any criticism of his beliefs, of the very religion that is condemning him. That is so messed up! Anthony respected the right of anyone to hold whatever religious beliefs they chose to, but it angered him when those beliefs were the source of shame and guilt and pain, as in the case of Jacob. He had been taught all too well to hate himself, and how could anyone have a happy and healthy life when they believed that they deserved to be hated by themselves, the world, and by God? Try as he might, he could not understand how a person could embrace a belief system that condemned that person to eternal damnation just because of who they loved or slept with.
To be fair to Jacob, Anthony knew he had been indoctrinated with these ideas since birth, so he couldn't blame him for holding on to these beliefs; they were all he had ever known. He himself had struggled with the same inner conflict that Jacob

was experiencing, but had ultimately resolved it by the time he was a teenager. So he knew firsthand the pain that his young neighbor was attempting to deal with. He would either have to find a way to help him, or just avoid him altogether, although he would prefer the former. I'd really like to have him in my life if I could, he thought. There's a very likeable guy underneath the surface if he can just get past his self-loathing.

CHAPTER FIVE

Jacob lay in his bed that night, staring blindly at the ceiling. He was so angry with Anthony that he couldn't even think. Anthony had no right to question Jacob's deeply held convictions. Everyone he had ever known believed the same way he did, and they couldn't all be wrong. Could they? Anthony was the first person he had ever met who believed differently. He said he didn't believe in God or the Bible, but exactly what did he believe in? Suddenly, he needed to know. He jumped out of his bed and threw on a tee shirt and his old blue flannel pajama bottoms. Hesitantly he stepped out of his back door and looked over at his neighbor's house. The lights were still lit on the covered deck, but he couldn't see Anthony anywhere. Quietly he tiptoed over to the fence enclosing Anthony's backyard.

"Anthony?" he called softly.

"Jacob?" Anthony replied. "What are you still doing up?"

Jacob walked through the gate and up the three steps to the deck. The cover to the hot tub was folded neatly against the back of the house and Anthony was sitting chest high in the bubbling water.

"I couldn't sleep," Jacob confessed.

"Look, I'm sorry about what I said," Anthony told him. "I didn't mean to offend you. It's just that I hate to see someone in pain, and you, my friend, are in a lot of pain."

"I'm not in any pain," Jacob said in a confused tone.

"Not physical pain," Anthony told him. "I'm talking about emotional and spiritual pain."

"Like I said, I'm not in pain."

"Okay," Anthony replied easily. "Come on, get in the hot tub."

"No, no, that's okay," Jacob said nervously. "I'm fine."

"Come on, it will help you relax," Anthony said with a grin. "And you look like you really need to chill out. I promise I won't attack you. And no more talk about religion."

Jacob studied his face for a few seconds, and then boldly stripped out of his tee shirt and pajama bottoms until he was standing on the deck in his new white boxers. Oh, my god, he thought I'm standing outside in my underwear, at a stranger's house in the middle of the night. My parents would be so disapproving. I'm probably going to hell for just being here!

"Nice shorts," Anthony said with an appreciative smile. He was impressed with the way Jacob filled out those shorts, as well as his slim but muscular physique. A light dusting of brown hair covered his pecs and legs.

"You have a very nice body, Jacob," he added lightly. "Grab us a couple of beers from the fridge, will you?"

Jacob obliged and then stood uncertainly beside the hot tub.

"Come on, get in and let's talk."

Jacob somewhat reluctantly stepped down into the warm, bubbling water until he was able to awkwardly sit on a preformed seat.

"Have you never been in a hot tub before?" Anthony asked him, surprised.

"No, never," Jacob told him with a small grin.

"Oh, my god, you have been so sheltered, haven't you?"

Jacob gave him an annoyed look.

"I'm sorry, I'm sorry," Anthony said hastily. "I didn't mean anything by that."

Jacob allowed himself to relax a little.

"You're right," he admitted with a small smile. "I have been sheltered. I've never met anyone like you before, that's for sure."

"You mean because I'm gay?"

"Well, yes."

"Trust me, Jacob, you've met plenty of gay people," Anthony chuckled. "You just weren't aware of it.

"Maybe," Jacob acknowledged. "But it's not just that you're…gay; I've never met anyone who didn't believe in God and the Bible."

"Are you serious?" Anthony asked him incredulously.

"Well, everyone I know is from the church, except for kids from high school, but I avoided them as much as I could."

"I think it's good to know people of all kinds. Gay, straight, Christian, Jewish, Muslim, Hindu, atheist, Buddhist, white, black, brown, whatever."

"The only people I know are white and Christian," Jacob said thoughtfully. "You know, just people from our church."

"Well now you know a gay person who is a sort of Buddhist," Anthony chuckled, taking a sip of his beer.

"You're Buddhist?" Jacob asked unbelievingly.

"Well, I really like his teachings. They say more to me than anything I was ever taught in the Bible," Anthony admitted. "And I like a lot of Native American spiritual beliefs."

"But you've read the Bible?"

"Sure I have," Anthony said. "I was raised in the Christian church just like you."

"So, I don't understand. If you were taught about God and Jesus and heaven and hell, how can you turn your back on all of it?"

"I didn't turn my back on Christianity. I just couldn't relate to it, or it couldn't relate to me. I can't wrap my head around the concept of a God who supposedly gives us free will, but unless we follow a strict set of unrealistic rules and live unhappy lives, He's going to send us to eternal damnation. It doesn't make sense to me that a loving God would send anyone to hell, or that there even is a hell."

"So what do you believe in?" Jacob asked earnestly. "I really want to know."

The Man Next Door

"You've probably never read anything about Buddhism, have you?"

Jacob shook his head.

"Well, I'll give you a book about his life and his basic teachings. Now I'm not saying they're perfect, because he was just a man. He never claimed to be anything other than an ordinary guy. In fact, he said that if his teachings help you, great, and if they don't, that's okay, too. There is no guilt or shame or sin; it's not about that. It's all about doing what's right because it's good for your soul, not because you're afraid of eternal damnation. If you do something bad, like stealing, it ultimately damages your soul. He taught that we should only do the things that nourish our souls."

"But what about sin? Being gay is a sin," Jacob said with a frown.

"Why is it a sin?" Anthony asked him seriously.

Jacob took a drink of his beer.

"Because the Bible says so," Jacob recited instantly.

"So, then eating pork or shellfish, or wearing blended cloths are all sins. But owning a slave is fine, beating a woman is okay, and genocide is okay? You surely don't believe that, do you?"

"Of course not!" Jacob said with a frown.

"So you don't believe those parts of the Bible?" Anthony asked him.

"Well, they were written for a different time and culture," Jacob argued.

"That's exactly my point!" Anthony asserted. "And so was the part about gay people. You have to remember, these were primitive and ignorant people. They were very superstitious; they would believe anything they were told if they thought it came from a higher power."

Jacob looked at him thoughtfully for a moment, and then shook his head.

"I don't know," he said with a trace of sadness in his voice.

"I'm not saying give up on Christianity, Jacob. I'm just asking you to think for yourself. That's all. Question everything, no matter who says it, even if it comes from the pulpit. Ministers aren't infallible, you know."

He grinned mischievously at Jacob.

"You know, they say the only difference between a religion and a cult is the amount of real estate it owns."

Jacob looked at him with a frown, which soon gave way to a sheepish grin.

"That's a joke," he said. "Isn't it?"

"Yes, it's a joke," Anthony agreed. "But there is a certain amount of truth to it."

Jacob sighed and laid his head back on the headrest. He had to admit the warm, rushing water felt very good on his bare skin. He had never enjoyed a sensation like this before. In fact, he was beginning to realize he hadn't enjoyed much of anything before. Except for his music, of course. He had always enjoyed playing the piano, escaping into a different reality from the strict, unemotional world of his everyday life. But here he was, trying new things, and feeling new sensations he wasn't aware even existed.

"I don't know, Anthony," he said at last. "I don't know if I can give up everything I've believed in my whole life."

"Jacob, that's not what I'm saying at all," Anthony exclaimed, leaning forward and placing a hand on Jacob's knee. "There's nothing wrong with believing in something, unless that something is damaging to your soul. And from what I can see, and from what I remember from my own experience, your beliefs are doing just that. You have been in pain your whole life, but you're so used to it that you don't even feel it anymore. That's not a healthy way to live."

He sat back and studied the other man's face. "Just don't believe anything that damages your soul."

"But how can I tell if something is 'damaging' my soul?" Jacob asked forlornly.

"You'll just know. Think about the last time you did something you knew was wrong, like telling a lie. How did you feel afterwards?"

"I felt bad, I guess," Jacob shrugged.

"Why?"

"Because it was a sin."

"No, that's not it," Anthony told him. "It's because you knew you could have done better. That's why you felt bad; you knew deep down that it wasn't good for your soul."

"Okay, I guess I see that," Jacob nodded slowly.
"But being gay is a lot bigger than just telling a lie."
Anthony sighed and then made a decision. He
reached over and pulled Jacob gently forward by his
arm.
"Come here," he said softly.
He pressed his lips gently to Jacob's mouth for a
brief moment, then released him and sat back.
"Now, how did that feel?" he asked.
Jacob stared at him with a glazed look on his face.
"It felt really nice," he whispered. "It felt...I don't
know...kind of...beautiful."
"Now, you decide what that did to your soul,"
Anthony said softly.
Jacob continued to stare at him.
"I've never kissed a man before," he said
wonderingly.
Anthony frowned at him.
"What? No way!" he said, disbelievingly. "You've
never kissed a man?"
Jacob shook his head.
"Well, now it's up to you to decide if it was good
for your soul, or bad."
Jacob leaned forward and pulled Anthony to him.
"Can I do it one more time?" he asked.
Anthony nodded and he kissed him again, gently
and briefly. Jacob sat back in a daze. He looked up
at Anthony and swallowed hard.
"I'm not sure if it was good for my soul, but it
definitely wasn't bad."

The Man Next Door

As Jacob was leaving for his office the next
morning, wearing a well fitting pair of slacks, dress
shirt and shoes, and a stylish tie, he looked over at
Anthony's deck and backyard and smiled.
Surprisingly, he had had the best night's sleep he
could remember. He felt wide-awake and energetic
this morning.

He spent the morning in his office, looking at choral
music. He frowned at the dull choral arrangements
of some of the more common hymns. These
wouldn't do at all, he decided. He called the music
director from his home church in Indianapolis and
had her email him a list of music publishers with
some new and upbeat arrangements.

During his lunch break, he stopped by one of Green
Grove's two grocery stores and picked up a
shopping cart full of food. It was time to have some
real food in the house, he decided. He felt strangely
empowered as he payed for his groceries for the
first time in his life. He was actually acting like an
adult, and he liked it, he thought with a satisfied
smile.

He had put his groceries away and was standing at
the kitchen sink, eating a ham sandwich and looking
out the double window at Anthony's house, when a
sharp knock came at the front door. He swallowed
and yelled to the caller to come in. Wiping his
hands on a dishtowel, he walked through the dining
room.

"Hey, Jacob," Lance Martin said with a smile.

"Hi, Lance," Jacob said with surprise. "What are you doing here?"

"I told you I might stop by sometime," Lance reminded him. "I just wanted to see your place."

Jacob smiled and hugged him briefly.

"Well, I'm glad you did. Let me show you around, although there's not much to see."

Jacob showed him the kitchen, and then back through the dining room to the sparsely furnished living room. The front bedroom, just off the living room, was devoid of any furniture, so they walked on through the bathroom and into Jacob's bedroom. Lance complimented him on the house as they paused beside the bed. He reached over and hugged Jacob again.

"I'm so glad you are here, Jacob," he said as he released him, keeping a hand around Jacob's neck. "I mean, I'm glad you moved here."

"Thanks, Lance; that means a lot to me."

Before he could react, Lance leaned in and kissed him on the lips. Jacob tried to pull back, but Lance strengthened his hold on the back of his neck. Jacob remembered his first kiss from the night before with Anthony and finally stopped resisting. He returned the kiss, wrapping his arms around Lance. The sensation of kissing and holding another man overwhelmed Jacob's senses, and his knees gave out. Lance laid him back on the bed, putting his full weight on the younger man as he continued to kiss him ardently.

After a few minutes, Lance reached down and began groping him through his pants and Jacob pushed him away hard.

"No!" he panted, struggling to sit up as he caught his breath.

"I'm sorry!" Lance exclaimed, standing and straightening his clothes. "I'm sorry, Jacob. I got carried away."

He turned away, his face turning bright red.

"I was just so horny, and you're so handsome. I wanted you so badly," he said, glancing over at Jacob contritely. "I'm sorry. I'll go."

"Wait, Lance," Jacob said. "It's okay. But you're a married man!"

"I know," he nodded, unable to look at Jacob.

"So you're married, and you're…"

Lance nodded again and sat down heavily on the side of the bed. He looked sorrowful and lonely, while Jacob merely appeared confused.

"So if you're…you know, why did you get married?"

"It was expected," Lance told him, his eyes filled with sadness. "I didn't have a choice. Her parents and mine didn't leave either of us much choice."

"But why do you stay together if you're….not straight?" Jacob asked curiously.

"Are you kidding?" Lance laughed mirthlessly. "No one in the Martin family gets a divorce. Ever! And no one in the Martin family is gay, either!"

Jacob scooted himself up to sit beside him.

"How old are you, Lance?" he asked.

"I'm forty," Lance said. "Listen, I'm sorry I tried this. It was a really stupid thing to do, but sometimes I feel so alone, so desperate to be with someone."

His voice trembled as he spoke.

"But that's no excuse, and I hope you'll forgive me. Please don't say anything about this. I'd lose everything if anyone ever found out."

"Are you kidding?" Jacob gave him a wry grin. "I know I'm not married, but I'm kind of in the same boat as you. If people knew I was…gay, I'd lose everything, too. Not that I have as much to lose as you, but still."

"So I guess you sort of understand."

Jacob put his arm around Lance's shoulders.

"I do. Actually, this may sound funny to you, but I'm glad to meet another guy like me in the church, even if we do have to stay closeted. Makes me feel a little less alone."

Lance nodded in agreement. He looked over at Jacob sadly. Jacob looked at him kindly, and after a moment, Lance leaned over and kissed him again. Soon they were back in each other's arms, and this time, when Lance reached down between them, Jacob didn't stop him.

The two men continued to kiss and fondle each other for several minutes, until Jacob pulled away.

"I've got to get back to work," he said, slightly out of breath.

"Me, too," Lance agreed. He hesitated for a moment. "Could I... Would it be okay if I came by again sometime?"

Jacob nodded and smiled shyly. As he gazed at Lance, a thought occurred to him, and his smile slowly vanished.

"Lance, what about your wife?"

"She knows," Lance sighed. "She's always known, but she married me anyway because of the pressure we were both under. She isn't happy about it, of course."

"I don't understand why you stay together. Lots of people get divorces; it may be a sin, but it isn't uncommon. Surely your families wouldn't get that upset, would they?"

"You don't know our families," Lance said. "My dad would disown me in a heartbeat if Linda and I divorced. You'd have to meet him only once to understand. He owns seven investment offices, including the one here in Green Grove. I don't own anything, I just run it for him. I'd lose my job, my house, everything."

"Just for getting a divorce?" Jacob said doubtfully. Lance nodded sadly.

"You have to understand, Linda's family has a lot of money, even more than my parents. It all comes down to money, and power, and prestige."

"I guess it's kind of like the church," Jacob said thoughtfully. "If anyone knew I was gay, they'd take everything away from me, too. My parents own this house, and they'd probably disown me. I'd be left with nothing. I guess that isn't too different from your situation."

"You know," Lance said with a small smile. "I'm glad I came over here today. I'm sorry I came on so strong, but I couldn't resist you. You're so cute! I'm still horny, by the way."

The two of them laughed nervously.

"Can I come by again?" Lance asked.

"I hope you will," Jacob nodded solemnly.

CHAPTER SIX

Jacob didn't get much accomplished that afternoon in his office. He couldn't stop thinking about Lance, and how the two of them had kissed. It was a new experience for him. Anthony had kissed him sweetly and tenderly, but the passionate, desperate kisses he shared with Lance had awakened something in him. He felt a sexual desire so strong that he thought he might explode.
He remembered Anthony's advice about doing only those things that didn't damage his soul. At this particular moment in time, he found that he didn't care about his soul at all. He was too overcome with a lustful, physical desire; nothing else mattered.

The days passed by, and one afternoon as Jacob arrived home from work, Anthony was working in his backyard, wearing shorts, sandals, and a tee shirt. Jacob walked over and stood at the gate.
"What are you working on?" he called out.
Anthony looked up and smiled at him.
"Hey, Jacob," he greeted him warmly. "I'm just doing some weeding. Come on back and see my little serenity garden."
He waved him back, and Jacob crossed between the deck and garage to the area where Anthony was standing.
The serenity garden, as Anthony called it, took up much of the fenced backyard. It was a large oval area enclosed by a stone path. A small stream

meandered across the length of it, beginning with a large stone fountain on one end, and encircling a ten-foot tall red Japanese maple tree at the other. A small wooden footbridge crossed the middle of the stream. A large cement Buddha sat near the stream and tree, facing the back of the house and overlooking the water. Most of the rest of the area was filled with a variety of neatly trimmed shrubs and flowers. A few large rocks dotted the open areas between the plants, and a tall metal obelisk covered with purple clematis vines stood close to the right side of the bridge. A small cement patio on the opposite side of the garden held a couple of comfortable patio chairs, so the area could be enjoyed from either the deck or the patio.

"This is gorgeous, Anthony!" Jacob exclaimed with delight. "How did you do all of this?"

"I just had an idea, and so I put it down on paper and then built it," Anthony shrugged, pleased at Jacob's reaction. "I wanted something peaceful and serene, someplace I could just look at and enjoy."

"You did a beautiful job," Jacob said, in awe. "I am really impressed."

"Thanks! Say, what are you doing right now?" Anthony asked him.

"Nothing, I guess," Jacob shrugged. "Why?"

"I thought you might like to run up to the resale store and see what they've got."

"That would be wonderful," Jacob said. "Let me change clothes real quick."

He ran over to his house and was back in about ten
minutes.

"Wow, look at you," Anthony whistled. "I thought
you looked good all dressed up, but you're even
hotter in jeans. Are those new?"

He walked around Jacob and admired him from
every direction.

"Peter picked out new clothes for me," Jacob
admitted sheepishly. He had to admit he felt a
strange, new confidence in these clothes that he had
never known before. "He made me promise to burn
all of my old clothes."

"I think he gave you some good advice," Anthony
said with a laugh. "Come on, we'll take my truck.

They drove the short distance to the resale shop,
which had originally been a car dealership before
that business had relocated out on the edge of town,
and Anthony greeted the owner with a nod and a
warm smile.

"This is my new neighbor and friend, Jacob," he
said. "Jacob, this is Myra. She owns the store, and
she can find you just about anything you want.
Myra, Jacob is the new music director over at Grace
church."

Myra, a pleasant, rather heavyset woman of around
sixty or so with a pair of glasses hanging from a
cord around her neck, greeted them with a friendly
smile.

"Oh, the new music director," she mused, looking Jacob over thoughtfully. She turned to Anthony questioningly.

"New friend?" she asked with a raised eyebrow.

"Friend," Anthony said firmly, but with a grin. "And he desperately needs help with his new house."

Briefly, he described Jacob's house and furniture. Myra studied Jacob carefully as she listened and nodded.

"Well, let's look around, and you tell me if you see something you like," she said briskly.

She led them through the large store, pointing out items she thought would interest them, and selecting a few pieces of furniture that she insisted that Jacob buy. She and Anthony teased each other mercilessly as they walked, and Jacob laughed until his sides hurt.

"Here," she said. "Here's a gorgeous lamp you can't live without."

"No!" Anthony protested. "He doesn't want that god-awful thing. It's hideous!"

"What do you know, you old queen?" she retorted. "The only taste you have is the taste of the last dick you sucked or the ass you ate!"

"Well, at least I've sucked a dick in this decade!" Anthony responded with a grin. "You don't even remember what one tastes like!"

"Thank god!" Myra said dryly.

Anthony turned to Jacob.

"Myra was married once."

"Don't fucking remind me!" she said.

"It's just as well you don't like men," Anthony teased. "Most of them are afraid of you."

She brushed him aside and moved on, picking up items here and there, seemingly unaffected by the insult directed at her. They finally completed their tour of the store and she listed all the items the three of them had selected. There was a second bedroom suite, lamps, chairs, framed pictures for the walls, and several other pieces of furniture and bric-a-brac, all in excellent condition.

"I'm not sure I can afford all of this," Jacob whispered anxiously to Anthony.

"That'll be five thousand dollars," Myra said, looking over her glasses at him with a frown.

The color drained from Jacob's face.

"Don't do that to him, Myra," Anthony chastised her. "Do you want to give him a heart attack?"

He put an arm around Jacob's shoulders as he spoke.

"Oh, did I say five thousand dollars?" Myra said innocently, looking down to recheck her figures. "I meant five hundred dollars, darling."

She grinned at Anthony as Jacob's color began to return.

"She tried that with me, too," Anthony said with a laugh. "First rule of thumb with Myra is never believe anything she tells you, because it's probably a lie."

Jacob heaved a sigh of relief.

"Five hundred, I can afford, I think," he said with a smile.

"Are you sure?" Myra said over her glasses. "Let's make it four fifty. I don't want to take all of your money. And that's giving you a thirty percent discount just because I like you."

"Why don't you make it four hundred even?" Anthony suggested with a mischievous grin.

"Why don't you shut the fuck up, bitch?" Myra replied without missing a beat. "Okay, kid, you drive a hard bargain, so four hundred even it is. Now pay me and get the hell out of my store."

She winked at Anthony as Jacob wrote out a check. Once he had his receipt, they loaded everything in the back of Anthony's truck.

"Thank you so much, Myra," Jacob said sincerely, giving her an earnest hug. "I really appreciate all of this!"

"You're very welcome, my darling. It's the least I can do if you have to live next door to this hag." She gestured rudely to Anthony.

"I love you, Myra," Anthony said, kissing her on the cheek as they prepared to leave.

"Yeah, yeah, I love you, too," she responded. She watched them fondly as they got in the truck and drove away.

Jacob and Anthony spent a very pleasant evening arranging furniture and hanging pictures. By the time nine o'clock had rolled around, Jacob's house had undergone a dramatic transformation. He and

Anthony stopped and looked around with satisfaction. Instead of a few pieces of furniture scattered here and there against bare walls, the house appeared full and cozy and welcoming.

"I can't believe it," Jacob said as he looked around in awe. "I just can't believe it! This looks amazing, Anthony! You're amazing."

"It does look pretty good, doesn't it?" Anthony agreed, looking around with a satisfied grin. "And all for only four hundred bucks! Good old Myra."

"This was so nice of you," Jacob said. "Everyone here has been so nice to me."

"Well, that's because you're a nice guy."

"Let me do something nice for you," Jacob said. "Please."

"What did you have in mind?" Anthony said suggestively as he stepped closer to him.

"How about I cook us something," Jacob said. "I'm a pretty decent cook, and I bought a couple of ribeye steaks today."

"That sounds great, but you don't have a grill," Anthony reminded him.

"No, but the stove has a broiler."

"How about we take dinner over to my place," Anthony suggested with a grin. "I've got a grill." Together they gathered everything needed for their supper and carried it over to Anthony's house. Anthony lit the grill for him, and in a short time, Jacob set two plates in front of them at Anthony's round wooden kitchen table. Anthony had selected a bottle of his favorite Napa Valley Cabernet Sauvignon, and he poured a glass for each of them. "Try this," he said, handing one to Jacob.

"Oh, I don't know," Jacob said with a frown. "It's bad enough I've been drinking beer. My parents would completely disown me if they knew I was drinking wine."

"You're kidding, right?" Anthony said in a disbelieving voice. "They don't approve of wine? Even though Jesus turned the water into wine in the Bible?"

"Remember, I told you I was taught that alcohol is sinful," Jacob shrugged, frowning at him.

"So how do they explain the water into wine thing?" Anthony asked as he tried to smother a laugh.

"He was just showing his ability to do it," Jacob explained. "It wasn't for drinking. At least, that's what I was taught."

Anthony started laughing outright at that.

"Doesn't that sound the least bit crazy to you?" he asked.

"No," Jacob said, becoming a little annoyed. "It's what I was taught."

"So let me get this straight. Jesus turned the water to wine but no one was allowed to drink it. And then he poured it on the ground and wasted it. Does that sound like something he would do?"

"I don't know, Anthony, I wasn't there," Jacob said angrily. "Were you?"

"I'm sorry, Jacob, but it amazes me how some of you people will do anything to find fault with the world. Alcohol, gay people, dancing, you name it, it's all sinful."

He watched a scowl appear on Jacob's face, and raised his hands in a gesture of peace.

"I'm sorry, I'm sorry," he said with a grin. "Let's agree to disagree, okay?"

Jacob relaxed a little, and his expression cleared. As a conciliatory gesture of his own, he took a sip of wine from his glass.

"So, what do you think?" Anthony asked him curiously.

"I think I like it," Jacob admitted with a small smile. "How's your steak?"

"It's wonderful," Anthony told him. "You'll be in charge of the grill from now on."

He looked down at his plate and cut off a bite size piece of the ribeye.

"You can handle my meat anytime," he said as seriously as he could.

He looked up at Jacob's taken aback expression and finally burst out laughing.

"Oh, my god, you are so fun to tease!"

Jacob tried not to laugh, but finally gave in, and the two of them giggled companionably for a few minutes. They continued chatting in a friendly manner as they ate.

"So tell me about your job as a nurse," Jacob said as they cleared the table and Anthony poured them each another glass of the Cabernet.

"It's good," Anthony said easily. "I really love it. I work in pre-op, recovery room, and post-op out at the hospital. It can be stressful sometimes, but it's usually not bad. And I work with some really great people."

"How did you get into nursing?" Jacob asked him. "I mean, I usually think of a nurse as a woman, and you're so masculine and everything. Please, I'm not trying to be offensive, I really want to know."

"I wanted to do something that made me feel good," Anthony said simply. "You know how I told you the Buddhist principle of doing things that are good for your soul? This is one of those things that does that. Helping somebody feeds my soul, and makes me a happier person.

"Besides," he added with a grin, "it pays well, and I don't want to work in some desk job."

"You do seem like a happy person to me," Jacob admitted, shaking his head. "But I don't see how a person can be happy and not believe in anything."

"Who says I don't believe in anything? I believe in lots of things."

"Like what?"

"Come on, let's go get in the hot tub before I get all philosophical on your ass," Anthony chuckled, slapping him lightly on the abdomen.

Jacob followed him out to the deck, where Anthony proceeded to undress down to his tight navy blue underwear. With a quick motion, the cover over the water rose up against the wall of the house almost by itself. Jacob undressed a little less self-consciously than before, and then stepped carefully down into the warm water. Once he was settled, he looked up, startled, to see Anthony strip out of his underwear, climb down into the water, and settle into a seat next to him. A push of a button brought the water to a frothy, bubbly boil all around them. Jacob did his best not to stare, but the sight of Anthony's perfect and impressively sized manhood surrounded by dense black hair was almost more than he could stand.

"How can you do that?" he asked, looking up at Anthony's face.

"Do what?" Anthony asked, leaning back and spreading his arms along the top of the hot tub.

"Take off all of your clothes like that?"

"Um, the same way anyone takes off their clothes, I guess."

"I'm too modest for anyone to see me nak…without clothes on," Jacob admitted.

"You mean naked."

Jacob nodded shyly.

"Then say the word," Anthony said. "Say 'naked'."

"I can say it," Jacob protested.

Anthony stared at him unflinchingly as he waited silently.

"Naked!" Jacob said uncomfortably. "See, I said it."

"And now you're embarrassed because you said it. Am I right?"

"A little," Jacob admitted.

"It's not a dirty word, you know," Anthony teased him.

"I know, I'm just not used to talking about certain things. And I am definitely not used to being naked around another man."

"You shouldn't be modest," Anthony told him sincerely. "You have a beautiful body. And there's nothing to be ashamed of or embarrassed about by being naked. It's the most natural state of being that there is."

"I guess," Jacob said doubtfully. "I just don't think I could ever be like you. I wish I could, but I can't." He looked away.

"I really wish I could be like you," he repeated in a softer voice.

"You don't need to be like me, Jacob," Anthony told him. "Just be free enough to be yourself."

"I don't even know how."

"Sure you do. Go on, take off your shorts. I promise I won't look. A hot tub is meant to be enjoyed without clothes anyway."

Anthony turned away and looked out over the backyard. Jacob looked at him anxiously.

"I don't think I can," he said with a great deal of consternation.

"You can do it, Jacob. You can do anything if you just let yourself relax and enjoy life," Anthony told him earnestly.

He turned back and put an arm around the younger man's bare shoulders.

"This is a safe place. You can say or do anything here without judgment. I promise I will never judge you."

He squeezed the back of Jacob's neck with his big hand.

"Let's make a pact."

Jacob turned to look at him tearfully. He wanted so desperately to break out and be as carefree and relaxed as Anthony, but everything in his past fought mightily against that impulse. He had rarely felt so torn before between what he was comfortable with, and trying something new, probably because he hadn't tried much of anything new in his life until he moved here.

"You and I will never judge or criticize each other here, no matter what. How about it?" Anthony said.

Jacob nodded without saying anything. Quickly, before he lost his nerve, he raised his hips and slid his underwear off. With a shout, he raised them out of the water and hurled them into the backyard. Anthony sat back, laughing delightedly. Jacob sat back as well, looking stunned at what he had just done. Slowly, he turned and gave Anthony a horrified look.

"It's okay, Jacob," Anthony said quickly, his smile fading at the look on Jacob's face. "Don't panic, it's okay."

He leaned forward and took Jacob into his arms and held him tightly. Jacob buried his face in Anthony's broad shoulder as he clung to him. Anthony sighed. He understood that this was an important moment for Jacob. By doing something so trivial as sitting naked in a hot tub and throwing his shorts out into the backyard, he was making a symbolic gesture,

taking his first step out from under the stranglehold
of his parents and the only way of life he had ever
known.

Jacob pulled back from him and looked up at him,
his expression a mixture of sadness, terror, and
defiance. He stared into Anthony's eyes for several
seconds, and then slowly slid forward until he was
sitting in front of him. Anthony pulled him toward
him and slowly tilted his head as their lips met,
tenderly at first, and then deeper and more
intensely. Jacob pulled himself up onto Anthony
until he was straddling him, never breaking the kiss.
He wrapped his arms around Anthony as tightly as
he could, his desire growing rapidly until he felt he
couldn't contain it.

They kissed for several minutes, enjoying the
feeling of each other's bodies, pressed tightly
together. Finally, Anthony pulled back reluctantly.
He held Jacob at arm's length.

"You've never been with a man before?" he asked
quietly.

Jacob shook his head, unable to turn his gaze away
from Anthony's handsome face.

"Then, I think we should take things very slowly. I
don't want you to do something you're going to
regret," Anthony told him, brushing a damp lock of
hair from Jacob's forehead.

"I don't care if I'll regret it or not, Anthony," Jacob
asserted breathlessly. "I want to be with you."

"And I want to be with you, too," Anthony said.
"God help me, you are so beautiful!"

Jacob reached for him again, but Anthony held him firmly in place.

"But I don't know if you're ready for this, Jacob. I want your first time to be wonderful and special. Something you'll always remember."

"I want it to be with you," Jacob whispered.

Anthony studied Jacob's face for several seconds. Finally he took his hand and stood up, pulling the younger man up with him.

"Come on," he said in a husky voice.

They quickly dried themselves and, leaving their clothes still on the deck, walked through the house to Anthony's bedroom. Anthony directed him to lie down on the bed, and then slowly and seductively climbed on top of him, kissing and nuzzling his body as he moved up until he was laying full length on him. Jacob instinctively wrapped his arms and legs around Anthony as they kissed. Anthony rubbed his groin against Jacob's, grinding repeatedly for a few minutes. Jacob finally gasped.

"Stop, Anthony!" he cried out.

Anthony stopped moving, but it was too late. Jacob's body spasmed and he climaxed as Anthony lifted his body and looked down. He looked back up at Jacob and grinned.

"That didn't take long," he said.

"Oh, dear God, what have I done?" Jacob cried out, covering his eyes with his hand. "I shouldn't be here. We shouldn't have done this."

Anthony frowned and sat up, moving to straddle his body. Jacob struggled to get up, but Anthony sat down firmly on him, holding him in place.

"You didn't do anything wrong, Jacob," he told him. "Can't you see how beautiful this was?"

Jacob kept his eyes covered and shook his head.

"Look at me," Anthony said sternly.

Slowly Jacob removed his hand and looked up at him with tears in his eyes.

"I'm not going to let you make this a bad thing, Jacob," Anthony told him. "This was a good time shared between friends. No one did anything wrong here. So don't turn something wonderful into something shameful. Didn't you enjoy it?"

Jacob stared up at him and nodded slightly.

"Okay, then. Even if you can't see it right now, someday you'll look back at tonight and you'll see the good thing that happened here. I promise you."

Anthony leaned down and kissed him again for a few seconds, even though Jacob didn't return it. He climbed off of him and rummaged in a dresser drawer, pulling out a pair of underwear. He threw them to Jacob.

"Here, put these on. I'll go get the rest of our clothes," he said, walking out to the deck.

Jacob hurriedly put on the underwear and walked out to the kitchen. He could see Anthony walking unconcernedly naked in the backyard, searching for the underwear that he had hurled away earlier. He stepped quietly out onto the deck and picked up his clothes from the deck floor.

"I've got to go," he called out tremulously.
With that he ran through the gate and back to his
own house.
"Jacob!" Anthony stared at him, crestfallen, as he
ran away. "Don't leave!"
His foot touched something unfamiliar and he
looked down. Slowly he reached down and picked
up Jacob's still wet underwear.

CHAPTER SEVEN

Jacob carefully avoided his neighbor the rest of the week. Each morning he would peek out his back door and run to the side door of the garage as soon as he was sure Anthony was nowhere around. He would start his car in the garage as the big door opened behind him, then carefully back the car down the drive as he pushed the remote to close the door.

He just couldn't face Anthony again, partly because he felt like such a fool for reacting so badly after he had….you know. But the main reason he did not want to see him was because the man was just too much of a temptation. A temptation that he had failed to resist. As much as he tried not to think about him, the memories of their kisses and the feeling of their bodies intermingled in the hot tub and on Anthony's bed continued to fill his mind.

If he were to be truly honest with himself, he would have admitted how wonderful and incredible it had felt to be with him, and that he already had developed a strong affection and attraction for the gentle, handsome man. But that would mean admitting to having feelings that he wasn't allowed to have, according to everything he had been taught all of his life. Thus, the only thing he could do was to deny those feelings and avoid Anthony as much as possible.

He did admit to himself that the thought of avoiding Anthony made him feel sad and more than a little lonely. But what else could he do. No matter how much he tried to pray the gay away, God seemed to turn His back on him. Those feelings had grown to an unbearable level since he'd been in Green Grove, and no amount of prayer was helping. God must indeed be a cruel god to make him gay, torment him with temptation at every turn, and ultimately send him to hell for eternity for something beyond his control. How could a kind and loving god do this? Why should he even worship a god like that?

When he arrived home the next afternoon, he hurried to his back door after making certain nobody was around. There, tucked in between the storm and inside doors was a book, along with his neatly folded underwear. He picked them up and quickly went inside, locking the door behind him. He tossed the book and underwear on his bed and sat down at the Clavinova, turning the volume down so that he could play unheard by his neighbors. The soft music soothed him as he played for an hour until his cell phone rang. The number was unfamiliar to him.

"Hello," he said warily.

"Jacob? This is Peter, from Larson's. I just wanted to let you know your suits are back from the tailor. Can you come in sometime soon?"

"Um, sure, yeah, whenever," Jacob replied awkwardly.

"What are you doing right now?" Peter asked impulsively.

"Nothing, just practicing."

"Practicing, huh?" Peter said with a suggestive tone. "Well, practice makes perfect, so I should be an expert, right? We are talking about fucking, aren't we?"

He chuckled at his little joke.

"No, I mean I'm playing the piano," Jacob said with a frown.

"I know what you mean, sweetie; I'm just having a little fun with you."

"Oh," Jacob replied, unsure of what to say.

"Get your cute ass down here to the store right now. You'll want these suits for Sunday, I'm sure, so let's make sure they fit you. See you in a minute."

Jacob stared at the phone for a second and shook his head in a dazed manner. It was a bit unsettling to him to have someone talk so freely about sex, even joking about it like it was nothing sinful. And yet he had been taught his entire life was that sex, like everything else that was pleasurable, was evil and the devil's way of keeping people out of heaven.

Jacob stepped out of the dressing room in his new, exquisitely cut dark blue suit.

"Oh, just look at you!" Peter breathed. "Jacob, honey, you are gorgeous! I'm serious! Now put your shoes on so we can see where the pants break." Jacob did as he was told, and Peter nodded his approval at the length of the trousers.

"Does it really look okay?" Jacob asked, turning this way and that as he examined his reflection in the three-way mirror.

"Oh, my god, sweetheart, you are beautiful," Peter told him, putting an arm around him and looking in the mirror as well. "Just look at yourself. Hasn't anyone ever told you how handsome you are?"

"No, not really," Jacob admitted shyly, shaking his head. "I've always kind of blended into the background most of my life."

"Well shame on you," Peter told him, giving him a little squeeze. "You were born to stand out, like me. I mean, look at that face, and that body!"

"I'm not that…"

"No, honey, I was talking about me!" Peter teased. He smoothed an eyebrow and blew himself a kiss before bursting out laughing at his reflection. Jacob couldn't help but laugh, too.

"Honey, believe me, you are a dreamboat. Any guy would be lucky to have you."

"I wish," Jacob sighed. "It can't happen, though."

"Of course it can," Peter said, smoothing Jacob's lapel.

"No, it can't," Jacob reiterated. "I'm not allowed to be…you know."

"You mean because of the church," Peter nodded with a knowing frown. "That's what you're talking about, isn't it?"

Jacob nodded, turning away from his reflection as Peter studied him thoughtfully.

"You know what?" Peter said suddenly. "We're having some friends over tomorrow night for dinner. Why don't you come, too? Please?"

"Oh, I...I...I don't think so," Jacob stammered anxiously.

"What will you be doing tomorrow night? Sitting at home alone?" Peter said astutely. "That's not good, Jacob. No, you're coming over; I won't take no for an answer. Neil and I are just two blocks behind you. It's the big brick house on the corner over on Third and Washington. Dinner is at seven o'clock."

"I don't –"

"This will give you a chance to meet some new people," Peter insisted. "Carl and Edna will be there. You love them, so just say you'll come."

"Okay, I'll come," Jacob relented finally. "But I tend to be kind of quiet at parties."

"That's fine, Jacob," Peter told him kindly. "All I want you to be is yourself."

Jacob changed out of his new suit, remembering Anthony's advice to him to be himself, but before he could get dressed, Peter poked his head around the curtain.

"Just checking, sweetie," he said brightly. "I had to make sure you weren't wearing those god-awful underwear you had on the other day!"

Jacob spent Saturday morning working on music for the Sunday service with the other musicians. Since he was unfamiliar with their habits, he let the song leader, a heavy-set, cheerful man named Oscar, be in charge. Besides Oscar, there was a guitarist, trumpeter, cellist, and himself on the piano. The other four musicians were very friendly to him, and responded well to a couple of minor suggestions that Jacob brought up to improve their sound. After a few productive hours of practicing together, the five of them said good-bye and Jacob headed for his car. On the way out the door, he heard a feminine voice call his name, and he turned to see Linda Martin walking rapidly toward him.

"Jacob?" she called. "Have you got a minute?"

"Uh, sure, Linda," he said hesitantly. "How are you?"

Linda was an attractive brunette with impeccable makeup and jewelry, perfect hair, and expensive clothes. She smiled warmly at him.

"I'm fine, thank you for asking," she said. "I was wondering if I could ask you to do a favor for me."

"Of course."

"It's about Lance," she said.

Jacob's face turned pale.

"Oh?" he said hoarsely.

"There's something nobody knows about him, something he doesn't want anyone to know, but I think you are just the person who should know because I'm hoping you can help him with it."

"Wha...wha...what do you mean?" Jacob stammered.

"He loves to sing," she said with a smile. "He has such a beautiful voice, but he won't sing in front of anyone. He's too talented to keep it all to himself. I was hoping maybe you could bring him out of the closet, so to speak."

Jacob laughed nervously at her choice of words.

"You want me to help him with his singing?" he asked incredulously. "That's what you want me to do?"

"If you don't mind," she said. "You don't know him yet, of course, but I think the two of you could be great friends. He loves music, and he's so talented, just like you. I thought maybe you could give him some lessons or something to encourage him."

"I'd be glad to help, if I can," Jacob said, with a sigh of relief.

"I'll have him give you a call or come by your house, if that's okay?"

"Sure, Linda, that would be fine," he assured her.

Anthony arrived at Peter and Neil's house at six o'clock that evening to help with the party preparations. The three of them stood in the beautifully remodeled kitchen of the stately old colonial brick mansion on Washington Street.

"So have you met your new neighbor yet?" Peter asked curiously.

"Oh, I've met him," Anthony said as he grated cheese for the salads.

"And?" Neil asked, looking up at Anthony's tone of voice.

Neil was an attractive man of thirty-two with a creamy dark brown complexion and warm brown eyes. Anthony often thought he had the most beautiful smile of any man he had ever met.

"He seems like a nice kid – guy," Anthony shrugged. "Petey, you probably know him about as well as I do. He told me you picked out his new wardrobe. Great job, by the way. His clothes were terrible, weren't they?"

"Oh, my god, the worst," Peter said with a wave of his hand.

He finished putting the final touches on his homemade lasagna and placed it in the oven.

"He's kind of messed up, though," Anthony added.

"I thought he seemed very sweet. He just needs to get out from under his parents' and the church's thumbs for a while. He needs to live life. You know, have some experiences, have some sex, get in trouble, that kind of thing. He has no idea what life is all about yet, but he's young. He'll learn."

"He's not that much younger than we are, sweetheart," Neil told his husband. "Someone said he's twenty-six or so."

"Yes, he's young and he's very sweet. He's extremely likeable," Anthony agreed. "Too likeable! God, he's so adorable. But he's so repressed, so entangled in the most conservative ideas imaginable. That's what he's been taught, and that's all he knows. He has no idea what the real world is like. So here he is, on his own for the first time, and he's still being controlled by the church."

"Well," Neil said thoughtfully. "The church isn't all bad. Some of them have evolved. I mean, look at Carl and Edna. They're two of the nicest people in the world and they believe wholeheartedly in Christianity, and yet they have absolutely no

problem with gay people. They even went with us
to Gay Pride last year in Chicago."
Peter and he laughed together at the memory.
"You should have seen them, Anthony," Peter
exclaimed. "They were wearing rainbow beads and
hats and feather boas! I think they had more fun
than we did. My dad danced with so many guys at
the bars that night, it was a scream! And when we
took them into the leather shop, oh my god…!"
He howled with laughter.
"There was a guy trying on a leather jockstrap right
out in the open, and Mom told him she thought he
looked divine, but that he should go a cup size
bigger!"
The three of them practically rolled on the floor,
laughing at the thought of Edna and Carl in a leather
store in Boystown.
"Well, maybe your parents can get him to chill out,"
Anthony said as their laughter died down at last.
"I've tried, but he just freaked out on me."
"You didn't show him your basement, did you?"
Neil said, wiping the tears from his eyes.
He and Peter started laughing riotously all over
again.
"No, I didn't," Anthony chuckled. "Besides, my
basement is pretty tame compared to some places
I've seen."
Peter nodded in agreement.
"That's true, but I think it's still a bit much for our
little Pollyanna, so don't talk about sex when he
gets here tonight."

"He's coming?" Anthony said with a frown.

"Yes, I invited him," Peter admitted. "Why?"

With a sigh, Anthony told them about his encounters with Jacob, including how they had gone to bed together and the young man had been overcome with guilt before running home.

"He's probably still wearing your underwear and dreaming about you every night," Neil teased.

"No, I know for a fact that he's wearing his new underwear," Peter told them nonchalantly.

"And just how the hell do you know that?" Neil asked him, frowning and pointing a large knife at Peter across the center island.

"I wish I could tell you, darling, but you'd just get jealous," Peter said sweetly. "Let's just say there's more that goes on in those dressing rooms than just changing clothes."

"Yeah, sure," Neil laughed. "In your dreams."

Peter leaned across the countertop and gave him a kiss and an adoring smile.

"Who else is coming?" Anthony asked.

"Well, Myra, of course, so she can insult us all," Neil said, counting off on his fingers. "It wouldn't be a party without her. Jacob, the underwear whore. And I invited Elaine, my new secretary. I could see her and Myra really hitting it off, if you get my drift."

"Mom and Dad, and Lucas and Randall," Peter added. "I think that's everyone."

CHAPTER EIGHT

They continued to talk and laugh as they finished up their party preparations. Before they knew it, seven o'clock had arrived. Peter and Neil ran up to their bedroom to dress, while Anthony walked through the large, airy rooms downstairs to make sure everything looked just right. He was passing through the large two-story entry hall when the doorbell rang. He called up the grand staircase to Peter before opening the heavy front door.

"Oh," Anthony said awkwardly. "Jacob, come on in."

He stepped aside to let the young man in, and then closed the door behind him.

"How are you?" he asked.

"Fine," came the terse reply.

Jacob looked all around him at the grand house, everywhere except at Anthony.

"Peter!" Anthony yelled up the stairs again. "Neil! You have a guest."

To Jacob he said, "Would you like something to drink?"

Jacob shook his head silently.

"Fine," Anthony said. He disappeared through a doorway at the back of the foyer, leaving Jacob standing alone, looking around awkwardly.

Peter hurried down the stairs a few minutes later, just as the doorbell rang again. He greeted Jacob with a hug and then welcomed Myra, who smiled happily when she saw Jacob standing off to the side.

"Jacob, I didn't know you'd be here," she said cheerfully. "Did you come with Anthony?"

"No," he said. "He's here, but we didn't come together."

She frowned at him, but said nothing more as Neil came downstairs. Carl and Edna arrived a moment later, and there was a flurry of hugs and kisses all around before Neil guided them all to the formal living room. Jacob looked around in awe at the elegant furnishings. There were thick Persian rugs, gold framed pictures and mirrors, and an assortment of traditional furniture interspersed with various Victorian pieces. A huge walnut secretary stood against the wall opposite the enormous, intricately carved fireplace. A shiny, long black piano set in front of the tall front windows. In spite of the large size of the room, it felt cozy and inviting.

Anthony acted as bartender, making sure everyone had a drink of their choice. Except for Jacob, of course, who politely refused when his hosts offered him a variety of alcoholic beverages.

"Oh, come on, Jacob," Edna said cheerfully, holding up her glass. "Have a drink. Try a Cosmo. It's my favorite."

He smiled shyly and shook his head.

"No, I think you're probably a martini man," Carl said, putting a fatherly arm around him.

"I'll just have some iced tea," Jacob said.

The last three guests had arrived, so Peter ushered everyone into the large dining room, where a long table that could accommodate more than a dozen chairs around it dominated the center of the room under an enormous crystal chandelier. All but ten chairs had been removed for tonight's gathering, and place cards sat on little brass easels in front of each lovely china and crystal place setting. Neil sat at the foot of the table, with Myra to his left and Elaine, a very quiet Asian woman, to his right. Peter sat at the head of the table, with Lucas on his left, and Randall on his right. Edna sat next to Jacob in the middle, with Carl and Anthony opposite them. Peter introduced Jacob to Elaine, Lucas, and Randall.

"This is our new friend, Jacob."

There were polite nods and smiles all around.

"Jacob is the new music director at Mom and Dad's church. I understand he's very talented. And he has exquisite taste in clothes. Don't you, Jacob?"

He smiled teasingly at him.

"Yes, I do," Jacob grinned bashfully. "Thanks to you and Carl and Edna."

"Well, Mary, you know what they say," Peter said, holding up his martini glass. "Sometimes it just takes a fairy."

They all laughed, and soon the conversation was flowing easily as the delicious food was being consumed and more drinks were served. Carl and Edna kept Jacob involved in the conversation, laughing and teasing with him all evening.

Somehow the conversation came around to the topic of coming out of the closet. Anthony told his heartwarming story of how he came out to his parents, and Lucas and Randall told their more painful tales of being disowned, and in Lucas's case, actually physically kicked out of the house as a teenager. Neil's parents had been very supportive of him and his younger brother who also happened to be gay. Myra's parents had passed away before she came out, and Elaine preferred not to talk about her experience.

"Well, our Peter didn't have any problem coming out to us," Edith said with an affectionate smile at her son. "He just told us, very matter of factly, that he was gay, and then proceeded to educate us on everything we needed to know. We accepted it immediately once we understood the facts."

"How could I be anything but gay?" Peter asked with a mischievous grin. "I mean, you named me Peter Johnson, for god's sake! Could you possibly have thought of a gayer name than that? I had no choice but to be gay! Peter? Johnson?"

Loud laughter filled the room until the guests had to wipe their eyes with their napkins. When it had died down, Lucas spoke up. He was an attractive dark haired man of about forty-five who strongly resembled George Clooney.

"What about you Jacob? You're the youngest person here, so what was your experience like?"

Jacob looked down at his plate uncomfortably.

"I, uh…I'm not out," he said quietly.

"That's okay, Jacob," Myra said in a very understanding voice. "You don't have to come out until you're ready."

"That's right, son," Carl added. "It's on your terms."

"He's right, but it's a very healthy thing to do," Anthony added, not looking at Jacob. "Living your life in the closet is not good for anyone."

"Well, then I guess I'm not as healthy as you," Jacob said in an annoyed tone, glaring at Anthony across the table.

"I'm just saying, it is damaging to our spirits when we try to live a lie," Anthony responded with a frown.

"I'm not Buddhist, Anthony," Jacob retorted. "I'm Christian, so I don't need your religion to teach me anything."

"Buddhism isn't a religion, Jacob, it's a philosophy!" Anthony said heatedly. "If you'd read that book I loaned you, you would know that."

Neil cleared his throat loudly while the others looked at Anthony and Jacob uneasily.

"Are we all ready for dessert?" he asked brightly. "Come on, Anthony, help me serve the cake."

"What was all that about?" Neil asked him as they ladled the slices of chocolate cake onto gold trimmed china plates.

"Nothing," Anthony sighed. "I'm sorry. I shouldn't have said anything. I just want him to think for himself, and to learn that there's a world outside of the church. But I guess he's too far gone. He's so deep in the closet, so repressed, that I don't know that he can ever find his way to a happy life."

"He's got to decide what's best for him by himself, Anthony," Neil reminded him gently. "No one can do that for him."

"I realize that," Anthony acknowledged. "But he *isn't* thinking for himself. That's the whole problem. He only knows what he's been taught and he accepts it all without question. I just want more for him than that. He'll never be able to lead a happy life as a gay man until he can be honest with himself."

"Do you have a thing for him?" Neil asked, licking a bit of chocolate frosting off of his finger. "I don't mean to pry, but it seems like you like him."

"I do like him," Anthony admitted. "Very much, in fact. But I'm not going to get involved with somebody who is that messed up. He's got too much emotional baggage to be in a relationship." He sighed and shrugged his broad shoulders. "It's too bad, too," he added. "Because he is really hot!"

The conversation around the dining table resumed its loud and enthusiastic manner as the guests enjoyed their dessert. As Peter and Neil cleared the table, the guests stepped through the French doors leading out to the patio and rectangular inground pool. Carl acted as bartender at the verdigris wrought iron and glass bar located near the far end of the pool. Myra and Elaine seemed to have found some common interest, and they took up seats in a secluded alcove near the back of the extensive gardens beyond the pool. Carl and Edna were having an animated conversation with their son-in-law, Lucas, and Randall, while Anthony stood moodily sipping his glass of Chardonnay, staring at the ripples moving across the crystal clear water. Jacob walked slowly along the paths intersecting the lush, colorful gardens, admiring the beauty of the plants and outdoor sculptures in the waning light of the warm summer evening. He kept his hands in his pockets as he strolled along.

Such lovely people, he thought. Peter and Neil seemed like a perfect couple, as though they were meant to be together. He frowned at that thought. They were two men, who shouldn't be a couple, according to all that he had been taught. And yet, as he observed them tonight at the table, he couldn't help but feel that they belonged to each other, just as much as Carl and Edna belonged together. And Lucas and Randall, though he had just met them, seemed like very nice, respectable men. He looked over at Myra and Elaine chatting happily together, and it suddenly dawned on him that these two women were gay as well. He had never met lesbians before, so the realization came as a big surprise to him. They seemed just like any other women he had met, although he didn't know anyone who cursed like Myra. This was all so new to him. He was surrounded by gay people, and none of them were the despicable monsters that had been described to him his whole life. They weren't to be feared, or scorned, or pitied, or hated. If God hated these people, then He was wrong. These were lovely, friendly, warm, caring people, and they had gone out of their way to make him feel so welcome tonight.

He sighed. Nothing was making sense to him. Something was wrong with the whole picture. It didn't appear to him that these people were evil sinners. Yet that's what Pastor Paul and the church thought they were. And the church reinforced that idea frequently, as if they were desperate for the world to believe them, and not the evidence right in front of their faces. These were good people; he could feel it in his innermost being. So if there was nothing wrong with these people, surely that meant that there was something wrong with the church. Teaching him that God hated these people, and therefore he should hate these people, and himself, simply couldn't be right, could it?

Why would God create gay people if he hated them and planned to send them to hell for the way they were born? Why would He bother to do such a thing? After listening to some of their stories tonight, he understood that they had had no more choice than he had as to whether they were gay or straight. It was just who they were, who he was. They weren't out to recruit anybody any more than he was. It was the way they had been born, so it made no sense that God could disapprove of them. He paused behind a tall evergreen shrub and looked around it until he could see Anthony standing beside the pool, looking down into the clear blue water. Dear God, he was so good looking! As he watched Anthony surreptitiously, he felt a friendly hand on his shoulder.

"Do you like our gardens?" Peter asked him, looking over at Anthony as well.

"Oh, they're really beautiful!" Jacob said sincerely. "Did you do all of this?"

"Well, Neil and I did it together. Once the patio and pool were in, we came up with the plan for all of this. We wanted it to feel like an old English garden."

They both looked around at the flowers, shrubs, and trees appreciatively.

"It's gorgeous, and so is your home," Jacob told him.

"We did most of that as well. Neil is an excellent carpenter, and I love to design and plan, so it was a match made in heaven."

"Do you really believe that?" Jacob asked him earnestly. "I mean, you two are so perfect together. But…"

His voice trailed off as he realized he didn't even know what he wanted to ask.

"Yes, absolutely," Peter said warmly. "I do believe we were meant to be together. There's no doubt in my mind. I love him with all of my heart. I mean, just look at how adorable he is."

The two of them looked over to see Carl put an affectionate arm around his son-in-law as their small group laughed together at something Neil had said.

"But don't you worry about going to hell?" Jacob asked him seriously.

"No, I don't," Peter told him, looking him straight in the eye. "Look, Jacob, I've been where you are. I understand the struggle you're going through. We all do. We were all raised to be good straight Christian boys and girls. But there comes a time when you have to decide if what most churches teach about being gay is right or wrong. I came to that point in my life a long time ago, when I finally knew there was nothing wrong with me, that I wasn't an evil sinner for loving another man. I knew that the church was absolutely dead wrong about people like me."

He took Jacob by the shoulders and looked directly at him.

"You have to make that decision for yourself. No one can do it for you, because everyone has his or her own spiritual path. What's right for me may be totally wrong for you, and vice versa. But do it soon, Jacob. Don't live your whole life in misery and fear. Find out what works for you spiritually and follow that path. Question everything, and don't take anything for granted. When you sit in that pew tomorrow, listening to that sermon, I want you to ask yourself if what he is saying feels right to you. Don't just accept it blindly, okay?"

Jacob nodded, looking over at Anthony.

"You know what, I think maybe Neil and I will come to church tomorrow for your first Sunday."

"Oh, that would be great, Peter," Jacob said enthusiastically. "Thank you!"

"Anthony is very handsome, isn't he?" Peter said, following his gaze. He placed an arm around Jacob's shoulders. "Get to know him, Jacob. I promise you, he will be worth your time."

That night, Jacob sat up in bed reading the book that Anthony had left for him until he finally fell asleep. In his dreams, he saw the Buddha and Anthony sitting together in Anthony's serenity garden. As he watched, a sudden gust of wind created a swirl of leaves and flowers around the two men. When it finally dissipated, the two men were gone. He ran to where they had been sitting moments before, frantically searching, looking up into the sky. 'Anthony! Anthony!' he cried over and over, 'Come back!' With a start, he awoke and looked around his bedroom, feeling a little sad, and suddenly very lonely.

Jacob sat down apprehensively at the beautiful black grand piano on the platform at Grace Community Church for his first Sunday service. Pastor Cal gave him a warm introduction to the congregation who applauded and smiled at him. Jacob looked out at the crowd and was pleased to see Carl and Edna along with Neil and Peter sitting in the third pew. They waved when they saw him looking at them, and he gave them a broad smile.

The Man Next Door

After the music portion of the service, Pastor Cal stepped up to the lectern and began his sermon. His topic was sin, not surprisingly, but he had a slant on it that Jacob had never heard before. Pastor Cal warned against the dangers of sin, as Jacob expected, but then he gave a definition to the word that surprised Jacob. He told the congregation that many of the times that the word sin was used in the Bible, it actually originally meant 'a missed opportunity'.

A missed opportunity to do the right thing, Jacob thought. But what exactly was the right thing? Obviously, stealing something was missing the opportunity to not steal. The same with telling a lie, or cheating, and so on. That sounded very much like what Anthony had been trying to tell him about doing things that were good for his soul, and avoiding the things that were bad. But how did it apply to him, he wondered, to his situation? Was he missing the opportunity to try to be straight? Is that the lesson he should learn here? He shook his head as he tried to understand.

Jacob stood beside Pastor Cal and his wife while the congregation filed past them as they exited the building. He smiled as dozens of smiling people introduced themselves to him, congratulated him on a service well done, and shook his hand. Peter and Neil hugged him tightly as they left, chatting and laughing like old friends. He hugged Carl and Edna, who showered him with praise for the wonderful music during the service.

When everyone had left, he walked back to his office to pick up his keys from his desk. As he turned around, he glanced up to see Pastor Cal looking at him from the office doorway with a serious expression.

"Yes, sir?" Jacob said guardedly.

"I see you know Peter Johnson," the pastor said abruptly.

"Yes, I met him when his parents took me to get some new clothes at Larson's. And I met Neil last night at dinner. They were very nice."

"I realize you're new here, Jacob," Pastor Cal said. "But there are certain places and people you may want to avoid in the future. Of course, you wouldn't know, but there is a…a bad element in town. Not just Green Grove, of course, but everywhere."

"A bad element?" Jacob said, becoming annoyed.

"Yes, you know what I mean."

"No, I'm afraid I don't."

"Peter is a homosexual," the pastor said quietly, looking over his shoulder to make sure they were alone.

"So, I guess that means that Neil is, too?" Jacob said wryly.

"Yes, they both are. I don't really approve of that whole interracial thing, either. They live together in that big house on Washington. I recommend that you stay away from them, and your neighbor as

well. That Miller boy. Anthony, I think his name
is."
"But, why? They seem like very nice people."
"That's just how they get you," Cal said eagerly.
"They pretend to be nice, ordinary people, and the
next thing you know, they're trying to convert you
to their perverted, evil way of life."
"I see," Jacob said gravely. "Well, thanks for
warning me. Excuse me, I'm having lunch with Carl
and Edna, and I think they're waiting for me."

Carl sat at the head of the table in the Johnson's
lovely red brick ranch house on the edge of town,
with Edna sitting to his left.
"That was a very nice service this morning," he
said. "I believe everyone was very impressed with
you, Jacob."
"You really are talented, Jacob," Peter agreed, as
Neil and Edna nodded.
"I don't know about that, but I do love music,"
Jacob said modestly. "And I love to play."
He looked at Peter and Neil with an odd expression
on his face.
"What?" Peter grinned at him.
"Oh, nothing," Jacob said shyly. "I'm just so glad
that I met all of you. Thank you again for all you've
done for me. You're all so wonderful."
"Yes, we are," Peter agreed with a grin. "I can't
deny it! And we think you are, too."
Jacob frowned at him suddenly and looked away.

"What's wrong, Jacob?" Edna asked in a concerned voice.

Reluctantly, he told them all what Pastor Cal had said to him after the service.

"That son of a bitch!" Neil exclaimed, throwing his napkin down on the table.

"Well, what did you expect?" Peter said. "Those people have told lies about us for so long that they believe them. They won't rest until they have the rest of the world against us, too!"

"It doesn't matter what they think, dear," Edna told her son soothingly. "You know that."

"I know, Mom," Peter said with a frown. "But that doesn't mean that I have to like it. And I guarantee you I will never set foot in that church, or any other church again."

"Well, Jacob, don't you listen to Pastor Cal, or anyone else who tries telling you that these boys are evil," Carl told him gravely. "You know better than that!"

"I know that," Jacob agreed with a nod. "But how can the whole church be wrong?"

"Oh, you'd be surprised," Edna said. "Just because everyone thinks something is true doesn't make it so, dear. Remember that."

Jacob looked through his kitchen window that evening trying to see over into Anthony's backyard. The wide garage door was up and there was a light in his garage, but Jacob didn't see Anthony anywhere. He stepped out onto the back porch, slamming the door loudly and looked around casually at his own backyard. Every few seconds, he would sneak a peek over into his neighbor's yard. He cleared his throat loudly, but there was still no sign of Anthony.

As he turned to go back into the house, Anthony stepped out of the garage.

"Hey," Jacob called out eagerly to him.

Anthony nodded at him with a frown but said nothing as he continued up the deck steps and into the house. Jacob stared after him for a few seconds, and then slowly walked back into his own house.

Anthony had made a decision after the party at Peter and Neil's house. He was well aware of his growing attraction to his new neighbor, but realized that any possibility of developing a relationship with him was hopeless. Until Jacob resolved his own issues it was useless to try. Even his attempt to help him find some spiritual peace had ended in disaster, with Jacob running back to his house like a scared rabbit. It was best if he gave the young man some space and kept his distance, he thought. So that's exactly what he planned to do. Perhaps if he were out of the picture, Jacob would sort things out on his own.

All of his studies into the philosophical world of Buddhism helped calm his mind. Everything would work out the way it was supposed to with Jacob. There was no need to worry about it, or anything else, for that matter. Usually, that was no problem for Anthony. Worrying really wasn't his style, with his easygoing manner and calm demeanor that he had inherited from his parents. Still, Jacob had already become important to him, for reasons he himself didn't fully understand. Obviously he was attracted to the handsome new neighbor, and he found that he liked him very much, too. Perhaps that's all it was, but he also felt a sort of connection with him that he couldn't explain.

CHAPTER NINE

Pastor Cal handed Jacob a stack of homemade paperback booklets the next morning.

"Here are your new lesson books," he told him. "You'll be teaching the adult singles Sunday School class starting next Sunday. You can use your office for a classroom."

Jacob looked down at the name on the front of the booklet on top of the stack. 'Waiting for Marriage: The Grace Community Church Guide to Being Single'.

"Are you serious?" Jacob gaped at him. "I'm not married! I'm one of the adult singles."

"Exactly, so you know how they feel," Pastor Cal said, patting him heartily on the back.

Jacob watched him walk away with a dumbfounded look on his face. With a sigh he sat down at his desk and leafed through one of the folders. You've got to be kidding me, he thought. I am exactly the wrong person to teach straight people this stuff about marriage. It's almost comical, he thought with a wry smile.

He spent the rest of the morning preparing a lesson plan for his new class. After reading through the whole book, he decided it was pretty much all about abstaining from sex until God gave His okay, ostensibly with a marriage license issued by the state of Illinois.

At lunchtime he parked on the street in front of his house and hurried up the front porch steps. Anthony walked through his front lawn at that moment toward his own front door. Jacob waved to him, and Anthony nodded grimly at him but kept walking. With a sigh, Jacob turned the key in the lock and stepped into his living room. He ate a sandwich at the kitchen sink, and then took his bottle of soda into the dining room and sat down at the Clavinova. Just as he began to play, a knock came at the front door. Suddenly feeling hopeful, he hurried into the living room and pulled the door open.

"Hi, Jacob," Lance said with a small smile. "I hope I'm not bothering you."

"No, not at all," Jacob said warmly.

He was pleased to see him, but couldn't help feeling a little disappointed that it wasn't Anthony knocking on his door.

"Please, come in."

Lance stepped into the house and looked around in surprise.

"Wow, you've done some redecorating since I was here last," he said. "This looks really nice."

"Thanks," Jacob said, pleased. "Myra at the resale shop and my neighbor helped. In fact, they pretty much did it all, so I can't take any credit for it. But it does look nice, doesn't it?"

"Yes, it really does," Lance agreed. "Very inviting."

"I talked to your...Linda, and she said you are quite the singer," Jacob told him as they sat down on the comfortable sofa. Wow, he is so good looking, he thought.

"I know, she told me she talked to you," Lance said sheepishly. "I'm actually kind of embarrassed that she did."

"Was she right?"

"Yes, I do love to sing," Lance nodded. "But I have no idea if I'm any good or not. I've never sung in public."

"Well, come on, let's hear you," Jacob said, leading him into the dining room. He sat down at the Clavinova. "I've got tons of sheet music. Look through this stack and pick out something."

Lance glanced through the assortment of songs and pulled one out that was familiar to him.

"What about this?" he asked, handing the music to Jacob.

"'Music of the Night'?" Jacob said, a little surprised.

"I'm a huge Broadway fan," Lance grinned.

"Me, too," Jacob said. "I love this song. Let's give it a try."

He arranged the sheets of music carefully in front of him and began to play. Hesitantly at first, Lance began to sing the beautiful song in a rich baritone voice. After several bars, Jacob stopped playing and looked around at him with an awed expression on his face.

"Wow, Lance, you have a beautiful voice. I mean, really beautiful! I can't believe you've never sung in public before."

Lance grinned shyly.

"Really? You're not just saying that?"

"No, not at all; you are really good. Let's go all the way through the song."

Jacob turned back to the music and began again. Lance's rich voice filled the room once more. When they finished, Jacob looked up at him and held up his arm.

"Look, goose bumps," he said with awe. "That's how good you are, Lance."

Lance rubbed Jacob's arm with his hand, causing the hairs on the back of Jacob's neck to stand up.

"You really think I'm that good?" he said quietly.

Jacob looked up at him silently. After a moment he stood up and took Lance's hand in his. Lance looked down at their joined hands in surprise.

"I really do, Lance."

They looked at each other for several seconds.

"Can we…can we go to your bedroom, Jacob?" Lance asked in a husky voice. "I really need to be with you."

Jacob nodded slightly, and then Lance led him into the next room. He removed his coat and tie, and then kissed Jacob lightly while the younger man unbuckled his belt and kicked his shoes off. After he had removed his clothes, Lance pulled back the blankets on the bed and took Jacob's trembling hand. Seconds later they were kissing and pressing their bodies together, with Lance laying all of his weight on his quivering partner.

"Relax, Jacob," he said soothingly. "Just relax and enjoy this."

Jacob nodded quickly a few times and swallowed hard. What am I doing, he asked himself? I'm about to have sex with a man, and a married man, at that! Guilt and shame started to build instantly in his mind until he was almost overwhelmed, but he abruptly pushed them away. To hell with it! I'm going to enjoy this. I don't care what the consequences are, and I don't care if I do go to hell for this! I want this; I need this. I've needed this for years, to be with another man. The church be damned!

For the next hour, Lance and Jacob kissed passionately, breaking apart only when Lance took him in his mouth, and then when Jacob awkwardly repeated the act on Lance. Jacob's senses were shocked to the point of overload when Lance's mouth engulfed him, and in spite of his best efforts, he found himself climaxing quickly. Lance held him in his mouth firmly until his spasms gradually subsided. Finally he released him. He rose up and smiled down at Jacob, before leaning down and kissing him again.

Jacob worked hard to keep his regret at bay, determined not to repeat that embarrassing scene between him and Anthony. Oh, Anthony, he thought sadly. How I wish I could go back and change how I reacted to you that night, and tell you how much I want to be with you. He pushed all distracting thoughts away and focused on Lance. He reached between them and took him in his hand, reveling in the feeling of the manly flesh he was holding. Within a few moments, Lance's body convulsed and he buried his face in Jacob's neck as he erupted onto the young man's body. He collapsed at last onto Jacob, panting heavily.

"Oh, my god, Jacob," he said when he could speak. "Thank you!"

Jacob held him tightly, with tears in his eyes.

"No, it's me who should thank you, Lance," he said softly. "You're the first man I've ever really been with."

In spite of himself his mind turned ruefully once again to the night he had run away from Anthony after their brief tryst in Anthony's bed. Technically, that had been his first time, but he had left there feeling only intense guilt and shame. This time, he refused to allow those emotions to dominate him. Instead, he decided to experience the positive emotions that he normally kept pushed down, like enjoyment, contentment, happiness, and pleasure. Pleasure, he thought. What was there in his life that actually brought him pleasure? His music, of course, that was a given. But what else? His family? The church? No. His family and his church brought him a certain sense of security and continuity, but he couldn't honestly say they brought him pleasure. The only pleasure he could remember feeling, other than his music, was when he had recently spent time with his new friends, most of which were gay. And while Carl and Edna were not gay, they were definitely gay-adjacent! And of course, riding the motorcycle with Anthony had been a very pleasurable and exciting experience for him as well. So as he lay in his bed with Lance, he allowed himself to feel content and even a little pleased with himself. He had finally, after twenty-six long years, been with a man, and it was wonderful!

"Oh, my god, you're kidding, right?" Lance exclaimed incredulously.

"Well, there was this sort of other time, but it didn't go very far," Jacob told him evasively. He was too embarrassed to tell him the truth.

"I hope you enjoyed it," Lance said softly.

"It was wonderful, Lance," he said honestly. "I think it was probably the most wonderful thing I've ever experienced."

"You are such a beautiful man, Jacob," Lance told him, kissing his chest.

"No, I'm not," Jacob blushed. "But you are."

He shifted to look down at Lance.

"So, we need to talk about your singing. You have one of the most beautiful voices I've ever heard."

It was Lance's turn to blush.

"I'm serious," Jacob continued. "You have to do something with it. Let's at least have you sing a solo in church."

"Oh, I don't know," Lance said uncertainly. "I don't think I have the confidence to sing in front of anybody except you."

"Come on, I have an arrangement of 'Abide with Me' that is absolutely gorgeous, and you have the perfect voice for it. It will be great for your first solo, because it isn't too challenging, and yet it's still really beautiful."

He hopped out of bed and picked his underwear up off the floor. He looked at Lance's frowning face with a grin.

"Come on!"

Jacob and Lance practiced every day that week during their lunches. Some days, much of their time was spent in bed together enjoying each other's bodies, while other times they concentrated more strictly on the music. As before, Jacob's inherent guilt and remorse threatened to overwhelm him each time they were together, but he suppressed them as best he could. He was more than impressed with Lance's natural musical talent, and knew enough about vocal technique to offer him a few tips to improve his performance. On Friday, they met at the church so that Lance could sing in front of a microphone in the large auditorium. His anxiety began to subside as Jacob continued to pour praise upon him. Carl and Edna were passing through the empty building, looking for Jacob, when they heard the glorious voice coming from the sanctuary. When they realized who was singing, they hurried up to him and congratulated him on his impressive talent.

"Why, I had no idea you could sing, Lance," Edna exclaimed delightedly. "That was absolutely beautiful!"

"Very nice, Lance," Carl added, shaking his hand.
"You've got to join the choir. We need you!"
It was as if a light had come on in a darkened room
as Lance's face radiated a happiness that Jacob had
not noticed before.
This is one of those things that Anthony was talking
about, he realized with a start. Singing was feeding
Lance's soul. He suddenly understood a little of
what Anthony had tried to tell him, and what he had
read in the book he had loaned him. Lance's life
was fairly unpleasant, what with all the pressure he
was under from his family, hiding who he really
was, and living a lie in a false marriage. Those
things were all hurting him, damaging his soul. But
singing was bringing him joy and happiness.
Singing was good for his soul, and Jacob was
pleased to be part of something that was truly
helpful to someone else for the first time in his life.
It made him feel good about himself.
He smiled at the Johnson's as they continued to
heap praises on Lance. They were such dear people.
Leave it to them to make Lance feel good about
himself.
"What are you two doing here?" Jacob asked them
when they finally paused to take a breath.
"Well, we came to talk to Pastor Cal," Carl began.
"And we set him straight on a few things," Edna
added.
She laughed gaily.
"Maybe straight isn't the right word," she said,
lightly nudging her husband's shoulder.

He began laughing with her, and soon all four of them were laughing together, although Lance's expression indicated he didn't quite understand what they were laughing at.

"Anyway, we brought him all kinds of information, just like Peter did with us years ago. Did you know that you can find just about anything on those Internets?" Edna told them. "I was amazed, but Neil showed us how to, what's the word, dear? Googly? Ask Googly?"

"It's Google, Edna," Carl told her with a hearty laugh. "Not Googly!"

"Well, whatever it is, we took it all to Pastor Cal. And while we were here, we wanted to ask you to lunch."

"You come, too, Lance," Carl added quickly.

"Thanks, I'd love to," Jacob said eagerly. "Come on, Lance."

"No, I really should get back to the office," Lance protested.

"Oh, to hell with the office," Carl said cheerfully. "I should be at the office, too, but it's such a beautiful day, I'm playing hooky."

"You know, Carl," Jacob said with a frown. "I don't even know what you do for a living."

"Oh, he's president of the bank, dear," Edna told him. "But he does it just for fun, and because they won't let him retire. They need him too much. He's kept it running smoothly for years."

"You remember Lucas?" Carl said. "You met him the other night at Peter and Neil's."

"Yes, I remember him," Jacob nodded. "He and Randall came together."

"Oh, they're not a couple," Edna told him. "They're both single."

She looked at Lance appraisingly.

"Well, anyway, Lucas is my vice-president. He actually does most of the work, while I take home the big paycheck," Carl laughed loudly at his little joke.

"You probably know Lucas, Lance," Edna said. "Since you're in investments, I'm sure you've had dealings with him."

"I know of him," Lance nodded. "But we've never actually met in person."

"Oh, he's such a nice young man," Edna told him, taking his hand and patting it lightly. "You really should get to know him better, dear."

"I'll be sure to do that," Lance said somewhat awkwardly.

She pulled Lance along with her and Carl put a hand on Jacob's shoulder as they ushered the two men out to their BMW.

"What are you two hungry for?" Carl asked them.

"I could eat a hamburger," Jacob suggested and Lance nodded in agreement.

Carl and Edna looked at each other, and then said simultaneously, "The bowling alley!"

"They have the best hamburgers in town, my darlings!" Edna said with a happy smile.

Lunch at the bowling alley was delicious, and the four of them laughed and chatted gaily. Most of the conversation focused on Lance's newly discovered talent. Jacob told them about him singing 'Music of the Night' for him and how it had given him goose bumps.

"I can imagine," Edna said, looking back and forth between them thoughtfully. "You two have become good friends, haven't you?"

"Yes, Jacob has been a godsend for me," Lance stated with a smile.

"That's nice, dear," Edna said with a slightly worried look on her face.

They all looked up as a tall, attractive man stepped up to their table.

"Lucas, what a nice surprise," Carl exclaimed, standing and pulling out a chair for him. "Please join us."

"You told me to come, Carl," Lucas said as he sat down, clearly confused.

"Oh, yes, of course I did," Carl said easily. "I'm just glad you're here. You've met Jacob already, but do you know Lance Martin?"

"We've talked on the phone a few times," Lucas nodded. He reached out and shook Lance's hand firmly. "Nice to finally meet you in person, Lance."

"Same here," Lance replied.

Lucas was looking quite dapper in his expensive gray suit that complimented his perfectly groomed, slightly salt and pepper hair. The two men eyed each other somewhat shyly.

"Lucas lives a few doors down from us," Edna told
them. "It's such a beautiful home, and he has it
decorated so nicely. You'll have to see it sometime,
Lance."
"I'd like that," Lance said, a little shyly.
Lucas smiled at him, and then looked quickly away.
His eyes met Jacob's, and he was surprised to see a
small frown on his face.

Sunday morning, a small group of teenagers and
young twenty-something's met in Jacob's office for
their 'Waiting for Marriage' class. He greeted them
all warmly, and after introductions were made, he
instructed them to open their books. The thirty
minutes passed quickly, and Jacob was surprised at
the enthusiasm his students had for the subject
matter. He felt inadequate to answer some of their
questions, but he had to admit he enjoyed their time
together. Afterwards, an athletic looking young man
of about seventeen held back as the others left the
room.
"I really enjoyed the class, Mr. Porter," he said
shyly.
"Please, I'm not old enough to be a 'Mr.'. Call me
Jacob," he smiled warmly at the teenager. "I'm glad
you liked it. I don't feel very qualified to teach
anyone about marriage, but I guess I'll learn right
along with all of you."
"I don't think I'll ever get married," the teen said
wistfully.

"Oh, you might," Jacob said. "You're so young, you have no idea what the future holds."

"I already know I won't," the young man said.

Jacob looked at him thoughtfully.

"What's your name again?"

"Brandon."

"Well, Brandon, don't make up your mind about your life right now," Jacob advised. "You never know."

"You seem to have it all figured out," Brandon said.

"Oh, you've got to be kidding!" Jacob exclaimed with a derisive snort. "I don't have anything figured out. I'm probably the last person to give anyone advice on being an adult."

"I don't have anything figured out, either," Brandon admitted.

"Well, if you ever need to talk, let me know," Jacob said kindly. "Maybe between the two of us, we can figure it out together."

CHAPTER TEN

Lance stood nervously in front of the congregation as Jacob began the introduction to 'Abide with Me'. His voice shook ever so slightly as he began to sing, but it became stronger and more self-assured as he continued through the beautiful old hymn. Jacob gave him an encouraging smile from where he sat at the piano. Normally after a solo, the congregation rewarded the performer with a solemn 'Amen', but when Lance finished singing, the audience broke out into spontaneous applause. He looked over at Jacob in surprise, and Jacob gave him a smile and the thumbs up sign.

After the service, Jacob stood at the door as expected, greeting the congregation as they departed. He stopped by his office and then slipped quietly out the back door of the church. He went home, changed his clothes and heated up a microwave dinner. He watched for any signs of life over at Anthony's house, but it appeared deserted. Soon he was back in his car. For some reason, he felt a need to get out of town, away from everything and everybody. It was a beautifully warm sunny day with a gentle breeze blowing from the northwest. He headed west until he came to another highway. He turned north and just drove, enjoying the green fields of corn and soybeans that lay on either side of him. Eventually he came to the town of Dixon. Just past the downtown, the highway turned to the northeast and he followed it as it mirrored first the eastern, then the western shore of the Rock River. The scenery became less open fields and more wooded as he drove. As he came around a sharp bend, he noticed a sign that said 'Castle Rock State Park'. He braked sharply and turned into the paved drive.

He got out of the car after parking in the small deserted parking lot and walked over to where the ground sloped gently downward. The wide, gently moving river lay immediately before him, curving its leisurely way from the northeast to the south. This is so beautiful, he thought delightedly! I wonder if people know this is here. As he looked around he spied a sign with an arrow pointing to an opening in the woods. Curiously he walked over and began to climb the long wooden path as it wound upward through the trees. He continued to climb until at last he emerged from the tops of the trees onto an enormous outcropping of sandstone with a number of large wooden platforms built on top of it. He walked on until he was standing on the highest platform, where he stopped and leaned against the wooden and metal railing, looking around in awe and delight. The whole Rock River valley lay before him. There were canoes and speedboats moving up and down the broad shining river far below him. He waved wildly and was pleased when a boater looked up and waved back cheerfully. All around the river as far as he could see were woods. He turned his back and leaned against the railing as he closed his eyes and took a deep breath of the fresh, sweet smelling air. It was all so beautiful here, he thought contentedly. In the distance he could hear an engine slow and eventually come to a stop. He tried to look down through the trees to the parking area below, but couldn't see anything through the dense foliage. After looking around for several more minutes, he slowly descended the wooden path through the trees to the parking lot. A shiny, black Harley Davidson motorcycle sat near the river on the far side of the paved lot, alongside a similar size ivory colored Honda Goldwing. Beyond them to the south, Jacob noticed another narrow wooden path partially hidden in the trees. Curiously he walked to the water's edge and looked to his right. He didn't see anyone, so he walked hesitantly along the path as it rose gradually through the woods. Several yards along the way he observed a small outcropping of stone, bordered by a low stone wall overlooking the water. Two men dressed in black leather were standing side by side looking out at the water. As he watched they turned and came down the narrow path toward him, laughing cheerfully. As they neared him, he gave a start as he recognized Anthony, who noticed him at the same time. Immediately the smile left his face and he held out an arm in front of his companion.

"Jacob, what the hell are you doing here?" he asked with a frown.

"Nothing, I...I just found this place by accident," Jacob said with a bit of nervousness in his voice.

"Oh," Anthony replied tersely. "Well, I'll see ya." He moved to step around Jacob, but the other man stopped him.

"Hi," he said in a friendly voice. "I'm Keith." He reached out his right hand toward Jacob, who grasped it briefly.

"I'm Jacob."

He looked this stranger up and down with a frown. Tall, dark hair, handsome, athletic, young, with a beautiful smile. An irresistible smile, dammit!

"Oh, right, the next door neighbor. I've heard all about you. You work in a church. You're a music director or something."

"Right," Jacob said briefly, looking over at Anthony furtively.

"Well, it was nice to meet you," Keith said with a smile.

He and Anthony continued walking back to the parking lot, and in a moment burst out into loud laughter. Jacob's face and ears suddenly felt hot, and he knew he had turned bright red. He could only imagine what Anthony had said about him to make them laugh so heartily. He probably told him about him tossing his underwear into the backyard, or how he had run tearfully home that night. Oh, my god, he thought, they're really having a good laugh at my expense. I must look like a complete idiot to them! And just look at Keith, so tall and handsome. How could he hope to compete with someone like that? Not that Anthony would ever be seriously interested in him anyway.

He watched them stroll away with Anthony's arm around the younger man's neck. Sadly he walked on to the outcropping of rock and sat on the low stone wall. Tears fell from his eyes as he remembered lying in bed with Anthony, when that beautiful man had tried to make love to him. Was it his fault that he was so confused and torn, that he had so many hang-ups? Sure, he had been with Lance since then and had managed to reconcile the guilt that still threatened to overwhelm him at times, but that first night with Anthony had come when he was totally unprepared to deal with it.

He also remembered some of the Buddhist teachings he had read in Anthony's book. They actually had been helpful, and had brought him some much-needed comfort during the last week. They made a lot of sense to him, and he appreciated the way they taught valuable lessons without any judgment or condemnation. He actually had begun to feel rather good about himself as he read and reread various passages, or at least not as guilty.

He knew he looked like a fool to Anthony and Keith, and that they had probably laughed over the image of him running home that night. He dropped his head into his hands and let the tears flow for a while. But finally, he wiped his eyes with his sleeve and walked back to his car. The two motorcycles were still parked side by side. He looked around but didn't see Anthony or Keith. With a sad sigh, he got in his car and headed home.

Late that night he lay in his bed, rereading the Buddhist book from Anthony. Many of the passages were soothing to him, and he felt a little better when he put it down. After he had turned out the light, he felt hot as he tossed and turned. He checked the thermostat in the dining room, and with a restless sigh stepped out onto his small back porch. The night air was cool, but humid. It felt better to him than the house, so he sat down on the back steps and looked around at the dimly lit backyard.

Laughter carried through the night air, and Jacob looked around curiously. He walked over through his gate onto the driveway and saw Anthony and Keith sitting in the hot tub on Anthony's deck, talking and laughing together. He watched them for a moment, and then turned away. Slowly he walked back to his own yard and closed the gate behind him.

He lay in his bed, still feeling hot and a little queasy. Why was it so hot in here? The air conditioning was on, but the house still felt stifling to him. He closed his eyes and tried to forget about how he felt. It shouldn't matter to him who Anthony dated because he barely knew the man. He certainly didn't have a future with him, so why did he care so much that Anthony thought he was a neurotic fool? Why did he care about Anthony at all? He could never have a relationship with someone like Anthony anyway.

After an hour of trying not to think about Anthony he drifted off into a restive sleep. He awoke before dawn, feeling a little cooler, but still nauseated, with a dull ache in his lower abdomen.

With a weary sigh he crawled out of bed and turned on the shower. He leaned against the shower wall for a few minutes, holding his right side.

Summoning his strength, he finished his shower and dressed for work. He opened the refrigerator door, but closed it quickly as the sight of food made him feel even queasier than before. He lay down on the couch and closed his eyes.

A noise outside woke him an hour later. He looked at his watch and quickly gathered his things together and headed out the back door. As he reached his gate, a wave of nausea hit him and the pain in his lower abdomen suddenly sharpened. He held on to the gate as he doubled over in pain and he broke out into a sweat. He took a few deep breaths and carefully straightened up to see Anthony hugging Keith as he sat on his motorcycle. Keith started the big machine and put his helmet on. With a wave, he glided down the driveway and onto the street.

Jacob pretended not to see Anthony as he tottered weakly to his car.

"Hey, what's wrong?" Anthony called to him.

"Nothing's wrong," Jacob answered, trying to hurry and open the car door. "I'm fine."

"The hell you are!" Anthony exclaimed, moving over to hold the car door closed. "You're sick, Jacob."

He placed a cool hand on Jacob's warm forehead as Jacob leaned against the car.

"You've got a fever. What else?" Anthony asked sternly.

"I...I have a pain," Jacob mumbled, holding his right side.

"When did it start?" Anthony asked him, his voice sounding concerned.

"During the night, I guess," Jacob said as he winced with pain.

"Come on, I'm taking you to the hospital."

Jacob felt too sick to argue with him as Anthony guided him into his garage and opened the front passenger door of his big truck. He doubled over once again and cried out with pain. Anthony picked him up carefully and set him in the front seat.

"I'll be right back, Jacob."

He ran into the house, grabbed his wallet, phone, and keys and hurried back to the truck. He drove them quickly to the hospital, calling Peter on the way from the truck speakerphone. Once there, he helped Jacob to the ER, pausing long enough to tell Barbara in registration to open the electronic doors for them since he had both arms around the young man. She looked alarmed as she immediately pushed a button on her desk.

Eric, a big, burly ER nurse, helped Anthony quickly get Jacob onto a gurney in a private exam room. They helped him out of his shirt and tie and into a hospital gown before more ER personnel arrived to start an IV of Lactated Ringer's solution, draw blood, and obtain vital signs. Eric kindly asked both of them about Jacob's symptoms, typing all of their answers into his bedside computer. When he had finished, Barbara approached him and had him sign several papers. A few minutes later, the ER physician entered the room and shook Jacob's hand. "Jacob, I'm Dr. Mac," he introduced himself. His real name was MacHenry, but he was known by most of the community as Dr. Mac.

"What seems to be the problem today?" he asked in a concerned voice as he released Jacob's hand and looked up at Anthony. "You're running a slight fever, I see."

Jacob winced again, drawing his knees up in pain. Anthony quickly filled Dr. Mac in on the events of the morning that had led them to the hospital. Dr. Mac nodded.

"We're going to do a few tests, Jacob, to find out exactly what is going on, okay?" he said in a gentle voice. "Do you have any family here?"

"No," Jacob said, shaking his head. "Just Anthony." He avoided looking at Anthony as he spoke.

"Okay, just relax a bit. We'll get you a little something for the pain. When was the last time you had something to eat or drink, Jacob?" Dr. Mac asked.

"Yesterday evening," Jacob said as he tried in vain to look composed and unconcerned.

Dr. Mac nodded and patted him on the arm before leaving the room.

"Am I going to be okay, Anthony?" he asked, his voice trembling slightly.

"Of course you are," Anthony quickly reassured him. "You'll be fine."

Jacob reached out for his hand and Anthony grasped it firmly.

"I'm a little scared," Jacob admitted, squeezing his hand tightly. "I've never been in a hospital before."

"It will all be fine, Jacob," Anthony told him confidently.

"Will you stay with me?"

"Absolutely, I'll be right here," Anthony said gently. "Don't worry about that."

Jacob nodded and smiled weakly with relief. He laid his head back on the pillow.

"Is it my appendix?" he asked.

"We'll have to wait for Dr. Mac, but I'd say it's very possible."

Jacob nodded again as Eric returned holding a needleless syringe.

"I've got a little pain medication for you, Jacob," he said in his kind voice. "It might make you a little sleepy."

He screwed the syringe onto a little blue port on the IV tubing and pushed the plunger slowly all the way in until the medication had been dispensed. Within ten minutes, Jacob was feeling a little better, but he refused to let go of Anthony's hand. He simply laid there on the comfortably padded cart, staring up at Anthony. He couldn't seem to look away from this beautiful man. For several long seconds, they looked deeply into each other's eyes, and Jacob felt a warmth growing in his chest, as though someone had wrapped him in a warm blanket. He realized it was probably just the medication affecting him, but the sensation was very real to him. Anthony smiled tenderly as he stared back at him.

"Anthony…" Jacob began, just as the radiology technician came into the room to take him to CT.

"Mr. Porter, I'm Karen, and I'm going to wheel you over to radiology," she told him with a friendly smile.

"Okay. Can Anthony come, too?" he asked nervously.

"Absolutely, if that's what you want," she said. Anthony knew almost everyone in every department of the facility, an advantage of working in a small community hospital. Karen winked at him as he helped her wheel Jacob's gurney through the service hallway to radiology. When the test was complete, they pushed him back to the ER room. Eric came to the door and signaled to Anthony.

"I'll be right back, Jacob," he said.

"There are some people out in the lobby who want to say a quick hello to Jacob," he whispered in the hall outside of the room. "Do you want to go talk to them?"

Anthony nodded and, using his ID badge, opened the electronic doors that opened into the ER waiting room. Carl, Edna, and Peter stood up anxiously as he approached them.

"Is he okay?" Edna asked with motherly concern.

"He's fine."

"What's wrong with him?" Peter asked with a frown.

Anthony considered the legal aspects of talking about a patient, especially since he was an employee of the hospital. But Jacob had told them that he was family, so he decided it was okay to tell what little he knew so far.

"He's got a fever, nausea, and right-sided abdominal pain."

"Appendicitis?" Carl asked in a knowing voice.

"That would be my guess," Anthony agreed. "But they're waiting on test results before they'll know for sure. He's had some medication to help with the pain, and he's resting. He asked me to stay with him, so I'd better get back."

"Tell him we love him," Edna said with a tearful look in her eyes. "I hate to think of him all alone. I'm so glad you're here. Promise me you'll stay with him, Anthony, dear."

"And we'll let Pastor Cal know what's going on," Carl added with a grim smile.

Anthony nodded and gave each of them a hug before returning to Jacob's room. He gave him Edna's message, and Jacob smiled sleepily.

Anthony sat down beside him on the edge of the gurney as Jacob reached for his hand again.

"Thank you, Anthony," Jacob said softly as he closed his eyes.

"I haven't done anything, Jacob," Anthony chuckled.

"You know what?" Jacob said opening his eyes enough to look directly at Anthony. "Call me Jake. I want you to call me Jake."

"Why?"

"Because I like you, Anthony," he said sadly, suddenly becoming tearful. "I really, really like you."

"Hey, now, don't cry," Anthony said gently. "I really, really like you, too, Jake."

"I'm glad," Jacob whispered just before he drifted off to sleep.

Eric came in and checked on them every ten minutes or so, smiling warmly at the sight of Anthony holding Jacob's hand while the ailing man slept. Dr. Mac came into the room just as Jacob was stirring.

"Jacob, how are you feeling?" he asked.

"I'm okay," Jacob said in a tired voice. "Do you know what's wrong?"

"It is your appendix, as we suspected. I'd like you to see Dr. Lee, our head surgeon. He's already seen your information and he'll be here in just a bit. Until then, we're going to get you settled into a more comfortable bed. How would that be?"

"That's okay, I guess," Jacob nodded apprehensively, gripping Anthony's hand a little tighter. "As long as Anthony can stay with me."

"Of course he can. You'll be in room 209. Eric will get you settled in just a few minutes."

Dr. Mac smiled warmly at him and left the room.

"Let me go let everyone know what's going on, if that's okay with you," Anthony suggested. "I'll see you in your room in a minute, okay?"

CHAPTER ELEVEN

Dr. Lee met Jacob in room 209 about thirty minutes later. Carl, Edna, Peter, Pastor Cal and Anthony were all there, surrounding the bed where Jacob was sitting up, trying his best not to look worried.

"Looks like we've got a party going on!" Dr. Lee said with a cheerful smile, shaking Jacob's hand. After all the introductions were made, he explained that Jacob's appendix did indeed need to come out, and that the plan was to operate around one o'clock that afternoon. Jacob swallowed nervously as he reached unself-consciously for Anthony's hand, unaware of the frown on Pastor Cal's face.

"After the surgery, you'll go to the recovery room for a while, and then back here. You should be able to go home in the morning."

Jacob nodded with a worried look on his face.

"And we'll all be right here the whole time," Edna said cheerfully, sensing Jacob's apprehension.

"Do you have any questions, Jacob?" Dr. Lee asked.

"No, I…I can't think of any right now," Jacob said.

"Well, you've got Anthony here in case you do think of any," Dr. Lee said with a smile. "I'm sure he could answer any questions you might have. But have him call me if you want to talk to me. Otherwise, I'll be seeing you in a couple of hours, young man."

Dr. Lee shook his hand and left the room.

"I think we should have a word of prayer," Pastor Cal said solemnly.

He moved up and squeezed between Anthony and Jacob, forcing them to release their handhold. He took Jacob's hand, closed his eyes, and began to pray, asking God to bring Jacob through this delicate operation safely and for a full recovery. Jacob, Carl, and Edna joined him when he finished with an 'amen'.

"I've got some things to do at the church," he said. "But I'll be back before you go into surgery."

Jacob nodded and smiled.

"Thank you, Pastor."

With a frown at Peter and Anthony, Pastor Cal left the room, followed by Carl and Edna.

Peter looked down at him with a smile.

"I'll stay, if you want me to, Jacob," he said kindly.

"I do, but you probably have to be at work, don't you?"

"Yes, but I can stay if you want."

"I'll stay with him, Petey, if you need to work," Anthony told him.

"Okay, I'll go to work, but I'll be here when you wake up, Jacob," Peter said, taking his hand and giving it a gentle squeeze. "Don't worry about a thing, Jacob; there's nothing to these operations these days, and Dr. Lee is very good, so you'll be just fine."

Jacob nodded and gave him a weak smile.

"Peter?" he began.

"Yes, Jacob?"

"What do you believe about heaven and hell?"
Peter looked up at Anthony for a moment and then turned back to Jacob.
"Well, I don't believe in hell, but I hope that there is a heaven. I like to think that we'll all be together again there."
"What about Neil?"
"Neil is a devout atheist," Peter told him. "Why?"
"I just wondered," Jacob said. "It doesn't matter." He sighed wearily.
"Did you know that there are over four thousand religions in the world?"
"No, I didn't," Peter shook his head. "What made you ask that?"
Peter looked at him with a frown until Jacob smiled up at him.
"Just that we all have our own paths to walk, don't we?" Jacob said.
"You've been listening to Anthony, haven't you?" Peter chuckled.
Jacob nodded and laid his head back on the pillow.
"And you, too. Thank you for coming, Peter," he said sincerely. "I really appreciate it."
Peter smiled and, bending down, gave him a friendly kiss on the forehead.
"I'll see you in a little while, my friend."
He turned and with a final wave, was gone. Jacob sighed and laid his head back on the pillow.
"You're all so wonderful," he said with a wistful look in his eye.

He thought back to the prayer that Pastor Cal had given.

"Did that prayer make you uncomfortable?" he asked Anthony curiously.

"What?" Anthony said, surprised. "No, of course not."

"I just wondered, since you don't believe in God."

"Jacob, I do believe in a Higher Power, I just don't call it 'God'. And I think prayer is a good thing. It sends positive energy out into the universe," Anthony told him with a small frown.

Jacob looked at him thoughtfully.

"I read that book you loaned me," he said. "Twice."

"Really?" Anthony said, sitting down in a chair beside the bed. "I'm surprised. I mean, I didn't think you'd approve of it."

"It was very interesting," Jacob admitted. "I liked the things it said. I always thought Buddhists worshiped Buddha as a god, but you were right. He was just a man, and he didn't pretend to be anything else. I don't really understand the whole 'nirvana' thing, but the rest of it made a lot of sense to me."

"I don't understand it all, either," Anthony said with a grin. "But for me, it's a wonderful philosophy that makes more sense than anything else I've ever been taught. And that's the secret, Jacob – I mean Jake – finding what makes sense to you, whether it's a religion or a philosophy, or whatever. There is no right or wrong to any of it, because, like you said, we all have our own path. It's just finding what gives you peace."

Jacob smiled when Anthony corrected himself. It
somehow made him feel closer to the man, knowing
that only he would call him Jake instead of Jacob.
"I thought I had all the answers. But now I think
there's a lot I don't know. Maybe I don't know
anything! Well, at least I'm starting to learn," Jacob
said, taking Anthony's hand.
"That's a huge first step, Jake."

Jacob climbed aboard the gurney that the two
surgery nurses brought to his room. They checked
his ID bracelet and asked him a few questions.
"I'm Marilyn, and this is Carole," one of the pretty,
middle-aged women said with a warm smile.
"We're going to be with you in surgery, Jacob. So
let's go and get rid of that nasty old appendix!"
Carl and Edna gave him a quick hug. Peter, who
had returned during his lunch break, squeezed his
hand as Anthony stood nearby.
"We'll be right here when you get back, dear,"
Edna assured him with a smile.
"Are these your parents?" Marilyn asked him,
smiling at the older couple.
Jacob looked at them affectionately.
"Yes, they are," he said easily. "This is my family."

"Jake?" a distant voice called.
"Jake?" the voice repeated, a little louder.
He struggled to respond, but found he couldn't open
his eyes.
"Jake?"

He felt a hand jostle his shoulder lightly. Slowly, he opened his eyes slightly and looked up.

"Jake, you're in the recovery room," Anthony said with a kind smile. "It's all over. You did very well."

"It's already done?" Jacob rasped hoarsely.

He looked around vaguely. He was in a large, sterile looking room filled with gurneys and monitors and other medical equipment. Anthony was standing over him, wearing dark blue scrubs.

"Yes, it's all over with."

Jacob smiled in relief. He blinked his eyes several times, trying to get them to focus until Anthony helped him put on his glasses.

"Are you having any pain?" Anthony asked him.

He shook his head, a little surprised, and stared up at Anthony thoughtfully.

"Is Keith a nice guy?" he asked softly.

Anthony looked at him with astonishment.

"What in the world made you ask that?"

"I don't know," Jacob shrugged. "I was just wondering. He's very handsome."

"Yes, he is," Anthony acknowledged. "And he's a very nice guy."

"I'm glad."

Anthony chuckled and shook his head. In his years of experience as a recovery room nurse, he knew that patients coming out of sedation often said humorous or off the wall remarks.

"Anthony?"

"Yes, Jake," Anthony said, as if he were speaking to a small child.

"I think you're really handsome, too," Jake said, reaching out with his hand. "I could fall in love with you."

"Is that right?" Anthony said, taking his hand as he smiled indulgently at him.

Jacob nodded wearily.

"I'm serious," he said as he stared up into Anthony's kind eyes. Suddenly, without warning, he felt his throat tighten and tears well up in his own eyes.

"Don't cry, Jacob," Anthony said, becoming concerned. "Are you sure you're not having any pain?"

Jacob wiped his eyes and shook his head.

"I'm fine," he lied. "Just fine."

That evening, practically everyone he knew in Green Grove was gathered around his bed in room 209. There was much laughter and confusion as everyone tried to talk to Jacob at once. He tried to listen to them all, but finally gave it up with a tired smile. The kind nurse had given him something for pain in his IV, and it had made him comfortable, but also sleepy. Several church members also stopped by briefly to wish him well as the evening went on. Around nine o'clock that evening, Carl clapped his hands to get everyone's attention.

"Come on, everyone, let's let Jacob get some sleep," he said.

Jacob thanked them all sincerely for their kindness to him.

"Dinner at our house Saturday night?" Neil said, as he and Peter kissed him on the forehead. "It's the Fourth of July weekend, you know."

Jacob nodded eagerly.

"We'll check on you tomorrow morning, dear," Edna said, grasping his hand as if she never wanted to let it go. He squeezed her hand affectionately and smiled.

Myra, Lucas, and Lance and Linda said their goodbyes as well. Anthony ushered them all out the door before turning back to him.

"Are you feeling okay?" he asked in a concerned voice.

"I'm fine," Jacob said.

"You know, you've become very popular in the short time you've been here," Anthony said with a grin.

"They're all such wonderful people," Jacob said earnestly. "I already love them all."

"You're all wonderful," he added, a little shyly.

"Thanks," Anthony chuckled. "We think you are, too."

A frown suddenly crossed Jacob's face.

"What?" Anthony asked. "Are you in pain?"

"No, I was just thinking that Pastor Cal told me to stay away from all of you."

"Oh, I see. He thinks we're a bad influence on you, huh?"

Jacob shrugged at first, but then nodded.

148

"It doesn't matter what he thinks. What do you think?" Anthony asked him curiously. "Do you think we're all evil?"

"No, no, of course not!" Jacob said assertively. "Not at all."

"So if we're not evil, then do you think we're all going to heaven?"

"Maybe, but I'm not sure," Jacob said honestly. "I can't see how God could send such nice people to hell. That would be wrong because they don't deserve that!"

"I have to agree with you on that," Anthony chuckled lightly.

"There's so much I don't understand anymore," Jacob sighed tiredly. "It's giving me a headache."

Anthony laughed out loud.

"But at least you know you don't know everything anymore. That's real progress in just a short period of time. I'm proud of you, Jake."

"That's another thing," Jacob said thoughtfully. "I never liked the name 'Jake'. But when you say it, it sounds different to me. I like it when you call me that. I wonder why that is."

"I don't know," Anthony replied with a grin. "When you figure it out, you let me know."

Once Jacob was sound asleep, Anthony stopped at the nurse's desk and spoke to Jacob's nurse, a friend of his. He made her promise to call him immediately if Jacob woke up during the night, or he needed him for anything at all. He stopped back at the door of Jacob's room and gazed at him with affection.

What was it about this young man that made it impossible to stop thinking about him? Obviously he was very attractive; that was a given. He looked so handsome, lying there asleep in the bed. Maybe it was his vulnerability and his innocence. He had evidently done some serious thinking about the things the two of them had talked about, which actually surprised Anthony. All too often, it seemed to him, people who were so profoundly indoctrinated in a religion usually refused to even consider the possibility that other ideologies could be right, too. It was much easier to just assume that they were right, and everyone else was wrong. He'd seen it too many times. But perhaps Jacob would be different. Perhaps he would be able to open his mind, as it seemed he was already attempting to do. He certainly hoped so, because he was finding it very difficult not to care for him.

By six o'clock the next morning Anthony was sitting in the chair beside Jacob's bed. About ten minutes later, Jacob opened his eyes and looked around groggily. He slowly began to remember the events of the previous day, and he lifted his blanket and hospital gown to look at the three small gauze bandages on his abdomen.

"How do they look?" Anthony asked, bending over to look as well.

"Oh, you surprised me," Jacob said, startled. "I didn't know you were there."

He looked over at him curiously.

"Did you stay here all night?"

"No, I went home for a while after you fell asleep. How are you feeling this morning?"

"Actually, not too bad; just a little sore," Jacob said. "When can I go home?"

"Dr. Lee will want to see you, and if he says it's okay, you can go home later this morning."

"Good. I want to sleep in my own bed tonight."

Dr. Lee arrived just after breakfast, followed by Carl and Edna. He was pleased with Jacob's progress and, after changing the dressings on his abdomen, quickly wrote out his discharge orders.

"I want someone to look in on you today from time to time," Dr. Lee said sternly.

"Don't worry," Anthony assured him. "I'm right next door. I'll stay with him, or I might even have him stay with me for a day or two."

"That would be excellent, Anthony," Dr. Lee said with an approving smile.

An hour later, his three friends had him safely deposited on his couch with strict instructions to call them immediately if he needed them. Carl and Edna said they were going to do his shopping for him, so they hurried off to the store.

"Are you sure you're okay?" Anthony asked solicitously. "I have a few clients this morning, but I'll be over to fix you some lunch around noon." Jacob assured him that he was fine. After Anthony left, he took a pain pill and was soon fast asleep. He awoke sometime later to hear noises coming from his kitchen. As he sat up carefully, a knock came at the front door. He started to stand up, but quickly sat back down.

"Stay there," Anthony said sternly, wiping his hands on a dishtowel as he came into the room. "I'll get it."

"Oh, hi," he said to the visitor.

"I'm here to check on the patient," Pastor Cal said, brushing past him and into the living room. "What are you doing here, anyway?"

"I'm looking after the patient," Anthony said evenly. "I am a nurse, you know. It's what I do."

"I can send some of the ladies from the church to take care of you, Jacob," the minister said, looking directly at Jacob. "He doesn't need to be here."

"They don't need to do that, Pastor," Jacob said quickly. "Anthony is right next door, and besides, I want him here. He's my friend."

He smiled at Anthony, who winked at him and grinned.

"I think it would be more appropriate if your fellow church members looked after you," Pastor Cal said firmly.

"More appropriate than a registered nurse?" Jacob asked with a frown.

"Well, of course, that's up to you," Pastor Cal shrugged. "I'm a little concerned that you haven't talked to your parents about your surgery. In fact, they said you haven't called them at all since you left home."

"I know, I'm sorry," Jacob said contritely. "There's just been so much going on. I'll be sure and give them a call to let them know I'm okay."

"They already know you're recovering well," Pastor Cal informed him. "I gave a full report to Pastor Paul this morning, and he told them for you."

"You called Pastor Paul?" Jacob said with surprise. "What did he say?"

"He was a little disappointed to hear that your parents hadn't heard from you, of course. But I told him you were fitting in nicely at Grace."

"Thank you, that's nice of you to say," Jacob said dryly. "Of course, you know they could have called me, too."

Pastor Cal ignored him while Anthony chuckled.

"Well, I'll be going," the pastor said, turning to look at Anthony with a frown. "I'll send some ladies over with some food."

Anthony opened the door for him.

"Bye, Calvin," he said cheerfully. "Jacob and I will be right here if you need us."

He shut the door after the big man had left and burst out laughing.

"Be quiet, he'll hear you," Jacob whispered loudly, trying not to smile.

"Wow, he really disapproves of me, huh?" Anthony said with a grin. "The big, bad gay neighbor!"

"He doesn't think I should be around any gay people. He said you'd influence me to become gay."

"I think you were already there before any of us had a chance to 'influence' you," Anthony said dryly.

"I know," Jacob agreed.

"I made you some lunch," Anthony said. "Are you hungry?"

"Did you make enough for both of us?"

"No, I just made it for you."

"Well, I can't eat very much, so you eat some of it, too," Jacob said, carefully and slowly standing up.

"Where are you going, Jake?" Anthony asked him.

"Bathroom," Jacob said, pointing at the bedroom.

"Do you need some help?"

Jacob felt a sudden thrill up his spine.

"Sure," he said.

Anthony grinned and put an arm around his waist, guiding him through the bedroom to the bathroom. At his first touch, Jacob felt himself instantly become aroused. When they got to the bathroom, Anthony tactfully left him standing in front of the toilet and retreated.

"I'll wait for you out here," he said.

After a few minutes of waiting for his arousal to subside, Jacob relieved himself and allowed Anthony to help him back to the sofa. He tried to concentrate on anything else to get his mind and groin off of his handsome neighbor as Anthony brought him a bowl of soup and a grilled cheese sandwich.

"This is so nice of you, Anthony," Jacob said appreciatively.

"No problem," Anthony waved his words away.

"Here, eat half of this sandwich," Jacob said. "I can't eat all of this."

They ate together for a few minutes in silence.

"How come you haven't called your parents?" Anthony asked curiously. "I thought you were pretty homesick when you got here."

"I'm not sure," Jacob said, chewing his half of the sandwich thoughtfully. "I should miss them and want to talk to them, shouldn't I?"

"I would think so," Anthony agreed, watching him closely.

"But I don't really miss them," Jacob admitted. "I haven't missed talking to them."

"Why not?"

"I'm not sure," Jacob said slowly. "Maybe because…"

Anthony waited.

"I've started to think they aren't very nice," Jacob continued, surprising himself at what he was saying. "Everyone here has been so wonderful to me, so kind. I've felt more love coming from people here in a few weeks than I ever felt at home. Carl and Edna, Peter and Neil, Myra.

"And you," he added, blushing furiously.

"They are some pretty terrific people," Anthony agreed. "They're very loving, and it's impossible not to love them in return."

"You've all made me feel better about myself than I ever have in my whole life."

Anthony smiled warmly at him as he leaned forward and caressed Jacob's cheek with his hand. "We care about you, Jake," he said simply.

"I care about you, too, Anthony," Jacob said, covering Anthony's hand with his own. His eyes teared up. "Maybe someday…"

"What?" Anthony said gently.

"Uh, nothing," Jacob said, shaking his head as he remembered watching Keith and Anthony hugging. "Nothing at all. This soup is really good, Anthony." He sat back on the sofa, pulling away from his touch and staring at his half finished bowl of tomato soup.

CHAPTER TWELVE

Pastor Cal was true to his word, sending several women from the church to stop in frequently the rest of the afternoon and evening. Anthony left to work with some clients but returned that evening after he had mowed Jacob's lawn for him. Jacob thanked him profusely for all that he was doing as he met him on the back porch. The two of them sat down on the steps.

"I really need to get a mower of my own," he said.

"Well, until you do, you can use mine, or I'll mow for you. It doesn't take more than a half hour to mow and trim, and I can do your lawn when I do my own. It's not a problem."

"I feel like I'm taking advantage of everyone here," Jacob said regretfully. "You, the Johnson's, Myra, Peter and Neil. You keep taking care of me and I haven't done anything for you."

"Jacob, we aren't doing anything we don't want to do," Anthony said, stripping off his sweaty tee shirt and wiping his forehead with it. "And no one expects anything in return."

Jacob stared at his glistening hairy chest for a moment before he replied.

"I know, but it's so different from how I was raised. No one has ever treated me so nicely before."

"What about your family, or the church you grew up in?" Anthony asked with a frown.

"Well, I've kind of always been a little invisible," Jacob said with a cheerless smile. "People usually don't notice me. At least, they never have, until I moved here, that is."

"That's surprising," Anthony said. "I think you're very noticeable."

"Hey wait, I've got something for you," Jacob said suddenly.

Carefully, he stood up, using Anthony's shoulder to balance himself. He went into the kitchen and returned a moment later with two cold bottles of Miller Lite. With a grin he handed one to Anthony as he sat down gingerly on the top step.

"Jake, I'm impressed," Anthony said with a short laugh. "You never stop surprising me. But you know, you shouldn't mix alcohol with pain medication."

"Well, I won't tell my doctor if you won't," Jacob chuckled. "Anyway, I'll just have a couple of sips."

They clinked their bottles together and each took a drink as they spent the next several minutes in a companionable silence. Jacob reveled in the sight of Anthony's beautiful body and pungent smell.

"There's plenty of food in the house if you're hungry," Jacob said after a while. "The ladies from the church have been coming all afternoon. I guess Pastor Cal thought they'd scare you away."

Anthony laughed at that.

"Well, don't worry about that. I don't scare that easily," he said. "Come on; let's eat some of that divinely inspired food. Maybe I'll get religion from eating it!"

They laughed conspiratorially as they went into the kitchen and began dishing out the various foods onto a couple of plates.

"Oh, my god!" Anthony said suddenly. "I should have gotten cleaned up and put a shirt on. Here I am all sweaty and without a shirt, you probably think I'm disgusting."

"You don't have to worry about that," Jacob admonished him. "You're not disgusting at all; you're perfectly fine."

He longed to tell Anthony he was more than fine, that seeing him half naked and covered in perspiration, looking and smelling very masculine, was actually not the least bit disgusting to him, but was in fact quite a turn on. However, he tried to act nonchalant as he looked at him casually.

"You don't have to do anything special just for me," he added, trying to concentrate on keeping his hand from shaking as he ladled out food.

When they had finished eating, Anthony cleared the table for them and washed the few dishes they had used.

"You didn't eat enough," Anthony chided him with a frown as he stood at the kitchen sink. Jacob stood up slowly and picked up a dishtowel to dry the dishes as Anthony handed them to him, one by one.

"I still don't have much of an appetite," Jacob said. "But it's getting better."

He felt a little hot as he set the plate in his hand down and leaned against the counter.

"Are you okay?" Anthony said, giving him a look of concern as he dried his hands. "I think you might have a fever. You're a little flushed."

He placed one hand on Jacob's shoulder and the other on his forehead.

"You'd better take a couple of pain pills and go to bed," he said firmly. "Come on."

He guided the protesting Jacob to his bedroom and helped him undress down to his underwear.

"Oh, my god," Anthony said with surprise. "You're wearing my underwear?"

"Oh, am I?" Jacob said, suddenly embarrassed, his face turning red. "I just picked up the first pair I found."

He was not about to admit that he had purposely put Anthony's underwear on, and that wearing them made him feel closer to the gorgeous man.

"Oh, I see," Anthony nodded knowingly. "Well, they look really good on you, Jake. Now get in bed and I'll get you a couple of pain pills."

He left the room and returned in a moment with two pills and a bottle of cold water from the refrigerator.

"Here," he said, handing the items to Jacob, who obediently swallowed the pills. "It's not surprising that you have a slight fever, especially at night, but I want to keep an eye on it. I'll be back in the morning to check on you, but call me tonight if you need me. I'll have my cell phone right beside my bed."

Jacob lay down under the covers and looked up at Anthony wearily.

"I'm sorry to be so much bother to you, Anthony.
I'll bet you're sorry to have me as a neighbor."
"Of course not! I'm glad you moved in next door,
Jake," Anthony told him with a frown. "Don't be
silly."
"I'll go turn out the rest of your lights," he said.
"I'll be back in a minute."
Jacob sighed and stared at the ceiling. In spite of
feeling a little under the weather, his desire for
Anthony was becoming more and more intense.
Looking at his half naked body was practically
unbearable, and touching his bare skin was almost
like experiencing an electrical shock. He wanted
nothing more than to do all kinds of intimate sexual
things with him, but even as he thought about how
wonderful that would be, the picture of Keith came
into his mind, and he suddenly was overcome with
sadness.
Anthony returned and looked down at him kindly.
"Are you okay?" he asked as he noticed the
expression on Jacob's face. "Is it pain?"
"No, I just wish..." Jacob broke off as he thought
about Anthony being with Keith. If only things
were different.
"What, Jake?" Anthony said, sitting down on the
bedside next to him.
"I wish things were different, that's all," Jacob said
quietly.
Anthony stared at him for a moment, and then
slowly bent down and kissed him gently on the lips.
Jacob put his arms around him and kissed him

passionately for several seconds. But eventually, he pushed the other man away and turned to his side.

"What's wrong, Jake?" Anthony asked. "Don't you want to kiss me?"

All that guilt must be overwhelming to him, he thought, shaking his head. If only he could get past the senseless shame his religious background had pounded into his head.

Jacob nodded slightly.

"Of course, I do," he said tremulously. "But I can't, not as long as…"

Not as long as you're with Keith, he thought sadly.

"Okay, Jake," Anthony sighed. "Living with all that guilt and shame is a hard thing to do. I hope that someday you'll be able to move past it, but that has to be your decision. It's up to you."

He stood up and turned out the bedside lamp.

"I'll see you tomorrow. Good night."

Jacob slept until late the next morning. He walked wearily into the bathroom, and then went into the kitchen for something to drink. He took a drink from a bottle of soda and stretched carefully. He actually felt pretty good this morning, just a little tired and stiff. He felt his forehead and decided his fever was gone as a knock came on the front door. He walked over and opened it, not realizing he was wearing nothing more than his underwear. Actually, wearing Anthony's underwear.

"Lance, it's good to see you."

"I just wanted to check on you," Lance said with a grin. "How are you doing?"

"I'm fine, just a little sore," Jacob assured him with a smile.

"Good," Lance said. He stepped forward suddenly and kissed him on the lips. Jacob put his arms around him and kissed him back for several seconds, then pushed him away gently.

"I'm sorry, but I'm not up to that right now, Lance," he said.

"I should say he isn't!" a voice barked from the kitchen doorway. Jacob looked up to see Anthony standing there, looking at them with a scowl on his face.

"Oh, my god!" Lance exclaimed, looking like a deer caught in the headlights of a car. "I'll see you later, Jacob."

He turned on his heel and hurried out the front door. Jacob turned to give Anthony an embarrassed look.

"What the hell was that all about?" Anthony asked angrily. "What was he doing, checking your temperature with his tongue?"

"Nothing, he just kissed me," Jacob said lamely.

"Yeah, I got that when I saw you sticking your tongue down his throat. Are you and he fucking?" Anthony asked incredulously. "Please tell me you are not fucking him, Jacob!"

"No, I'm not," Jacob said. "We haven't done that yet. We've just messed around a little."

"So you're having an affair with a married man?" he said loudly. "A member of your church?"

"It's not like that, Anthony."

"That's exactly what it's like! So you can fuck a married guy over and over, but you're overcome with all this Christian guilt when you're with me one time?"

Jacob looked at him pleadingly.

"Oh, my god! And here I thought you were getting your act together," Anthony spat. "You're even more messed up than I thought you were!"

"No, I'm not," Jacob told him. "I did have all that guilt that night I was with you, but I'm learning…trying…I'm trying to get past all that."

"Well, you're doing a hell of a job of getting over it, sleeping with a married man, and standing in your living room kissing him. I tried to kiss you last night and you pushed me away."

Anthony walked back into the kitchen and returned moments later with a bowl of soup and a ham sandwich. He set them down heavily on the old wooden trunk that they had bought together at Myra's store, which now served as a coffee table.

"Here's your lunch," he said, turning away abruptly. "Maybe all that activity will help you get your appetite back!"

"Anthony, will you listen to me?" Jacob cried. "Please!"

Anthony ignored him and strode angrily toward the kitchen. Jacob stood perfectly still until he heard the back door slam loudly. With a stunned expression on his face he stumbled back to the sofa and sat down gingerly. He looked at the food in front of him for a moment, pushed it away, and then picked up the bottle of pain pills. He downed two pills with his soda, and then lay back down with his back to the room.

CHAPTER THIRTEEN

Jacob didn't see Anthony the rest of the week, except through his kitchen window. He didn't venture outside unless he knew Anthony had gone to work, or was in his basement with clients. Lance apparently was keeping his distance as well. The Johnson's stopped by everyday for a few minutes to check on him, but he was in no mood for a cheerful visit with them. Peter and Neil stopped by on Thursday evening to bring him a casserole for supper. The three of them walked into the kitchen together.

"I'm glad you and Anthony are getting along," Peter said as he and Neil prepared a plate for him.

"Yeah, me, too," Jacob said quietly, not looking at either of them.

They looked at each other briefly, and then back at Jacob.

"Oh, god, what happened?" Peter said with a sigh. "Everything seemed fine at the hospital."

"Nothing, it is fine," Jacob lied. "Don't worry about it."

"Come on, tell us," Peter tried again.

"It's nothing. He just found out what a messed up idiot I am," Jacob said jokingly, trying to lighten the mood.

"Everyone is a messed up idiot, Jacob," Neil said dryly. "All of us. You can't be any worse than the rest of us."

Jacob just shook his head.

"You're still coming Saturday night, aren't you?" Peter asked with a frown.

"Will he be there?" Jacob asked, still avoiding eye contact with either of them.

"Yes," Peter nodded. "I think Keith will be there, too."

Jacob visibly cringed as he leaned against the counter with his head down.

"Look, I'm not feeling very well, you guys," he said quietly. "I think I'll go lay down. Thanks for bringing me dinner. You're the best."

He hugged them both very quickly and walked into his bedroom and closed the door.

"What was that all about?" Peter asked with a baffled expression.

Jacob returned to work on Friday morning. There was the music to prepare for the Sunday service, a scheduled choir practice at four o'clock, and he had his Sunday School class to prepare for as well.

His work kept him busy, and the day passed quickly enough. He ate his lunch at his desk, rather than go home and risk seeing either Lance or Anthony. Pastor Cal was out of town, so he had the church mostly to himself.

At five o'clock, he knew he couldn't delay it any longer, so he drove home and parked in the garage. Once again, he was playing a hiding game with Anthony as he hurried into the house. A few minutes after he arrived home, a knock came at the front door. He opened the door cautiously to see a

167

tall young man standing there holding a couple of canvas bags.

"Hi, Mr. Porter, I mean Jacob," he said. "It's Brandon, remember?"

"Of course, Brandon, come on in," Jacob said, opening the storm door for him. "How are you?"

"I'm fine," Brandon said as he stepped into the living room. "Mom asked me to bring you supper tonight."

"That was very nice of her," Jacob told him. "Come on."

They carried the bags to the kitchen and set them on the small round table.

"There's enough food here for an army," Jacob exclaimed. "Do you want to stay and eat with me?"

"I probably shouldn't," Brandon said, hesitating.

"Oh, come on," Jacob said cajolingly. "Please, stay. I feel like some company."

"Okay," Brandon said with a shy grin.

Together they unpacked the fried chicken, potato salad and baked beans. Jacob got some plates and silverware from the nearby cabinets and set the table.

"You'll have to thank your mother for this," Jacob said as he took a small bite of potato salad.

"I will," Brandon said with a smile. "How are you feeling?"

"I'm good," Jacob told him. "Still moving a little slower than usual, but getting better."

"That's good."

"So tell me about yourself, Brandon. Are you still in high school?"

"No, I graduated in May," he said. "I'm going to the U of I this fall to study computer science, even though my parents aren't too happy about it."

"Why on earth wouldn't they be happy about that?" Jacob asked curiously. "I would think they'd be thrilled."

"It's not a Christian school," Brandon said simply.

"Oh, I see."

"They don't want me exposed to bad influences," Brandon continued. "If they only knew!"

"Knew what?" Jacob asked with a frown.

"Nothing."

"Well, tell me some more about you," Jacob said, tactfully changing the subject. "Do you have a girlfriend?"

"You're kidding, right?"

"No, I wasn't, but maybe I should be?" Jacob said, giving him a confused look.

"I don't have a girlfriend, and I never will have a girlfriend," Brandon looked at him meaningfully.

"Oh," Jacob said as the realization sank in. "Oh! You mean you're…"

"Is everything we say just between us?" Brandon asked gravely.

"Absolutely!"

"Then, yes, I'm gay," he said, taking a deep breath and letting it out shakily. "Oh, my god, I can't believe I just told someone that! Especially someone who works for my dad!"

169

Jacob's face turned a shade whiter.
"You mean," he gulped, "your dad is…"
"Pastor Cal."

"So no one knows you're gay, except me?" Jacob
asked Brandon.
The teenager shook his head.
"Who could I tell?" he asked. "All the people I
know are mostly from the church. My sister and I
were home schooled, you know, to keep us away
from the bad influences, so I don't know too many
other people my age. I just thought maybe you'd
understand."
Jacob regarded him for several seconds.
"You mean…because I'm gay?" he said hesitantly.
Brandon nodded.
"I figured you were, but I wasn't sure. Thank
goodness you are!" he said. "I've wanted to tell
someone for so long! You have no idea!"
"Believe me, I understand. I've never told anyone I
was gay. But everyone here has figured it out
anyway."
"So your family doesn't know, either?" Brandon
asked him.
"No, they'd disown me if they knew," Jacob said,
surprised by the question.
"But you know, they're so wrong to be like that,"
Brandon said earnestly. "You're a great guy. You're
talented and good-looking, and you're so nice. They
don't know what they're missing by not knowing
the real you."

"I don't think they would see it that way. As far as they're concerned, all gay people are going to hell."

"You don't believe that, do you?" Brandon said.

"I'm not sure anymore," Jacob said honestly. "Before I came here, I would have said yes, but now I don't know."

"You've got to be kidding!" Brandon exclaimed. "You're a gay man, and you believe that crap about gay people going to hell? How can you do that?"

Jacob blinked at him in surprise.

"You don't believe it? Even after you've been taught it your whole life?"

"No, of course not!" Brandon said sharply. "I know God better than that. He made me gay, so why would He send me to hell for that? It's like going to hell because you have brown hair, or you're tall, or whatever!"

"Wow, I'm impressed," Jacob said. "I've struggled all of my life with being gay, and here you are, younger than me, and you've got it all figured out."

"No, I don't have anything figured out," Brandon told him, shaking his head. "But I do know that God doesn't send people to hell for being gay. I've always known that."

"Well, if you've got that figured out, you're a long way ahead of me," Jacob said sincerely.

"I just don't know how I'll ever have a boyfriend," Brandon said with a trace of sadness in his voice, "unless I never see my family again, because I guarantee you, they'll never accept it."

"I know how you feel," Jacob said. "I'm in the same situation."

They sat in a companionable silence for a while as they ate.

"You know who might have some good advice for you?" Jacob said thoughtfully. "Carl and Edna Johnson. Their son, Peter, is gay. You can trust them completely, and they have no problem with it at all. They've been so kind to me, too. I think they've even had some conversations with your dad on the subject."

"The Johnson's have a son?" Brandon said. "I didn't know that. I've never heard anyone talk about him."

"Well, now you know why! The church doesn't approve of him. You should talk to them, Brandon. They're a whole lot smarter than I am. And you should meet Peter and Neil. They're two of the nicest guys I've ever met. They live in that huge brick house on Washington Street. Peter works at Larson's, and Neil is a lawyer over in Dixon, I think."

He shook his head and laughed shortly.

"Your dad already told me to make sure I stayed away from them."

"Oh, really?" Brandon said, clearly annoyed as he thought about his dad. "Where's all that Christian love he's always talking about?"

"Apparently, sometimes that only applies to other Christians," Jacob said with a sigh. "But Carl and Edna are the real thing. They don't judge or condemn anyone, the way true Christians are supposed to act. And they're two of the happiest people I've ever met! They're way happier than my parents are, that's for sure!"

"I think I need to get to know Carl and Edna a little better," Brandon said thoughtfully.

Jacob studied his new friend for a few moments. "There's a party at Peter and Neil's house tomorrow night. I wasn't going to go, but it might be a good place to get to know the Johnson's and some other like-minded people. If you want to go, you can be my guest. It starts at seven."

"That would be fantastic, Jacob!" Brandon exclaimed. "Thank you!"

"Just remember, it will have to be a secret, I'm afraid."

"Believe me," Brandon said with a wry grin. "I know how to keep a secret!"

Anthony took his garbage out to the bins near the back corner of the house, next to the driveway. He looked up when he heard a screen door close squeakily on its hinges. He walked down the driveway to where a small compact car was parked close to the street under Jacob's tall maple tree. Just as he reached the front corner of his house, he saw Jacob and a tall, well built young man standing on Jacob's front porch in the darkening evening. The stranger gave him a long hug before turning and running down the front steps to his car. He stepped back into the shadows as the car's headlights came on. Jacob waved good-bye and then turned to look at Anthony's house. He stood there staring for several moments, and then his shoulders slumped and he shuffled back into the house.

So who was that, Anthony wondered? Probably another trick. Wow, Jacob sure gets around! But it was none of his business, he told himself, whether he slept with one married guy, or a hundred guys. In spite of how much he had grown to care about Jacob over the last few weeks, he had to make himself realize that he was just a neighbor, not his boyfriend. Hell, he wasn't even a friend anymore. He walked back toward his backyard, when he heard the roar of a motorcycle coming down the street. He turned in time to see Keith pulling into his driveway on his Honda. He walked up to him as he climbed off the big bike and gave him an affectionate hug. As he turned to walk through his gate, he looked over and saw Jacob staring out at him from his kitchen window. The light suddenly went out as he watched, and with a sigh, he turned back to his visitor.

Jacob lay in bed that night, staring at the ceiling thoughtfully. What an interesting young man was Brandon, he thought. He was so young, but he had already made peace with himself and with God about being gay, as opposed to himself, who was still kind of a mess. Was there any reason that he couldn't reconcile his faith and his sexuality, too?

For the first time in his life, he prayed that night to God for help in accepting who he was, rather than begging for forgiveness and moaning and crying with guilt. As he prayed, he immediately felt a sense of satisfaction and relief. Somehow, he knew he was on the brink of an important turning point in his life, as far as his faith was concerned. In spite of what he had been taught all of his life, he was coming to understand that being gay was not a sin. Perhaps the way gay people were demonized by people in the church was where the real sin was. It was all a little hazy to him at the moment, but he felt like he was beginning to see the light.

CHAPTER FOURTEEN

Brandon came by Jacob's house a little after six o'clock the next evening. He was wearing a nice pair of black slacks and a royal blue shirt.
"You look really nice, Brandon," Jacob told him. "Give me a few minutes to get ready."
He stepped into the bedroom to change clothes.
"How did you get to be so comfortable with being gay at such a young age?" he called out to the other room.
Brandon leaned against the doorframe leading to the bedroom.
"A lot of prayer," he said dryly.
"What did you pray for?" Jacob asked curiously.
"At first, it was for God to take it away and make me straight," Brandon admitted. "But when nothing changed, I started praying to understand why I was this way. And that's when I started getting answers."
"Really?"
"Oh, yeah," Brandon nodded vigorously. "It all became very clear. There wasn't anything wrong with me at all. I was just the way God wanted me to be. Maybe my family refuses to believe that a person can be gay *and* a Christian, but that's their choice. I can't change them or their way of thinking, so I just pray for them."
"I'm beginning to see that, too," Jacob said, straightening his shirt as he came out into the dining room. "Can I ask you a personal question?"

"Sure," Brandon nodded.

"Did you freak out the first time you had sex with another guy?"

Brandon broke out into loud laughter at the question. When he had recovered himself, he shook his head.

"No, I didn't," he said. "Why, did you?"

"Yeah," Jacob said sheepishly. "It was wonderful and beautiful, but I was dealing with so much denial and guilt, and I was scared to death. I acted like a huge idiot."

He looked at Brandon sadly.

"And the worst of it is, I scared away a really great guy," he said. "Someone I believe I could have fallen in love with. I think I regret that more than anything else I've ever done."

"Is it someone here in Green Grove?" Brandon asked. "Anyone I know?"

"I doubt it," Jacob told him, hesitating for a moment. "It's my neighbor Anthony. You'll meet him at the party tonight. He's the reason I wasn't going to go."

"Can't you explain it to him?" Brandon asked. "Maybe he'd understand."

"No, I don't think so," Jacob shook his head. "He's got a boyfriend now. There's more to it than that, but let's forget it for now and go to the party."

Peter and Neil welcomed them warmly in the foyer of their lovely old home.

"We're so happy to meet you, Brandon!" Peter said.

He looked at Jacob and winked.

"Honey, he's too adorable!" he whispered loudly, wrapping an arm around the teenager.

"Peter!" Jacob exclaimed with an annoyed smile, as Brandon blushed furiously. "He's here to meet other gay people! He's not my date."

"Okay, darling, whatever you say," Peter said. "I'm just glad you're here. I thought you weren't going to come because of you know who."

"I'm here for Brandon," Jacob told him. "I want him to get to know you and your parents. He needs all the support he can get with his home situation."

"Of course, Brandon," Peter assured him. "We are here for you, whatever you need. Now come on, everyone's already here. Come meet everyone."

He linked arms with them and propelled them into the living room where everyone was chatting and laughing over drinks. He quickly introduced Brandon to Elaine, Myra, Lucas, Randall, Anthony, and Keith. Carl and Edna knew him from church, of course. They embraced him and told him how happy they were to know that he was coming out of the closet. The other guests agreed heartily with Carl and Edna and welcomed him with warm smiles and hugs. Anthony scowled at Jacob, who carefully avoided his eye, but greeted Brandon in a friendly enough manner.

"So, Anthony, you and Jacob are neighbors?" Brandon asked, as Neil handed him a soft drink.

Anthony nodded in a noncommittal fashion and looked away, as if he would rather not be reminded of the fact.

"You'd never know it, though," Keith interjected with a chuckle. "He hides away in that house; we never see him."

Jacob's face turned red and he stared at the floor.

"Jacob's just had surgery," Peter reminded everyone. "Of course he's been staying indoors and taking it easy lately."

"Hardly," Keith grinned. "From what Anthony says, old Jacob here isn't taking it easy at all. He's a very 'active' boy."

He used his fingers as quotes to indicate that the word 'active' was being used in a less than desirable way.

"Keith," Anthony said warningly.

"What?" Keith said. "That is what you said. You said he's –"

Anthony pinched his shoulder sharply with his hand to make him stop talking. He turned back to Brandon.

"You two know each other from your church, I take it?" he said with a frown.

"Yes, he teaches my Sunday School class, 'Waiting for Marriage'," Brandon told him.

Keith burst out in raucous laughter at the name of the class, while the others, excluding Carl and Edna, tried in vain to hide their laughter as well.

"Oh, my god!" he gasped. "That's too fucking hilarious! 'Waiting for Marriage'? You're kidding, right?"

"No, I'm not kidding," Brandon said, looking around at them with a frown, apparently not understanding the joke.

"Come on," Keith laughed. "You've got to be joking! A gay guy trying to teach a bunch of straight church kids about marriage? What the fuck does a closeted gay guy know about marriage? He could probably teach them about sucking a dick, but not marriage! That's crazy!"

He laughed long and loudly at the idea while the others either turned away to hide their smiles or looked uncomfortably at the floor. After a minute or two of this Keith looked at Jacob and put a hand to his mouth.

"Oh, I'm sorry, man," he said contritely as he tried to contain his laughter.

Jacob's face was red and scowling. All the pleasure he had been feeling at being part of this group disappeared in an instant.

"I'm sorry, Jake, I mean Jacob," Keith said. "No insult intended. But I can just picture you sitting in front of a class trying to tell them…"

He burst out laughing helplessly once again.

"That's enough," Carl said reprovingly. "There's nothing funny about Jacob teaching a Sunday School class."

He moved over and placed a protective arm around Jacob's shoulders. Jacob looked around the room, pausing to gaze intently at Anthony's face for an instant before staring down at the floor. Anthony was still trying to hide his smile, too, he noted, along with the rest of his new friends, except for Carl and Edna. He suddenly felt sick to his stomach with embarrassment and humiliation.

"Well, I think dinner is just about ready," Neil said loudly. "Come on, everyone. Let's eat!"

Together with Peter, he ushered them all into the large dining room, where the long dining table was covered once again with beautiful china and crystal and silver, just as it had been the last time Jacob had been here.

Jacob lingered in the doorway for a moment, then excused himself and hurried to the bathroom.

"Jacob," Peter called after him. He paused to glare at his guests for a moment, focusing his attention finally on Keith, and then turned to follow Jacob. Edna gave Keith an angry look as well as she hurried after her son.

"What?" Keith said, spreading his hands and grinning innocently. "You have to admit that's pretty damn funny. I mean, the idea is insane! And I apologized, didn't I?"

"Look," Brandon said heatedly. "Kevin, or Keith, or whatever the hell your name is, I don't know who you are, but how dare you embarrass Jacob like that! You have no idea the hell he's been through! He's trying to work out who he is, and he doesn't need an asshole like you making everything worse by laughing at him."

"I said I'm sorry," Keith said, becoming annoyed. "What more do you want, kid?"

"What I want is to beat the shit out of you, but I'll settle for you shutting the fuck up!" Brandon yelled as he stormed from the room.

Jacob stood at the sink in the small, beautifully decorated bathroom under the staircase, frowning at his reflection in the gilded mirror. Peter tapped on the door before pulling it open. He placed a hand on Jacob's shoulder.

"Come back to dinner, Jacob," he said gently. "Don't let what Keith said bother you."

"It wasn't just Keith, Peter!" Jacob lashed out angrily. "Everyone was laughing at me. I'm just a joke to all of you, aren't I?"

"Of course you're not!" Peter said reassuringly. "No one thinks you're a joke."

"You all do! I saw you all try not to laugh," Jacob told him. "Even you, Peter! It's bad enough knowing what Anthony thinks of me. I already know how he hates me! Oh, my god! I can't stand being the butt of everyone's jokes, too."

He brushed tearfully past Peter into the foyer and ran into Brandon and Edna as he walked to the front door.

"Please, Jacob, dear," Edna said consolingly. "They didn't mean to laugh at you. Keith is a foolish young man who speaks without thinking. Don't mind what he says."

"That's right, Jacob," Brandon said. "The guy's an asshole!"

"He is an asshole. But he just said what everyone was thinking," Jacob said bitterly.

"Please, Jacob," Peter said. "I know you're upset, but –"

"I'm not going back in there, Peter," Jacob said angrily. "I can't, knowing what you're all thinking. I'm just going to go on home. Look after Brandon here, and make sure he stays and gets to know your parents."

"Jacob," Brandon began. "I'm not going to stay if you aren't."

"No! I mean it, Brandon. Tonight was about you getting to know Carl and Edna and Peter and Neil, so stay here and have a good time. I'll…I'll probably see you tomorrow."

"Jacob, please…"

Jacob wiped his eyes and opened the front door, quietly closing it behind him as he stepped out into the warm July evening, leaving Peter, Edna, and Brandon frowning at each other.

Okay, maybe I overreacted, Jacob thought as he walked home, trying not to cry. But it had been so humiliating to watch a whole room full of people – people that he thought loved him – laughing at him because of some insensitive remarks spoken by an arrogant asshole like Keith. Why did Anthony want to be with someone like that? Because he's handsome, and he's probably really good in bed, he supposed. He probably has no crazy hang ups about sex, either. Anyone would look good to Anthony after what Jacob had put him through that fateful night that he had run away from him. The night that he had ruined his chances with Anthony. If only Anthony could see how much he had grown in just a few short weeks. It wouldn't matter anyway, he thought sadly, after the incident with Lance in his living room.

He hadn't seen Lance since then, and he really didn't care if he did anyway. Anthony was right; he shouldn't be sleeping with a married man. It hadn't felt like a big deal to him at first, when he was thinking only with his libido. But Linda seemed like such a nice person, and she was already in a bad situation. He didn't want to make things worse for her. He could understand Lance's feelings about his marriage, since it was not so very different from his relationship with the church. But Linda deserved better. Come to think of it, they all deserved better. Lance, Linda, and himself. The only way that could happen is if Lance and Linda stopped hiding the truth and dealt with it honestly. He needed to be honest as well, he told himself. He unlocked his front door and stepped into the dark house, just as his cell phone rang in his pocket. He pulled it out and shut it off without looking to see who was calling.

The next day, Sunday, he called Pastor Cal and told him he wasn't feeling well. He wasn't ready to face people again after his humiliating experience last night. Instead, he spent the morning looking on the Internet for everything he could find on Buddha and his teachings. Although he didn't understand much of it, he found a considerable amount of common sense in the lessons the Buddha had taught. He also spent a lot of time in prayer and meditation. Now that he had stopped praying to be 'cured' of his sexuality, his prayers seemed much more authentic and meaningful to him.

He returned to work on Monday, and the rest of the week went by quietly. He concentrated on his work at the church with his office door closed, and went home each afternoon, hiding his car in the garage and pulling down the blinds on the windows. A few times there were knocks on his front and back doors, but he stayed in his bedroom at the back of the house while the rest of the house remained dark. He didn't want to see any of his former friends. Perhaps someday he would be able to face them and be cordial, but that was not possible right now. His feelings were too hurt. He had opened up to these seemingly lovely people only to find himself the object of their scorn and ridicule. They'd probably been laughing at him all along. His ego was just too fragile to take such rejection right now, especially with everything he was feeling about Anthony, as well as his ongoing spiritual struggle. His self-esteem had indeed grown far beyond anything he had known before, but with just a few words from

his neighbor's boyfriend, it had deflated as quickly
as a balloon being stuck with a pin.
Peter and the others could never understand that, he
thought. They were all happy, well-adjusted people,
who weren't struggling with the inner turmoil he
experienced every moment of his life. He knew he
was a neurotic mess, but at least he was making an
honest effort to move beyond the fears, the shame,
and introversion that had been his constant
companions ever since he could remember.

CHAPTER FIFTEEN

On the next Sunday Jacob taught the lesson that was laid out for him for his class, carefully avoiding eye contact with his students as much as possible. He noticed that Brandon was absent, and he wondered why. Perhaps he had joined in the laughter the group had probably shared openly after he left Peter and Neil's house that night. When his class ended, he quickly headed for the sanctuary to line up his music for the service. He avoided looking at the congregation, and focused on the music and his fellow performers. When the musical portion of the service had concluded, Jacob took a seat at the end of the front pew nearest the piano. He looked around surreptitiously and was astonished to see Brandon, Peter, Neil, Lucas, Randall, and Myra sitting together several pews back. They were all staring at him when he looked their way, but he frowned and quickly looked away. What the hell were they all doing here, he thought angrily? Was it really necessary to mock him further? Is that why Brandon didn't come to class, so they could all meet and laugh at him?

"The sermon for today is called 'Sexual immorality and the Bible'," Pastor Cal said in solemn tones from the pulpit. "Friends, what we have in our community is an epidemic of sexual immorality." He continued speaking against the evils of premarital sex and adultery for several minutes. When he had exhausted those topics, he brought up the ultimate sexual sin of homosexuality, telling his parishioners to beware of the evil gay people in Green Grove. He spoke of grossly 'unnatural' acts, extreme promiscuity, and how gay people would recruit young children to be gay, since they couldn't reproduce themselves. Jacob grew more and more annoyed as he listened to the false information being taught from this supposed man of God. A true man of God would not be spreading lies, he thought angrily, but most of the words he was spewing forth Jacob knew to be definitely untrue. How strange, he thought as he listened to this fount of lies, that people like Pastor Cal and Pastor Paul thought that all gay people were obsessed with sex, when it seemed to him that those two thought more about sex than anyone else he knew. Why did they care so much about controlling what people did in their bedrooms? He didn't care what anyone else did with his or her sex lives; he was only concerned with his own.

As Pastor Cal continued what Jacob could only call a tirade, he gazed around at the congregation curiously. Some people seemed to be hanging on to every word, but the majority looked uncomfortable, while a very few seemed downright annoyed. As he looked around, he saw Carl and Edna and a couple of other people stand up and sidle down their pews until they reached the center aisle. Peter and his group, except for Brandon, stood up as well and headed for the door. Before she turned to head up the aisle toward the main doors, Edna turned to look at the pastor.

"Shame on you, Pastor Cal!" she cried angrily. "Shame on you for saying such things about something you clearly know nothing about. You're standing up there telling these people nothing but lies!"

She looked around at the congregants.

"And shame on all of you for sitting there listening to this nonsense."

She turned her back on the pastor and followed her husband and the other people out the doors. Jacob's jaw dropped as he watched this encounter, hardly believing what he was seeing.

Pastor Cal looked taken aback for a moment but then shook his head disapprovingly at the departing group.

"How sad! There are none so blind as those who will not see," he intoned piously.

That did it, Jacob decided angrily. He couldn't, wouldn't, take it anymore! Summoning all the courage he could muster, he stood up and glared at the man standing self-righteously behind the pulpit.

"Edna is right!" he exclaimed loudly, his voice trembling. "Everything you're saying is untrue; you're a liar, Pastor Cal, and you don't know what you're talking about! You're just trying to spread hate! And you're the one who chooses not to see!"

He turned and walked up the aisle along the sidewall and out the same doors that his friends had exited through moments before. He ignored the stunned look of the people sitting in the pews as he passed them. When he reached the lobby area, his courage failed him and he leaned against a nearby wall as his legs seemed unable to hold his weight. The door opened again behind him, and he turned to see Brandon run tearfully from the sanctuary and out the door to the parking lot. He took a deep breath and headed for his office to grab his keys. Then he ran out the back door, jumped in his car, and roared out of the parking lot with tires squealing.

Brandon watched first Edna, and then Jacob confront his father with tears in his eyes. They were all so brave, he thought! Edna and Carl and the rest of them. And Jacob, too! As his father stood in front of the assembly looking stunned, he jumped up and ran out into the lobby. His vision was blurry with tears as he continued out into the warm, sunny day. He looked around the car-filled parking lot until he saw a small group of people standing near Carl and Edna's big sedan. Carl called out to him when he saw him standing there, unsure what to do. Edna was comforting the group as Brandon ran up to them.
"You should have seen him!" Brandon gasped. "Jacob stood up after you all walked out and told Dad he was a liar, just like you, Mrs. Johnson!" There were gasps of surprise from each of his new friends.

"Jacob called him a liar? In front of everyone?" Peter repeated disbelievingly. "No, he didn't!"

"Yes, he did," Brandon said with an emphatic nod. "You should have seen it!"

"I can't believe it," Neil said. "Jacob's such a little mouse."

"NO!" Brandon shouted at him. "Stop calling him names and stop laughing at him! What is wrong with all of you? He's not a mouse. He's very brave. Do you know how scared he was to even come to Green Grove? How hard it was for him to go to your party that night? He did that for me, even though he knew his neighbor would be there. He's trying so hard to learn and grow, and then to be laughed at by you, his friends? After what happened that night, I'm surprised he didn't just pack up and leave."

"Yes, but it was nothing; he couldn't even take a little joke at his expense," Randall interjected with a frown. "He shouldn't have run away."

"No, Randall, you're right; he shouldn't have run away, damn it! But you have to understand that it wasn't a little joke to him," Peter said. "Not with all he's trying to deal with. Look, we are his friends, and we came here to support him and show him that we love him. Brandon, you know we didn't mean to laugh at him, don't you? None of us would hurt him for the world."

"But you did hurt him," Carl spoke up. "He thought he could trust all of you, and he thinks you let him down. I know you love him, and it was great that

191

you all came here this morning, but it's going to take more than showing up here to regain his trust."

"I still can't believe he had the guts to stand up in front of everyone and call the pastor a liar," Myra said, shaking her head. "Good for him. I'm really impressed."

"The boy's got nerve, after all," Randall agreed.

"Oh, dear," Edna said with a concerned voice. "Carl, what about his job?"

"I don't know," Carl said with a shake of his head. "He probably doesn't have one any more."

As they continued to talk, Brandon looked around at all of them with a frown.

"Where is Jacob, anyway?" he asked with concern. "He didn't come out here?"

"No, we haven't seen him," Peter said, looking around as well. "He must have stayed in the church."

"I think we should go find him," Neil said. "He shouldn't be alone right now."

As they turned and started to walk back toward the building's front doors, a car roared past them from behind the church. It careened along the edge of the parking lot, scattering gravel as it skidded onto the street. With a squeal of its tires it sped away.

"Well," Lucas said with a sigh. "There he goes."

The group stopped and looked at each other with worried expressions on their faces.

Jacob drove as quickly as he could to Castle Rock State Park. He felt a desperate need to get away

from Green Grove and the only place he could think
of to be alone was along the Rock River. He parked
the car in the same place in the deserted parking lot
as before and got out. His knees felt weak when he
stepped out of the car as he realized the enormity of
what he had just done. Pastor Cal must have already
suspected he was gay when he told him to stay
away from Peter and Anthony, and he himself had
probably just confirmed it. Oh, my god, he thought,
leaning against the car, I really did it; I called my
boss a liar in front of the whole congregation. He'll
fire me, and then he'll tell Pastor Paul that I'm gay!
Pastor Paul will tell my family, and then everyone
back home will know that I've disgraced them. I'll
be disowned, he thought, turning pale; I'll lose
everything!

He slowly climbed the steps on unsteady legs to the
top wooden platform, high above the trees, and
looked out over the broad, lushly green Rock River
valley. He took some slow, deep breaths, trying to
calm himself with the beauty and serenity of the
panorama before him. Finally he turned and
slumped against the wooden railing, sliding down
until he was sitting on the floor, oblivious of the
new suit he was wearing.

What would he do, he wondered? Where would he
find a job? Someplace to live, too, since he was
certain his parents would take his house away, the
house that they had bought for him. No job, no
home, no money, no family, and now no friends.
Tears began to flow as he thought about the party at

Peter and Neil's, the snide remark from Keith, the ensuing laughter, Anthony's obvious distaste at the very sight of him, and now a future devoid of any hope. He didn't know how long he cried, but when he finally dried his eyes on his sleeve, he looked up and was startled to see a man sitting quietly on the wooden bench across the platform from him, studying him thoughtfully. Quickly, he pulled himself together and stood up, shaking himself to straighten his new suit.

"Hey, man, don't go away on account of me," the man said. "You looked like you were having a real moment there."

Jacob looked at him more closely. He couldn't tell if the man was thirty, or sixty; he seemed almost timeless. He had short, tousled brown hair, a sun weathered brown face with a rough graying beard, missing front teeth, and he was wearing a pair of ragged jeans, dirty tennis shoes, and an old flannel shirt over a stained gray tee shirt.

"I'm sorry, but I should go," Jacob mumbled.

"You shouldn't," the stranger told him. "This is one of the best places to figure things out, and it looks like you've got something big to figure out."

Jacob nodded slightly.

"Well, sit back down there."

The man pointed to where Jacob had been sitting on the floor of the wooden platform.

"Go on, sit back down," he said again.

Reluctantly, Jacob slowly sat back down, never taking his eyes from this strange man.

"Now, you can talk about it if you want; I'll be glad to listen," the man said with a grin. "Or you can just tell the sky and the river and the trees. They're the best listeners you'll ever find. I come here to work things out all the time, and I always get my answer."

"I wish someone would give me some answers," Jacob told him.

"Are you a minister or something?"

Jacob looked at him in surprise.

"It's Sunday and you're wearing a suit," the man explained. "I just kind of figured."

"I'm a music director at a church in Green Grove. Or at least, I was," Jacob said, shaking his head. "I'm not sure what I am now."

"Okay," the other man nodded.

"I called the pastor a liar," Jacob admitted, unsure why he was telling this stranger anything.

"Whoa!" the man said, taken aback for a moment. "Is he a liar?"

"Yes," Jacob said simply. "He said some untrue and very unkind things about...some people I know. And he said it to the whole congregation. I couldn't just sit there and take it anymore."

"So you did what you thought was right," his new friend said, watching him closely.

"I thought so at the time, but now I'm not so sure. I've probably lost my job and everything I ever had, not that I had a lot to begin with."

"No, you did the right thing, son, if you stood up for what you believe."

He watched Jacob for a few moments.

"Do you believe in what you stood up for?"

"Yes, I think so, but it's kind of complicated. It goes against everything I was ever taught."

"It's not complicated, and it doesn't matter what you were taught. What does your heart tell you?" the man asked gently. "I know that sounds corny to a young man like you, but your heart is already telling you the truth, or you wouldn't have had the nerve to stand up to your pastor."

Jacob looked at him thoughtfully.

"You think about that," he went on, standing up and smiling down at Jacob. "Close your eyes and listen. You already have your answer. It's right there." He pointed to Jacob's chest.

"Go on, close your eyes and sit there for a while. Don't think, just sit. That's all you have to do." Suddenly feeling very tired, Jacob did as he was told. As he sat there, feeling the gentle cool breeze and the warm sun on his face, he began to relax, and soon he felt a calm, peaceful feeling spread across his being. After what seemed like a few minutes of quiet meditation, he opened his eyes and looked down at his hand. For some reason he was holding a flat, smooth stone in his left hand. It was a curious purplish color and was perfectly rounded and as smooth as silk to the touch. He looked up to speak to his companion and was startled to see that he was all alone. The only evidence that someone had actually been there was another small, smooth river rock lying on the bench where the stranger had been sitting. Jacob looked at his watch and was astonished to see that almost two hours had passed since he first climbed the long wooden steps through the trees.

With a sigh, he stood up and straightened his clothes. He put the small, smooth stone in his pocket with a small smile. Taking one last look out at the beautiful scenery before him, he took a deep breath and descended the long flight of steps to his car.

When he arrived home, he was dismayed to see a couple of cars parked in his driveway and in front of his house. He parked on the street in front of Anthony's house and walked up his front steps. Carl, Edna, and Brandon stood up from where they had been sitting on the front porch waiting for him.

"There you are," Edna exclaimed with relief. "Jacob, we've been so worried about you."

"Brandon told us what you did," Carl told him. The three of them gathered around him, offering their sincere concern and understanding.

"I'm fine," Jacob told them, embarrassed by the attention. "I just can't believe I did it."

"But you did do it, Jacob!" Brandon said. "You stood up for what's right!"

He gave Jacob a quick hug.

"That took a lot of guts, man!" he said admiringly. "I'm so impressed!"

"Yes, it did, Jacob," Carl agreed with a warm smile. "I'm so proud of you, son. We all are."

He placed his arm around Jacob's shoulders affectionately. His kind sentiment brought unwanted tears to Jacob's eyes. Neither of his parents had ever said those words to him that he could remember, and though he had known the Johnson's only a short time, he felt closer to them than his own family.

"But what will you do, Jacob?" Edna asked with a frown.

"I...I don't know," Jacob said, feeling more than a little dazed as he contemplated an uncertain future.

"Don't worry about that, Jacob," Brandon told him. "You did the right thing, what you had to do, so it will all work itself out."

"Absolutely, dear," Edna said soothingly. "Don't worry about a thing."

CHAPTER SIXTEEN

Jacob sat at his beloved Clavinova late that afternoon, playing anything that came to mind, trying to soothe his over-stimulated nerves. After a few hours, he felt better, even as he kept looking at his phone, which he had finally turned back on, waiting for a call or text from Pastor Cal. Instead, a short knock came on the front door.

"Lance, this is a surprise," Jacob said as he pushed the screen door open.

"I know, I'm sorry," Lance said as he stepped into the living room. "I should have called. I just wanted to see how you are after what happened this morning."

He stepped closer and hugged Jacob.

"I'm okay, I guess," Jacob said. "Still a little shell shocked. I can't believe I did that."

"I couldn't believe it, either," Lance told him with a grin, releasing him. "But I was very impressed. I know I never could have done it."

"Well, I'm glad you're impressed, but all it means is that I'm more than likely out of a job."

Lance nodded sympathetically.

"You never know," he said. "The congregation likes you. And I want you to know it means a lot more than that to me, and probably a lot of other people. You and the Johnson's stood up for what you believe in, Jacob. Poor Pastor Cal was beside himself after all of you walked out."

"Poor Pastor Cal?" Jacob said with a frown. "The man was saying terrible lies about us, Lance."

"I know," Lance sighed. "He is obviously very anti-gay."

"It's the same thing I've been taught my whole life," Jacob said, becoming angry again as he remembered Pastor Cal's words, "and I just couldn't take it any more. When Carl and Edna stood up to him, and he made that snide remark about them, I realized how wrong people like him are, because there are no better Christian people in the world than the Johnson's. He's dead wrong! And I knew in that same instant that God has no problem with gay people at all. It's only religious and ignorant people who have a problem, and they're the ones spreading lies about people like us. They're the sinners, not us."

"You're right," Lance agreed, shaking his head sadly. "Just like my folks."

They sat down on the sofa.

"Mine, too," Jacob agreed.

"So what will you do now?" Lance asked.

"I have no idea," Jacob told him with a shrug of his shoulders. "Once my parents find out that I'm gay, if they haven't already, they'll probably disown me. They bought this house for me, so I'll probably lose it. Knowing them as I do, they'd never let me keep it."

"Is it in their name, or yours?"

"I'm not sure, come to think of it," Jacob admitted. "I've got the papers here somewhere. They put all kinds of legal papers together in a file for me."

"I'd check on that, if I were you," Lance advised. Jacob thought for a moment, and then lifted the lid on the old trunk in front of the sofa. He rummaged through it briefly before pulling out a thick folder. Together they looked through the papers that Jacob's parents had put together for him. There was a last will and testament, leaving everything Jacob owned to them, plus an advanced directive, naming them as his power of attorney for healthcare. They scanned the rest of the papers, but found nothing regarding the house.

"What about papers from your realtor?" Lance suggested.

Jacob pulled another folder out of the trunk.

"You really need to keep these papers in a fireproof safe," Lance told him reprovingly.

"I'll get one," Jacob said as he handed the folder to Lance.

"Here you go," Lance said as he scanned its contents. "This lists you as the sole owner of the house. The bill of sale has their names on it along with yours, but your name is the only one on the deed."

"So, what does that mean?" Jacob asked him.

"That means that you are the sole owner."

He continued to peruse the multiple pages in front of him.

"There's no lien on it, apparently," Lance said as he studied the documents.

"No, they paid cash for it," Jacob said, remembering. "They bought it at auction, and I remember they didn't pay very much for it."

"Well, then it looks to me like it belongs to you," Lance told him with a smile. "They can't take it away from you even if they wanted to."

"That's a relief, I suppose," Jacob said. "At least I'll have a place to live. So, I guess all I need is a job."

"You haven't heard from Pastor Cal yet?" Lance asked.

"No, but I'm sure I will," Jacob said dryly. He changed the subject. "So, how have you been? I haven't seen you for a while."

"I'm okay," Lance said unconvincingly. "I haven't stopped by because I didn't want to cause any problems between you and your neighbor."

"I appreciate that, but that ship has already sailed. He hates me, but at least you and I are still friends, right?"

"Of course," Lance nodded. "I hope we can still be more than friends."

"I've been thinking about that," Jacob said hesitantly. "I'm not sure we should have sex anymore, as much as I still want to. Not as long as you're married to Linda. It doesn't feel right."

"But you know my situation, Jacob," Lance said. "I'd get a divorce if I could, but I can't."

"I don't know, Lance," Jacob said. "I really care about you, and I love being with you. But…"

Lance grabbed him and kissed him hard. Jacob resisted and tried to break away from him. Finally, he relented and gave in to the passion and lust he was feeling. When they pulled away from each other at last, Lance looked at him hopefully.

"Would you be with me just one more time?" he asked quietly. "Now?"

Jacob looked at him affectionately, brushing a stray hair from his forehead. What the hell did he have to lose, he thought wryly? He nodded slowly and took Lance's hand in his, leading him to the bedroom. They quickly undressed and intertwined their bodies together on the bed for the next hour, passionately trying to satiate their longing for each other. Finally, they lay side by side in each other's arms, sweaty and exhausted.

"Isn't there a way, Lance?" Jacob asked after he caught his breath. "Can't you and Linda work something out? You both deserve to be happy. You could both still be with the people you're meant to be with."

"The only way would be to get a divorce, and my dad would never stand for that."

"Lance, I'm no one to be giving advice, believe me, but maybe it's time to stand up to your dad," Jacob said. "I mean, I stood up for myself for the first time in my life today, and it felt really good. Not that I wasn't terrified when I did it. Hell, I'm still scared to death of what's going to happen. But I'm still glad I did it."

Lance looked over at him thoughtfully.

"You're a lot braver than I am, Jacob," he said, shaking his head. "It's too late for me."

"Stop it! Why would you say that?" Jacob said indignantly. "You're still young. You're handsome and sexy and fun to be with. It's not too late, and I don't want to hear you say that ever again."

"Honestly, I don't know if I could be alone," Lance confided in him. "I've never been on my own before. It sounds lonely and a little terrifying."

"Maybe terrifying is good for us, Lance. Maybe we have to take a chance and stand up for ourselves for once. Besides, what's the worst that could happen?"

"I lose my home, my job, my family, my friends," Lance said dryly, standing and reaching for his clothes.

"Well, if worse comes to worst, I have a spare room you can stay in, and you'll still have me as a friend, along with the Johnson's. And don't forget Lucas," Jacob said.

"No, I haven't forgotten Lucas," Lance said with a small smile. "We've talked several times lately, and gone out for coffee a couple of times. He's a really wonderful guy."

Jacob felt a pang of jealousy for a moment, and then let it go. He knew that he cared for Lance as a friend, and they had a lot of fun together, but he knew deep down that they would never be anything more than just good friends. He also knew in his heart who it was that he was really in love with.

"See, you already have friends."

"I don't know, Jacob," Lance said doubtfully. "But I guess it's something to think about, at the very least."

Lance kissed and hugged him goodbye. Jacob stood at the front door and watched him drive away in his shiny black Cadillac CT6. With a sigh, he checked his phone again, but there were no messages and no missed calls from Pastor Cal. There were, however, several missed calls and a couple of messages from Peter. He dialed his voicemail and quickly deleted the messages without listening to them. He threw on some shorts and a shirt and wandered through the house, ambling aimlessly onto his back porch. A noise caught his attention, and he looked over at Anthony's house. Keith was standing with his arms around Anthony in the driveway next to his Honda Goldwing. They just can't keep their hands off of each other, he thought as a stabbing pain pierced his stomach. They talked briefly before Keith donned his helmet and climbed aboard the big machine. With a touch of a button he started the engine and guided the bike down the drive onto the street. Anthony watched him go for a moment before turning away. His gaze fell on Jacob, who quickly looked away and started back into his house. "Jacob, wait a minute!" Anthony called out to him. Jacob hesitated, trying to decide whether to pretend he hadn't heard him or not. Enough pretending, he thought. He turned back and looked at Anthony questioningly.

"Can you come over and talk for a minute?" Anthony asked him.

"What do you want to talk about?" Jacob called back with a frown.

"Will you just come over here?" Anthony said sternly, and then added more softly. "Please?"

Unwillingly, Jacob descended his back steps and walked through his gate. Once they were seated in the comfortable furniture on Anthony's deck, he spoke first.

"I never got to thank you for helping me after my surgery," he said, not looking at Anthony directly. "So, thank you."

"How are you doing?" Anthony asked.

"Fine," Jacob responded in a dull voice. "I guess."

"No pain, or anything?"

"No, I almost forgot I even had surgery until just now."

"That's great. I'm glad," Anthony said sincerely. "I knew you'd do just fine."

Jacob stared out at the serenity garden but didn't reply.

"Look, I wanted to apologize for the other night," Anthony said.

"Why?" Jacob said without turning around. "I already know what you think of me, Anthony, so I don't see any reason for you to apologize to me. I know that I'm just a joke to all of you. Especially you. Let's just forget it and go our separate ways. We don't need to be friends."

"Keith shouldn't have said what he said," Anthony stated.

"Oh, I see," Jacob nodded with a frown. "You're only apologizing for what Keith said. Gotcha."

He stood up to leave.

"Well, you know what? You can tell your precious Keith to go straight to hell, and the rest of you can join him. Peter, Neil, Myra, and the others. Oh, yeah, and especially you!"

"Jacob…" Anthony began.

"No, don't even bother, Anthony," he said as his anger grew. "You made it obvious before that you think I'm a horrible person for what I believe, and for fucking a married man. And you all made it extremely clear that night by laughing at me. But you know what's really a joke?" He threw his hands in the air. "I thought all of them were my friends. I cared about them so much, and I especially cared about… You know what? Never mind, because it doesn't matter now. It looks like Brandon is the only one not laughing at me."

"He's a little young for you, isn't he?" Anthony said, half jokingly.

"For god's sake, I'm not fucking him! He's only seventeen, he's just a kid!" Jacob yelled at him. "Damn it!"

"Wait. Did you just say 'fucking' and 'damn it'?" Anthony asked in surprise.

"Yes, I did, and let me say it again," Jacob said loudly, trying to suppress the angry tears that threatened to fall. "Fuck all of you!"

With that, he stormed away and ran into his own house.

What the hell was that about, Anthony wondered? He understood that Jacob was very hurt by what happened that night. But what was with the profanity? He had never heard Jacob swear before. In fact, he didn't think Jacob was even capable of using foul language. He picked up his phone and hit speed dial. When Peter answered, he told him about his conversation with Jacob.

"You don't know the half of it, honey!" Peter exclaimed.

He went on to tell him how his parents and Jacob had publicly stood up against Pastor Cal's anti-gay tirade that morning, and that Jacob had almost certainly lost his job. Anthony's jaw dropped as he listened.

"Oh, my god!" was all he could say when Peter had finished. "Jacob really did that?"

"Yes, he did. So what are we going to do?" Peter asked after a moment. "We all love him, and the last thing we wanted to do was to hurt him. If only Keith had kept his fucking mouth shut!"

"We can't blame Keith for all of it," Anthony reminded him. "Jacob saw that we were all trying not to laugh. He just took it that we were laughing at *him*, not that ridiculous class he was being forced to teach. His ego is really fragile right now."

"Well, it sounds like he's learned to accept a few things about being gay. Otherwise he wouldn't have stood up to that prick Hanson like he did, and in front of the whole church, too. Oh, girlfriend, I wish I could have seen it! You should hear Mom and Dad talk about it. They're so proud of him; they can't stop talking about it. And they're mad at all of us for that night, too, by the way. I've tried to call him several times, but it always goes to voicemail. It's clear he doesn't want to talk to us."

"He's hurt and embarrassed," Anthony told him. "I just wish he had told me about all of this. Although, why would he, after I yelled at him the way I did? Look, why don't all of you come over for a cook out next Saturday?" Anthony suggested. "Maybe we can get him over here."

"That's fine, but we need to do something before then," Peter said.

He agreed to call each of their friends before he hung up. Anthony slowly lowered his phone as he stared thoughtfully at Jacob's house.

It sounded like Jacob had come a long way in accepting his sexuality, and perhaps in reconciling it with his beliefs. Standing up to his pastor must have been an incredibly difficult thing for him to do, and yet he had done it, as difficult as it was for him to believe. No wonder he was so upset with all of them. He was struggling to overcome a huge spiritual obstacle, and he had been on the brink of success when they had seemingly mocked him for it. Of course they hadn't meant to mock him, but that was how it had appeared to Jacob. If only Keith had kept his mouth shut. He truly loved him, but sometimes he could just strangle that guy!

The call from Pastor Cal came that evening around nine o'clock.
"Hello?" Jacob said apprehensively, sitting up from where he had been lounging on the couch, staring at the ceiling.
"There will be a board meeting tomorrow night at the church at seven o'clock," Pastor Cal said without preamble. "You will need to be there."
"Okay," Jacob said calmly.
With a click, the call ended.

CHAPTER SEVENTEEN

Jacob tossed his phone on the sofa and stood up restlessly. He paced around his house and finally stepped out on the front porch. Old-fashioned streetlights gave Maple Street a warm, small town appeal, and he decided to go for a walk and think. He set out toward the downtown, walking slowly with his hands in his pockets.

By this time tomorrow night he would be unemployed from his first real job. He hadn't even made it two whole months yet and he'd already failed. He was surprised that he hadn't heard from his parents at all. In spite of the promise he had made to Pastor Cal that he would call them after his surgery, he had done no such thing. In fact, he couldn't help but wonder why they hadn't called him. Their oldest son was facing surgery in another state, and not a word from them? Oddly, he felt no obligation to call them. A thought had occurred to him back when this job in Green Grove had come up, and it resurfaced now. His parents had gone to great effort in getting him this job and buying this house; it was almost as if they were anxious to get rid of him. Of course, that idea was only in his head, but he couldn't help but wonder. And now that he was here, not a word from them in weeks. He also wondered if they had somehow figured out that he was gay, and that was why they wanted him away from their family and church. Perhaps it was unlikely, but he still wondered.

To tell the truth, he was actually glad to be away from his family. This was his first time on his own, and as terrified as he had been at first, he was delighted to be here. He had met Carl and Edna, who had made him feel truly loved and special for the first time in his life. Of course, he supposed his parents loved him, but it was a cool, reserved kind of love. He thought of Carl telling him how proud he was of him, and once again his eyes welled up. Had his parents ever praised him or hugged him? He assumed they had, but try as he might, he couldn't remember a single time.

He planned to pick up a newspaper in the morning and start searching the want ads. As long as his house was here, he would probably stay in Green Grove. He had no desire to go back to Indy anyway. Maybe Carl could recommend him for a job somewhere. He didn't really care what kind of job he found as long as he could pay his bills.

The thought of running into people from church, or Anthony, or Peter and the rest bothered him, but he would just have to find a way to avoid them as long as he was here. Ironic, wasn't it? Just as he was coming to accept his sexuality, here he was living in a small town where the chances of finding a boyfriend were pretty much nonexistent. Was this God's idea of a joke, he wondered? If it was, he didn't see the humor in it.

True, he had found a man he had come to care deeply about right next door, but he had screwed that relationship up royally before it ever had the chance to begin. And now Anthony was with Keith. He was very fond of Lance, but there was no chance of a relationship with him, either. Brandon was an adorable and sweet young man, but he was just a boy who would be leaving for college in the fall. The only other gay men he knew were Lucas and Randall, but he wasn't interested in them romantically, and vice versa. Besides, they regarded him as a fool.

His eyes welled up as his thoughts returned to Anthony. He was so incredibly beautiful. And he was kind and sweet and gentle. So manly, too. He pictured him in the full black leather outfit he was wearing at Castle Rock. He couldn't imagine anything sexier than Anthony in leather, unless it was him wearing nothing at all. He thought back to the night when Anthony had been all hot and sweaty from mowing the lawn, and the image and the memory of his masculine smell immediately made him hard.

Why, God? Why put him next door to the most beautiful man he could imagine, only to make him unavailable? He had to believe that God had a plan for him, but at the moment, he had no clue what that plan was. He had brought him here to this small town, only to have him fall in love with someone he couldn't have, make new friends that he lost in a matter of weeks, and begin a job that he had also lost. What the hell was going on? The only positive thing he could find in the whole ridiculous mess was his newfound peace with himself and with his sexuality. He found that he no longer feared God's wrath for simply being who he was. And in spite of the pain he was feeling with everything else, he felt more content and happier than he ever had before. He walked a little faster and couldn't stop a tiny smile from crossing his face.

As he continued walking through the downtown, he heard a motorcycle come up the street behind him. He looked over as it slowly passed by, but turned quickly away as he recognized Anthony. The bike continued on its way, and Jacob breathed a sigh of relief as he watched it turn right at the corner at the end of the block.

He kept walking and thinking until he eventually found himself in front of Peter and Neil's house. In the circular driveway sat Carl and Edna's BMW, Anthony's motorcycle, Brandon's compact car, and a couple of other cars that looked vaguely familiar. That's just great, he thought, they're having another party, but this time didn't even bother to invite him. Of course they didn't, he told himself, since they thought he was a fool, and he had made it clear that he wanted nothing to do with them. He had ignored Peter's calls, and even told Anthony they could all go to hell. So why would he expect to be invited? Still, it hurt deeply to know that his former friends, practically everyone he knew, were just a few feet away, laughing and drinking and having a marvelous time, and he couldn't be part of it. He choked back unwelcome tears and walked dejectedly the two blocks to his own house, feeling a sudden overwhelming loneliness.

The next morning Jacob sat on the padded bench in front of his Clavinova. He tried to concentrate on the music in front of him, but found that his mind kept wandering. There was just too much to think about, with the upcoming board meeting, finding a new job, Anthony, and his former friends. Every time he thought about Anthony and the others, he felt a sharp pain in his stomach. Finally giving up on playing, he dressed and walked to the downtown to buy a newspaper.

When he returned to his house, Brandon's small Ford was sitting in his driveway. Steeling himself, he walked up the front porch steps and greeted the young man cheerfully.

"I picked up a paper to start job hunting," he told Brandon as they walked into the house together. They walked into the kitchen and Jacob grabbed a soft drink from the refrigerator, handing one to Brandon as well. They went into the living room and sat down on the sofa.

"So how are you doing?" Brandon asked with concern. "You look exhausted."

"I haven't slept well for a few weeks," Jacob admitted. "But I'm fine. Don't worry about me."

"I am worried, and so is everyone else," Brandon told him.

"You mean Carl and Edna," Jacob said with a small smile. "I sure love those two dear people!"

"No, not just them," Brandon said. "I mean everybody."

"Hmm," Jacob shrugged. "So has your dad said anything about me, or the board meeting tonight?"

"No, he's not said much of anything to me since yesterday morning."

"Well, I guess I'll find out everything I need to know tonight," Jacob said grimly.

"I guess so," Brandon agreed with a worried expression. "So what kind of job are you going to look for?"

"Anything that will let me pay my bills. It doesn't matter what it is, really."

"Maybe Mr. Johnson has an opening at the bank?" Brandon suggested.

"I thought of that," Jacob admitted. "I'll ask him about it the next time I see him."

"I just saw their car over at Peter and Neil's on the way here. Why don't you go over and see him?"

"I don't think so, Brandon," Jacob said dryly. "I'm not going back there. Not after the last time."

"Why not?"

"I'll tell you, if you'll tell me how the party was last night," Jacob said pointedly.

"Party?"

"Don't, Brandon. I saw all the cars there last night when I was out for a walk," Jacob said.

"Oh," Brandon said briefly.

He looked at Jacob.

"You know, everyone is really sorry about what happened, Jacob. They really didn't mean to hurt your feelings."

"Yeah, whatever," Jacob said dismissively.

"NO!" Brandon said angrily. "Not 'whatever'! Listen to me! They weren't laughing at you, Jacob, they were laughing at the name of that stupid class. 'Waiting for Marriage'. You have to admit, it is kind of funny if you think about it. A gay man being told he has to teach a class to a bunch of straight people about marriage. I know how it looked to you that night because it looked the same way to me, too. I was furious! That's why I told that Keith guy off and threatened to beat the shit out of him. He was acting like a jerk, and the Johnson's told him so after you left. So did Peter and Anthony."

Jacob looked up at him sharply.

"Anthony stood up for me?" he frowned. "Against his own boyfriend?"

"Yes, he did. Everyone did. None of them think you're a joke, Jacob, honestly! They all love you very much. And that was no party last night. Peter called them – us – all together to try to figure out how to make it up to you. That's why we were all there at church yesterday morning. They wanted to show you how much they support you. And how much we all love you."

Jacob stared at him, stunned.

"That's why they all came?" he said. "I thought…"

"You've got to forgive them, Jacob. Peter and Neil and the rest. They really do love you, and they're very impressed and proud of you, too, especially after what you did yesterday morning. They were already proud of you before that, but now you're kind of their hero."

Jacob shook his head in wonder.

"They didn't come to make fun?"

"No, of course not! How could you think that? Peter and Neil understand what you're going through with the church. They're worried sick about you, too, especially since no one has been able to get hold of you. They feel really bad about this whole situation. They're afraid you'll leave Green Grove. We all are."

Jacob sat back on the sofa, wiping the dampness from his eyes. He covered his face with his hands.

"Oh, my god! I just keep ruining every relationship in my life. Damn it! Brandon, I misread all of this! I…I thought…I thought they were laughing at me, and I'm such a stupid mess, I couldn't handle it. I'm such an idiot!"

"No, you're not," Brandon said firmly. "I thought the same thing you did, and I told them so. But just because we were wrong doesn't mean we are idiots. If you had stayed that night, you would have realized it wasn't you they were laughing at. I can tell you, I know for a fact that they love you, they're proud of you, and they want to make it up to you." He took Jacob's hand in his.

"Now, are you going to do the Christian thing and forgive them, or do you want to be like my dad?"

The two of them chuckled as Jacob squeezed Brandon's hand affectionately.

"I need to call Peter, don't I?"

"The sooner, the better!"

After Brandon left, Jacob picked up his phone and started to call Peter. Before he pushed Peter's name on the screen to dial, he stopped and put the phone in his pocket. He grabbed his keys and walked the few blocks to Peter and Neil's house. Peter was just backing his small gray Audi convertible out of the garage as Jacob walked up the curving driveway. He stopped the car and smiled when he saw Jacob. As he got out of the small vehicle, Jacob ran over to him and hugged him. They stood like that for several seconds.

"I am so sorry, Peter," Jacob said earnestly.

"Why are you sorry, Jacob? You didn't do anything wrong," Peter chuckled, giving him an extra tight squeeze before releasing him. "We all owe you the apology."

"You tried to tell me…"

"You're feelings were hurt, and we're all so sorry that we caused that," Peter said.

"I thought you all were laughing at me."

"Now, listen to me a minute, and listen good!" Peter said, taking Jacob's chin firmly in his hand. "No one was laughing at you. Do you understand that?" Jacob nodded.

"I do now, thanks to Brandon. I'm so sorry I keep screwing everything up," he said.

"You're not screwing anything up, sweetheart. You thought we were laughing at you, and it really hurt your feelings. I'd have felt the same way. Anybody would be hurt if they thought their friends didn't respect them. But you need to understand and believe me when I tell you that everyone there that night, except maybe for Keith, loves and respects you very much."

"Well, not everyone," Jacob said wryly. "But there's nothing I can do about that, I guess."

"We *all* love you, Jacob. Including Anthony."

Jacob looked up at him with surprise.

"What happened between you two after your surgery?" Peter continued. "You were getting along so well."

"It's just another one of my screw ups," Jacob said lightly. "It doesn't matter anymore, anyway."

"Are you sure about that?" Peter asked with a frown. "Because I think it does matter."

"Well, anyway, I'm sorry I misread everything," Jacob said, changing the subject. "I love you guys more than anything in the world."

"I know," Peter said with a grin. "And I'm so impressed with you, you big strong man, you! Standing up to Hanson in front of everyone! Your balls must be the size of a bull's!"

They chuckled together.

"Not at all," Jacob said. "I was scared to death. But I just couldn't sit there and listen to that nonsense any more."

"So you do think what he was saying was nonsense?"

"Yes, I do," Jacob said sincerely. "I did a lot of reading and praying, and I knew in my heart that the things he was saying were all wrong, and he was just spreading hate, like all the other preachers I've heard all my life."

"I'm so glad to hear that, girl!" Peter said. "Now, what about your job?"

"There's a board meeting tonight at seven that I'm supposed to attend."

"I know. Dad told me. Oh, my god, what will you do if they fire you?"

"I have no idea," Jacob said with a shake of his head.

"You won't leave Green Grove, will you?"

"No, I'm not planning to, since my house is here," Jacob replied. "Lance said my parents can't take it away from me."

"Why would they do that?"

"Once they find out I'm gay I'm sure they'll completely disown me," Jacob shrugged. "Which is fine; I don't want to go back to Indy anyway. Everything – everyone – I love is here."

"Oh, darling, that's good news," Peter said, giving him a quick hug. "Now don't worry about that job. If worse comes to worst, I'll get you a job at Larson's. It doesn't pay much, but it will get you by for now."

"Oh, Peter, thank you!" Jacob said, giving him a relieved smile. "I might have to take you up on that, if you're sure."

"Of course I am! It does have its perks, you know. Every so often I get to see a cute young thing in his sexy underwear!"

Peter grinned and arched one eyebrow as Jacob blushed.

"Well, you were going somewhere, so I'll be on my way," Jacob said.

"We'll all be thinking about you tonight," Peter said as he dropped down into the seat of the convertible. "Now, don't worry about a thing. It will all work out the way it's supposed to."

"I know," Jacob nodded, trying to look nonchalant.

Peter reached out and took his hand.

"It really will, sweetie," he said gently. "Just believe that."

As soon as Peter got to work, he got on the phone and called everyone in their circle of friends, telling them about his conversation with Jacob. He called Anthony last.

"Hello, Petey," Anthony said into his phone.

"Are you busy?"

"No, I don't have another client for thirty minutes. What's up?"

"I just spoke to Jacob. He came over to the house."

"Really?" Anthony said, suddenly all ears. "What did he say?"

"Apparently, Brandon was able to get through to him and make him understand that we weren't laughing at him. I told him how sorry we all were and that we all love him."

"Well, that's a relief," Anthony said. "I'm glad. I hated the thought of him feeling hurt and alone."

"He's feeling much better now that we're all friends again. And based on what he said, it seems to me he's worked through a whole bunch of his issues with the church. He truly believes that Hanson was wrong. He looked less uptight and more relaxed than I've ever seen him."

"Did you invite him to the cook out on Saturday?" Anthony asked.

"No, I think you should ask him. So what happened after his surgery?" Peter asked abruptly. "You've never told me."

"It doesn't matter," Anthony said.

"I think it does," Peter said wisely. "Because I think you're crazy about him, and I'm pretty sure he's in love with you."

"What?" Anthony said. "Are you out of your mind? I tried talking to him and he told me to fuck off."

"He's trying to protect himself by pushing you away, that's all. You're both giving me the same lame story. 'It doesn't matter'. That just tells me that it does matter a lot to both of you."

"I don't know, Petey," Anthony sighed. "I guess you're right, it does matter to me."

"I know," Peter told him with a smile in his voice. "It's kind of nice to see you all worked up over a guy. You never used to be like that."

"True, except for that one time," Anthony agreed with a grin. "There was just one boy I ever fell in love with, back when we were in school."

"I remember, sweetie," Peter said. "I loved you, too, just like I do now. But you know we were meant to be best friends, not boyfriends."

There was a brief pause and then Peter sighed loudly.

"If only you'd been rich, or something," he added.

"You shallow bitch!" Anthony laughed.

"You got that right, honey!"

CHAPTER EIGHTEEN

At six o'clock that evening, Jacob sat anxiously on his sofa, dressed in slacks and a blazer. He tried in vain to relax for a while, but finally stood up and began pacing around the house. He tried to play the piano, but gave that up almost immediately and resumed pacing. At six thirty he decided to go ahead and drive over to the church. He could hide in his office until seven o'clock.

He grabbed his keys and headed for the garage. Anthony's Harley Davidson was parked in front of his garage. As Jacob stepped through his gate, Anthony emerged from the back door of his house wearing his full black leather motorcycle gear.

"Hey," Jacob said in a small voice, trying not to stare at the ruggedly handsome man.

"Hey," Anthony replied with a short nod in his direction. "You're all dressed up. Time for the big meeting?"

"How'd you know about that?" Jacob asked him with surprise.

"Peter told me."

"Oh, okay."

Jacob looked around uneasily for a moment.

"Well, I guess I'll see ya," he said as he moved to his car.

"You want a lift?" Anthony called after him.

"Thanks, but I'll drive."

"The motorcycle's all ready to go," Anthony said enticingly. "You just need your helmet."

Jacob looked back at him and was surprised and a little amused to see him already holding his extra helmet in his hand. He stared at the helmet for a moment and then raised his eyes to meet Anthony's. "Oh, what the hell!" he said finally.

"That's the spirit," Anthony grinned and handed him the helmet.

Once again, Jacob struggled with the chin strap, so Anthony stood in front of him, just inches away, and helped him with the final adjustment. This time, Jacob didn't try to avoid looking at him as he had done before. He stared freely at Anthony, admiring the masculine beauty of the man.

Anthony tried to hide his smile as he noticed Jacob staring openly at him. He finished adjusting the chin strap and then donned his own helmet. As before, he climbed aboard the big bike and extended a hand to Jacob, who reached out gingerly and then grasped it tightly. Once he was aboard he placed his arms carefully around Anthony's waist. When they started down the driveway, he slowly and hesitantly leaned against Anthony's back, wrapping his arms tighter around his torso. God, why does he have to feel so good?

Instead of heading downtown and up Market Street to the church, Anthony headed east out of town on the highway. He brought the motorcycle up to cruising speed as they emerged into the open countryside. Once again, Jacob felt a surge of elation and excitement rushing through him. He leaned back against the backrest and raised his hands into the air. For a few moments he forgot about the board meeting, the church, his parents, even Anthony, as he reveled in the pure joy of rushing through the warm, fresh, sweet smelling air of northern Illinois.

Anthony slowed the bike and rolled to a stop in the parking lot of the same fertilizer plant they had been to before. He climbed off and removed his helmet.

"Oh, my god!" Jacob said with delight. "I love this!"

"Do you?" Anthony asked with a happy grin.

"Oh, yeah! I want to learn how to drive a motorcycle! Will you teach me?"

Jacob quickly sobered as he realized what he had just said.

"I mean, maybe you could give me some tips or something," he said with an indifferent shrug of his shoulders.

"Sure, I'd be glad to teach you to ride," Anthony said eagerly. "You could ride with Keith and me." He noticed that the shy smile immediately left Jacob's face at the mention of Keith's name.

"Oh, well, that's okay," Jacob said with a frown. "I probably couldn't do it anyway. Just forget it."

"No, Jacob, I think you'd be great on a bike," Anthony protested.

"No thanks. You'd better get me back now. You can take me home if you want and I'll drive myself."

"No, I'll take you there," Anthony said. "And I'll take you home afterwards."

Why did I have to mention Keith, he asked himself angrily? Obviously Jacob is still touchy about the remark he made that night at the party. He just needs to get to know Keith to see what a great guy he is. With a sigh he climbed aboard the bike, strapped on his helmet, and pointed them toward town. He couldn't help but notice that Jacob held on to him much less on the way back to town.

Jacob got off the big motorcycle in front of the church doors. He handed the helmet to Anthony. "Thank you for the ride," he said. "It was wonderful. But I can get a ride home after the meeting, so you don't have to wait on me."

"I told you I'd be here to take you home," Anthony said firmly. "And I will be right here, waiting for you."

"Thanks, Anthony," he said in a small voice. Straightening his shoulders, he looked up at the imposing building and walked resolutely through the front doors. Alone.

Ten of the twelve board members were already seated in the conference room around the impressive rectangular walnut table that filled the room. A few of them rose from their chairs to greet him with a grave smile and to shake his hand, but most remained in their chairs. He noticed that Pastor Cal was not present, and neither was Carl. He stood beside the door for a few moments, unsure what to do, as Pastor Cal strode confidently through the door and took the seat at the head of the large table. He carried an enormous Bible with him, Jacob noticed.

A minute or two after Pastor Cal sat down, Carl and Edna entered the room, stopping to give Jacob a hearty hug.

"Edna, I'm afraid you are not a board member," Pastor Cal said with a frown. "And as such, I'm going to have to ask you to leave."

"Would you like to try and make me, Pastor?" Edna said sweetly, flashing him a winning smile.

She calmly sat down in a chair against the wall near the door with her purse in her lap as the board members whispered and grumbled among themselves.

"Suit yourself," Pastor Cal said gruffly. "Well, are we all here?"

He looked around the room until his gaze fell on Jacob.

"Mr. Porter, have a seat."

With great trepidation, Jacob forced himself to step forward and sit in the end chair, opposite the pastor.

"You all know why we are here," the pastor intoned solemnly.

"Good Lord, Calvin, this isn't a trial," Carl said.

"Carl, I know you mean well, but let's get through the facts of the situation before we open things up for discussion."

He cleared his throat and paused for effect.

"We are here to discuss the conduct of our music director yesterday. As I was delivering my sermon,

Mr. Porter openly defied me and God in front of the entire congregation."

"So when you say 'me and God', are you saying that you and God are on the same level?" Carl asked with the slightest hint of a grin on his face.

"No, of course not!" Pastor Cal said irritably.

"Okay," Carl said affably. "I just wanted to clarify that."

"Mr. Porter defied me and called me a 'liar'!" the pastor said, returning his attention to the other board members. "Isn't that right, Mr. Porter?"

Jacob nodded.

"Yes, sir."

"Ooh, ooh!" Edna said cheerfully, leaning forward and waving her hand. "Don't forget, I called you a liar, too."

"I haven't forgotten, Edna, believe me," Pastor Cal scowled.

Edna settled happily back in her chair.

"In addition, I'd like to point out that Mr. Porter has also been keeping company with certain people in the community, even though he was warned against it," the pastor added.

"What people?" a board member unknown to Jacob asked.

"Homosexuals," the pastor said. "The same ones who were here in the service yesterday."

"You mean my son," Carl said with just the slightest hint of anger in his voice.

"Yes, Carl, among others. I'm sorry, no offense intended. But it's not my fault that your son is one of them."

"It's no one's fault, Pastor," Carl replied heatedly. "Peter is exactly as God made him. And so are the rest of his friends."

"Now, that's where you're wrong, Carl," the minister said, tapping the book in front of him with his finger. "The Bible makes it clear that homosexuality is a sin."

"Excuse me, Pastor," Jacob said loudly as he stood up in front of his chair. "Why is being gay a sin, but we don't have a problem with the other things mentioned as sins in the Old Testament? Why is it okay to pick and choose what we want to believe?"

"I don't know what you're talking about!" Pastor Cal said huffily.

"Well, I do," Edna said, standing as well. "According to the Bible, eating shellfish or pork is a sin and wearing clothes made of mixed fibers is a sin. And yet we have no problem doing those things today."

"And at the same time, murder, rape, slavery, genocide, and incest are mentioned as sanctioned by God," Carl chimed in. "But who a person loves is a sin if it's someone of the same sex?"

"You have it all wrong, Carl," another board member said. "Those things were part of the Old Testament, and we live by the teachings of Jesus, in the New Testament."

"So why do you always use the Old Testament to condemn gay people?" Edna said loudly. "I'll tell you why. Because Jesus never mentioned homosexuality. He taught love and peace and forgiveness. He said not to judge anyone. Do you hear those words, Pastor? We are not supposed to judge anyone, gay or straight!"

She strode around the table and pointed her finger at Pastor Cal.

"You are judging my son and his friends without even knowing them. Shame on you and anyone else who does that! That's hardly being a Christian, Pastor. Is it?"

She waited as she stared at him, and then turned her attention to the rest of them.

"Well, is it?"

"No, it's not, Edna."

They all turned to see who had spoken. A thin, rather frail elderly man stood up with a small amount of difficulty. He leaned on the table and looked around at all of them.

"It isn't up to us to judge anybody," he continued in a hoarse sounding voice. "That is up to God alone. The only things we have to do, as far as I can tell from the Bible, are to love God and love each other. Simple as that."

He looked directly at the pastor.

"And I've got to tell you, Pastor, I'm not seeing any love here."

He gestured to Jacob.

"Sure, maybe this young man shouldn't have spoken to you the way he did. He probably spoke before he thought because he's so young. He'll learn. But at the same time, you shouldn't have been encouraging this church to judge people they don't know. Why, every one of us probably has a gay person in our own families. I know I do. My own brother is gay, and he's one of the finest people I know."

He pointed at the pastor.

"Even you, Pastor. You could have a gay person in your family. Would you judge them as harshly as you're judging these other people? Would you want some stranger judging a member of your family the way you judge them? I should hope not."

He took a few deep breaths as he looked around the room.

"I'm not saying being gay is right or wrong. How the hell should I know? It's not up to me, and it's not up to any of you to decide that."

He sat down heavily.

"I guess that's all I've got to say."

There was a long pause as the board members looked around at each other, suddenly unsure of themselves.

"Thank you, Charlie," Carl said at last, reaching over to shake the man's hand. "Those were the most Christian words I've heard tonight."

"Jacob, do you have anything to say in your defense?" a board member asked him.

"No," Jacob said. "I take full responsibility for what I did, and what I said."

"Jacob, why don't you step outside for a few minutes and let us discuss the matter," another board member suggested, giving him a friendly smile.

Jacob nodded and left the room, followed closely by Edna.

"So, what do you think?" Jacob said to Edna as they stepped into the tastefully decorated lobby.

"I don't know, dear, but at least Pastor Cal and the rest of them got an earful!" she said with a smile.

"And don't worry. No matter what happens in there, you don't have to worry about a job. Carl will see to that."

"They didn't even ask if I was gay," Jacob said with a perplexed expression. "I thought that would be the first thing they would want to know."

They sat down in a couple of comfortably padded chairs set against a nearby wall.

"Well, either they already know, or they don't want to know," she said. She changed the subject. "I see that young Anthony brought you over on his motorcycle."

"Yes," Jacob admitted, shivering slightly at the thought of riding with his arms around Anthony.

"He's a lovely young man, don't you think?" she said, watching Jacob's face. "Very handsome. Why, if he was straight and I was thirty years younger, look out!"

They laughed together.

"I can just see you on a motorcycle, Edna," Jacob teased.

"You'd be surprised," she said with a mysterious smile. "Carl and I were raised in the 60's and 70's, you know! You're too young, of course, but those were the days, Jacob. Free love, flower power, peace, marijuana. It was a great time to be young." She looked over at him with a warm smile.

"And you and Anthony are both so young right now. You need to enjoy it and be with each other," she advised. "I can tell how you feel about him. You like him very much. Maybe even love him?"

"I wish I didn't," he said, looking down at his hands in his lap.

"Now, why would you say that?" she frowned.

"He has someone, Edna," he said sadly. "He's taken."

"Really?' she said. "I didn't know that. Well, whoever it is, he won't be around long, because I think the two of you belong together."

"You already know his boyfriend –"

"Jacob," a voice called. "Will you please come in?"

"Wow, that didn't take long," he whispered to Edna as the two of them stood up and walked back into the conference room.

Pastor Cal looked at him with a scowl as he took his seat.

"Jacob, we want you to know that we like you very much, and we appreciate the work you're doing with the music here," the same man who had sent them out of the room said.

He hesitated for a moment and then continued.

"We don't want you to leave, so we've decided that you can keep your job on one condition. We want you to apologize to Pastor Cal. Publicly."

The room turned to look at Jacob, who slowly stood up and faced them.

"No," he said firmly. "I can't do that. I won't do it."

The board members whispered among themselves for a moment before Jacob continued.

"Maybe how I stood up to him wasn't the best way to do it. But it would be a slap in the face to everyone who has stood up for me since I've been here. These so called evil people that Pastor Cal was preaching against have been kinder to me, and more loving and supportive, than anyone I have ever known. I cannot betray them. I believe in them. They are my friends – my family."

"Are you certain you know what you're doing, Jacob?" the same man said.

"Absolutely!" Jacob asserted.

"I told you," Pastor Cal said with a condescending look at all of them. "I knew he wouldn't agree to that."

"Pastor Cal, I'll make you a deal," Jacob said suddenly, taking them all by surprise. "I will agree to apologize to you in front of the congregation on one condition. You apologize for the things you said, in front of the congregation. And you apologize to my friends who were here yesterday morning."

He turned away and strode to the door. He looked back at them for a moment.

"I'll give you until Friday to decide."

With those words, he walked confidently out the door and out of the building.

Once he was outside in the deepening twilight, his confidence wavered and he nearly collapsed on the paved parking lot. Anthony was leaning against the Harley, but stood up quickly when he saw Jacob walk through the door. He began to walk over to him, and then ran to catch him before he could fall.

"Oh, my god, Jacob!" he exclaimed. "What happened?"

"Can we just get out of here?" Jacob said tremulously. "Now? Fast?"

Anthony helped him to the bike and quickly helped him with his helmet. In a matter of seconds, the beautiful vehicle was gliding smoothly out of the lot onto Market Street.

Anthony parked the motorcycle in his garage and climbed off carefully. He took off his helmet and leather jacket and gloves and tossed them onto the workbench nearby. He helped Jacob unfasten his chin strap and then pulled the helmet off. Jacob alit shakily from the bike and the two of them walked to Anthony's deck. Once Jacob was seated on the settee, Anthony stepped inside and returned in a moment with a couple of beers. He opened one and handed it to Jacob before sitting down in the closest chair.

"Take a couple of drinks, and then tell me what happened," Anthony told him.

Jacob leaned back and took three big swallows from his beer. Before he could speak, however, they heard first one car, and then two more cars pull into the driveway. Anthony got up from his chair and looked around the back of the house.

"We're back here," he called to the new arrivals.

A moment later, Jacob was surrounded by Peter, Neil, Brandon, Carl, and Edna, who were all excitedly talking to him at once.

"Hold on, everyone," Anthony said loudly, squeezing in next to Jacob on the settee. "Give him a chance to talk."

"You won't believe it!" Edna said, barely able to restrain her excitement. "You won't believe what this boy did!"

"I wouldn't have believed it if I hadn't seen it for myself!" Carl exclaimed. "He was magnificent!"

"Well, tell us, for god's sake!" Peter practically shouted.

"Carl, will you tell it?" Jacob said weakly.

All eyes turned to Carl expectantly. He quickly proceeded to tell them about the meeting, finishing with Charlie's remarks.

"And then they gave him an ultimatum. Apologize or lose his job."

He looked affectionately at Jacob.

"Tell them what you said, Jacob," he said.
"I told them I wouldn't do it," Jacob said simply.
"Tell them the rest, dear," Edna prodded him.
He hesitated for a moment. Before he could speak,
Edna continued for him.
"He said he couldn't apologize because that would
mean betraying his friends. And then he gave them
an ultimatum. He said he would apologize if Pastor
Cal publicly apologized to his congregation and to
all of you."
They all turned to Jacob with a look of awe in their
eyes.
"Oh, my god, Jacob," Peter said incredulously.
"You are fucking unbelievable! I can't believe how
brave you are."
The others nodded enthusiastically in agreement.
"I think that's one of the bravest things I've ever
heard," Anthony said, clinking his beer bottle with
Jacob's.
Jacob looked at him wide-eyed and slowly broke
into a small grin.
"They have until Friday to decide," Carl told them.
He reached over and slapped Jacob on the knee.
"You know, next to my own son and Neil, I don't
know when I've ever been so proud of a young man
as I am of you right now."
Jacob looked back at him and was immediately
overwhelmed with emotion. He fought back the
tears as much as he could, but was not entirely
successful.

"Don't cry, sweetie," Edna said tearfully. "You'll make me cry, too."

Anthony wrapped a strong arm around him and held him tightly as Jacob buried his face in his shoulder for a moment.

"We're all so proud of you, Jacob," Neil said kindly. "That took real courage."

"You're incredible, Jacob," Brandon said. "No one can deny how tough you are ever again."

"That's right, Jacob," Anthony said softly.

Their kind words made it even harder for Jacob to control his tears. A few seconds later, however, he collected himself and dried his eyes.

"No one has ever…" he began. "You are all…"

He looked around at their smiling faces and shook his head.

"All of you are the incredible ones," he said sincerely. "Not me."

CHAPTER NINETEEN

After everyone had left, Anthony went inside to change out of the leather pants he was still wearing. He came back to the deck wearing only a pair of shorts and a ragged tee shirt carrying two bottles of beer, to find Jacob stripping out of his clothes under the dim lights strung over the deck.

"What are you doing?" he chuckled.

Jacob reached down and with a flick of his fingers lifted the hot tub cover.

"What's it look like?" he said with a tired grin.

He slid his underwear off and, after looking at them for a moment, threw them out into the backyard. He stepped down into the water and pushed the button that he had seen Anthony push before. He settled into the bubbling water and reached out for a bottle. Anthony leaned over and handed it to him.

"Are you getting in?" Jacob asked him.

Anthony set his bottle down and quickly stripped out of his clothes, throwing his underwear over his shoulder into the backyard to land beside Jacob's. He climbed down and settled in the warm water beside Jacob.

"So, how are you feeling?" he asked.

"I'm good," Jacob said, settling back.

"You're not worried about what the board will decide?"

"No," Jacob shrugged. "I'm really not. As long as I have you – all of you, I mean – I'm fine. Peter said he'd get me a job, and Edna said Carl would get me a job, too, if necessary. So I'll be able to pay my bills at least."

"So…you're planning on staying, no matter what happens?" Anthony asked casually.

"Yep!" Jacob said. "Lance looked at some of the house papers, and the house is in my name, so my parents can't take it away."

"Is that the only reason you want to stay?"

"No, of course not," Jacob said with a slight frown. "I want to stay because of Peter and Neil, and Carl and Edna, and Myra and Lucas and Randall and Brandon. They're more important to me than my own family. I don't want to think of my life without them."

Anthony waited a moment for him to continue, and then turned away.

"They're all coming over Saturday night for a cook out," he said. "I hope you'll be here."

Jacob nodded.

"It was part of a plan to get you to forgive us," Anthony explained.

"I'm so sorry. I'm past all that," Jacob said as his face turned red. "Brandon set me straight, thank God! I'm really sorry I messed everything up so badly. I took everything the wrong way."

"I'm sorry, too," Anthony told him. "I'm sorry for laughing at what Keith said, even though I wasn't laughing at you, just that stupid class. And I shouldn't have said anything about you and Lance Martin. It was none of my business."

"No, you were right about all of that."

"But I was wrong to criticize. You can sleep with
whoever you want. It has nothing to do with me."
Jacob looked at him sadly. If you only knew how
much everything has to do with you, he thought.
"I stopped sleeping with him, you know."
"Not because of what I said, I hope," Anthony said.
"Well, yes, sort of," Jacob admitted. "It seemed
kind of wrong, him being married and all. He's a
really great guy, but I couldn't stand having you
hating me."
"Hating you?" Anthony said, looking at him with
deep concern. "Oh, my god, is that what you
thought?"
"Well, yes," Jacob said. "Not that I could blame
you. I've been acting like a fool."
"You're not a fool. And I never hated you; I
couldn't hate you."
"Well, it doesn't matter anymore," Jacob told him,
avoiding eye contact with him.
They were silent for a while, each sipping their beer
slowly.
"So, what are you doing tomorrow?" Anthony
asked him.
"I don't know, now that you mention it. Maybe I'll
go talk to Carl or Peter about a job."
"Would you like to go for a bike ride?"
"Oh, wow! Yeah, that'd be great!" Jacob exclaimed
as his face lit up. "You don't have to work?"
"No, I have no clients tomorrow, and I only work at
the hospital two to three days a week now. We

could go up to Castle Rock, if you like, or wherever you want to go. You know, make a day of it."

"You would want to do that?" Jacob said. "I mean, spend the whole day with me? Just the two of us?"

"Sure, why wouldn't I?"

"I don't know," Jacob replied. "Maybe because I'm such an idiot."

"Hell, you're not an idiot. Look how far you've come in such a short time. You're not the same man that moved here a few weeks ago. I mean, you stood up to your minister, your boss, for preaching lies. And in front of the whole church, no less. And you stood up to the church board tonight. You've gone through an amazing transformation. I've got to say, I liked the guy you were before, but I love…I mean, I like the guy you are now even more."

"Thanks, Anthony," Jacob said with a shy grin. "Maybe there's hope for me yet."

The next morning Jacob walked over to the garage where Anthony was busy stowing various items into his second motorcycle, a deep ruby-red Indian Roadmaster with rich black upholstery and chrome accessories.

"Oh, my god," Jacob exclaimed, looking over the sleek and elegant lines of the big machine. "This is gorgeous, Anthony! I don't think I've ever seen anything so beautiful!"

Except you, he said to himself.

"Thanks," Anthony said with a grin, pleased at Jacob's appreciation of his most prized possession. "I've got to agree with you there."

He pulled out a black leather jacket from the garage closet and handed it to Jacob.

"Here," he said. "I want you to wear this. It's just a little tight on me, so it ought to fit you just about right."

Jacob took the jacket eagerly and quickly slipped it on over his navy polo shirt. It fit perfectly. He took a deep breath, imagining that he could smell a little bit of Anthony mingled with the rich scent of the leather.

"That really looks good, Jake!" Anthony said with a long whistle. "You are hot!"

He rummaged through a shelf at the top of the closet and pulled out a pair of black leather driving gloves.

"Now I just need the leather pants," Jacob joked.

"Actually, I've got a couple of extra pairs, if you want to wear them," Anthony offered, pulling out two pairs of leather pants on hangers. "I think one of these would probably fit you."

Jacob took the pair that seemed a little smaller than the other. He stepped behind the Harley and slipped out of his jeans and into the leather pants.

"How do they look?" he asked as he moved out into the open.

Anthony looked up at him and his jaw dropped.

"Oh, fuck, Jake!" Anthony exclaimed. "I mean, holy fuck! You look incredible in that outfit! I don't know if I can keep my hands off of you, or not!" He walked around the younger man and whistled appreciatively once again.

"I've never worn leather like this before," Jacob admitted, pleased at Anthony's reaction. "I feel kind of sexy wearing this."

"Believe me, you are incredibly sexy," Anthony told him. With or without the leather, he thought. "Here's a pair of boots you can wear. I'm afraid the tennis shoes just don't work."

Jacob happily put on the heavy black leather boots that Anthony gave him.

"Oh, Anthony, this is fantastic!" he practically shouted in delight. "I feel like a different person in these clothes."

"Well, you look amazing," Anthony told him sincerely, trying not to stare. He cleared the lump from his throat. "So, are you ready to go?"

"Sure, I'm ready whenever you are."

Anthony gave him a quick overview of the bike, as well as supplies and tools that should be carried at all times. Jacob listened carefully and repeated some of the lecture back to him so that he would remember it better. He was clearly fascinated with everything motorcycle related, and Anthony was delighted that he was proving to be such an eager student.

Once Anthony had completed his checklist, they climbed aboard the shiny, graceful bike and headed

west out of town. Jacob thrilled as they glided
along, as much by the ride as by the continuous
contact with Anthony's leather clad body.
Anthony passed by the entrance to Castle Rock and
drove another quarter of a mile or so to a large
parking lot, picnic area, and boat ramp next to the
wide, placid Rock River. He parked the bike and the
two of them walked past the picnic tables and the
neatly mown grass down to the water's edge. Such
beauty, Jacob thought contentedly, taking a deep
breath of the fresh air. The river curved very gently
here in its slow procession to where it eventually
emptied into the Mississippi at the Quad Cities.
"It's so beautiful here," Jacob sighed happily. "I
think this is the prettiest part of Illinois."
Not that he had even seen Illinois, he thought,
except a small portion of Chicago and the flat mid-
portion of the state.
"I'd have to agree. I've always loved this area
around the Rock River. Come on," Anthony said,
reaching out and taking his hand. "I'll show you
another pretty spot."
Less then twenty minutes later, Anthony drove into
the entrance of another state park. Jacob read the
rustic wooden sign as they drove by. White Pines
State Park, it read. They crossed a bridge over a
pretty little stream and took a left at the fork in the
road. They skirted some picnic areas on their left
and a tree-covered hill on their right until they came
to a point where the road dipped down and was
eventually covered by the same stream they had

previously passed over. Just before they would have entered the water, Anthony turned the motorcycle aside and parked it. They walked over to the stream where it had carved the rock on the far side into a tall tree and brush covered bluff. There were a few fishermen seated on the bank of the pretty little creek, and they nodded and smiled at them in a friendly manner as they walked along.

"What do you think?" Anthony asked him.

"It's wonderful," Jacob said. "I love this, especially being here on the bike with you."

"I'm glad," Anthony grinned at him.

They turned back and strolled leisurely back to the motorcycle.

"Do you want to try it?" Anthony asked him, pointing to the bike.

Jacob looked at him with surprise.

"Are you kidding?" he sputtered. "Shouldn't I start out on something smaller?"

"Come on, I'll be right there behind you. We'll only go a few feet. All you'll do is steer it a little at first."

Jacob shook his head nervously.

"I…I don't know if I should."

"Jacob, look at me," Anthony said, grabbing his arm and turning him.

Jacob looked into Anthony's clear, warm blue eyes.

"You can do this, Jake," Anthony said softly. "You can do anything you set your mind to. And I'll be right there with you."

Jacob nodded silently, mesmerized by his blue eyes and deep voice.

Anthony got on the rear seat of the bike and beckoned to Jacob, who gave him a nervous smile and then took the seat in front of him. Briefly, he showed Jacob again the clutch, brake, and throttle. Jacob nodded his understanding, and then Anthony took hold of the handlebars around him. Jacob placed his hands on the handlebars as well, as Anthony started the engine. Very slowly he allowed the bike to roll forward a few feet as Jacob carefully watched what his hands were doing. They stopped and Anthony put the transmission in neutral, allowing Jacob's hands to take the place of his own. Gently, he placed his hands over Jacob's and repeated his instructions once again. Jacob gave the bike a little gas and slowly released the clutch, as Anthony had done. The motorcycle lurched a little and Jacob quickly squeezed the clutch again. Taking a deep breath, he tried it again. This time the powerful machine glided smoothly forward several feet until he brought it to a graceful halt.

"Do it again," Anthony told him in a loud voice. They continued going around the long deserted parking area in circles, six or eight feet at a time. Jacob gradually started to relax and enjoy himself as he began to get the hang of it. Oh, my god, he thought. I am actually driving a motorcycle! In the driver's seat. Well, sort of. Less than two months ago I was living with my parents, terrified of life, and wearing drab, ill-fitting clothes. Now look at me. I'm living on my own, wearing a full leather outfit, and riding a motorcycle with a beautiful gay man! Look how my life has changed, and in such a dramatically positive way. True, I may not have a job, but who cares? Who, the hell, cares! Look, I can even swear a little! And I think I like swearing!

He finally brought the bike to a stop and took off his helmet.

"This is the most fantastic thing I've ever done!" he exclaimed joyfully. "I love it! I want to do more!"

"Let's do a little more after a while. I want to take you one more place," Anthony suggested.

Jacob nodded and climbed off so that Anthony could move forward to the driver's seat. He grasped Anthony's shoulder as he threw his leg over the seat and straddled it behind him. As usual, a shiver went up his spine at the touch. In a moment they were flying along the highway once more, between the rolling green fields and groves of trees. Anthony took them into the small picturesque town of Oregon, past the courthouse square, and across the bridge over the Rock River. He turned left onto the River Road and headed up a steep hill until he reached the entrance to Lowden State Park. They cruised slowly through the camping area and stopped near a picnic table.

Together they unpacked the lunch that Anthony had put together, slipped off their leather jackets and gloves, and sat down in the shade to enjoy it. A pleasantly cool breeze filtered through the trees.

Jacob prattled on continuously about the thrill of actually controlling the motorcycle while Anthony listened happily, enjoying the young man's enthusiasm.

"I never dreamed I'd be riding, even driving, a motorcycle," Jacob continued. "I still can't believe it! Just a few weeks ago I was so...so...uptight, I didn't know how to really enjoy anything, but I'm having so much fun now. Thanks to you, Anthony."

"No, you deserve all the credit. You're the one who opened your mind. No one did that for you."

They ate in silence for a few moments.

"What made you change your mind?" Anthony asked curiously. "I mean, about being gay and going to hell. You have changed your mind about that, right?"

"Yes, I have," Jacob replied, looking at him thoughtfully. "I know now that God made me the way I am, and being gay is nothing to be ashamed of or to ask forgiveness for. I don't have to spend the rest of my life alone. But what made me change my mind? Well, part of it was that book you loaned me. Part of it was Peter and Neil. And Brandon had a lot to do with it, too."

He paused to think.

"After I talked to Brandon, I stopped asking God to cure me of being gay, and started asking for understanding. Carl and Edna played a big part, too, of course. They're just about the finest people I know."

Anthony nodded in agreement.

"But I think most of the credit goes to you," Jacob said, looking at him with unmasked affection for once. "You made me think for myself for the first time in my life. I wouldn't have ever thought to question anything if it wasn't for you. You were right when you said we all have our own spiritual path to follow, and that everyone's paths are different."

He reached over and took one of Anthony's hands in his, admiring its masculine beauty.

"I owe everything to you."

Anthony squeezed his hand and smiled gently at him.

"You don't owe me anything, Jake, but I'm glad if I played a part. The most important thing to me is that you're happy with who you are."

"I'm getting there," Jacob said, discreetly wiping his eye. "I know I'm a nerd and all…"

"Most nerds don't wear leather and ride motorcycles!" Anthony teased him with a laugh. "I think that puts you in the 'cool' category now."

"Jacob Porter, cool?" Jacob said slowly. He suddenly grinned. "I like the sound of that."

He stood up and walked around the picnic table with a cocky smile on his face.

"Oh, yeah," he said seriously. "I'm cool."

Anthony burst into laughter, followed quickly by Jacob. Finally Jacob walked up behind him, bent over, and wrapped his arms around him.

"I think you're wonderful, Anthony!"

Anthony's expression became serious as he replied in a husky voice, "Not half as wonderful as you."

They drove on into the park and stopped to admire the huge Blackhawk statue set on a bluff one hundred feet above the river. They sat on the low ledge in front of the fifty foot Indian for a while, enjoying the view and each other's company. Finally, Jacob jumped up and looked down at Anthony.

"Come on, I want another driving lesson!"

Anthony drove them back to Green Grove, but instead of stopping in town, he headed straight east out of town until they came to the fertilizer plant parking lot they had visited twice before. The plant sat on the corner of the busy highway that led into town from the interstate, and a seldom-used highway called Old Church Road that extended five miles, ending at another connecting road. Anthony moved to the back seat again, and Jacob took the driver's seat. They proceeded as before, but this time, Anthony showed him how to shift gears so that he could control another aspect of the powerful machine. Jacob asked a few intelligent questions, and repeated back the information being taught, just to make sure he understood completely. Very slowly and cautiously, with Anthony's help, he put the bike in gear and pulled out onto the empty highway. Soon, he had them traveling along at thirty miles per hour, until Anthony signaled to him to stop.

"How are you feeling?" Anthony asked him. "Are you comfortable with everything?"

Jacob nodded with a wide smile on his face.

"It's fantastic!"

"Okay, let's go again, but this time I'm going to let go."

Jacob's smile faded slightly, but he nodded again and faced forward. With a determined look in his eye, and Anthony's arms around him, hands over his on the handlebars, he put the motorcycle in gear and glided slowly forward. He shifted gears smoothly until he was going forty miles per hour down the deserted road. Just as he was beginning to relax, he felt Anthony pull away from him slightly. His hands lifted off the handlebars, so that Jacob was in complete control of the big machine. Almost instinctively, he slowed down a little. But after a moment he slowly began to increase the speed up to forty-five miles per hour. By the time they reached the end of the road, Jacob felt a real connection with the motorcycle. It was beginning to feel comfortable and natural to him. He eased the bike into a large empty lot at the Horton Grain Elevator and gracefully made a wide u-turn. Once back on the highway, he accelerated smoothly until they were back to forty-five miles per hour. The bike rolled to a gentle stop at the fertilizer plant.

"Oh, my god!" Jacob yelled at the top of his lungs as he removed his helmet. "Oh, my god! I can't believe I did that!"

He kept yelling as he slid off the motorcycle and jumped up and down, punching the air as he yelled. Anthony took his helmet off as well and laughed. Without thinking about it, Jacob practically leapt into his arms and kissed him as hard as he could.

CHAPTER TWENTY

The next day, Jacob walked down to Larson's Men's Store. Peter greeted him with a smile and a hug. Jacob was still on an emotional high from his day with Anthony. He told Peter excitedly about how he had learned to pilot the motorcycle, how beautiful all the parks around the river were, and how much fun he had with Anthony.

"I'm glad to see you two are getting along again," Peter told him, enjoying the happy expression on Jacob's face. "You really like him, don't you?"

Jacob's smile faded as he nodded.

"I think I love him," he admitted.

"Well, you don't seem too happy about it, sweetheart," Peter observed. "Why not?"

Jacob shrugged his shoulders and he straightened a sweater that was folded haphazardly on a display table.

"I just wish…" he struggled for the right words.

Peter waited silently, watching him carefully.

"I just wish I hadn't screwed everything up in the beginning with him," Jacob said at last. "And now it's too late."

"Why is it too late?" Peter asked him, clearly confused.

"It just is," Jacob said sadly. "He's moved on."

He cleared his throat and forced himself to smile brightly at Peter.

"So, do you have any job openings?"

Peter frowned at him thoughtfully, shaking his head in a perplexed manner.

"Mary!" he yelled abruptly. "Get out here! Now!"

Mary Larson-Simmons, a tall, attractive auburn haired woman pushed a curtain aside as she emerged through a doorway from some back room.

"Will you please stop yelling at me, Peter?" she said good-naturedly. "I am the boss. I'm supposed to yell at you."

"Mary, darling, this is Jacob. Since you think you're the boss, give him a job," Peter said, putting an arm around him.

"You want me to hire someone I've never met, just like that?" she said with a hint of a smile on her face. "And just because you told me to?"

"Yes, of course I do. He needs a job, or at least he may need a job. We don't know yet."

"So, I'm supposed to hire your friend Jacob who may need a job, but who may not need a job?" she said with one eyebrow raised.

"Yes, now you're getting it," Peter smiled dazzlingly at her.

"Jacob, you're a friend of Peter's?" she said, turning her attention to him.

He nodded.

"I'm so sorry about that," she teased. "Do you need a job?"

"Well, I –"

"Here's the deal," Peter interrupted him. He proceeded to explain Jacob's situation, including how the board was supposed to make a decision on Friday.

"My husband and I have been to that church a few times," Mary said with a frown. "I'm sorry they put you in such a difficult position, Jacob. If you find that you need a job, come back next Monday and we'll put you to work. Okay?"

Jacob thanked her profusely before she returned to her office. He hugged Peter tightly.

"Oh, my god, what would I do without you?" he said.

"Well, for one thing, you'd probably have a better paying job than this!"

Peter called Anthony at work after Jacob had left and told him about the job offer.

"Well that's a relief," Anthony said.

"Do you have a minute?" Peter asked.

"Sure, I just discharged the last patient."

"I asked Jacob if he liked you, and he gave me a strange answer," Peter told him.

"What did he say?" Anthony asked hesitantly.

"He said he screwed everything up and that it was too late. He said you've moved on," Peter said.

"What the hell does that mean?" Anthony asked. "I haven't tried to get him in bed because I don't want him to feel pressured, especially while all this church stuff is still undecided. Is that what he's talking about?"

"I don't know," Peter said. "I was hoping you knew. He seems to think he doesn't have a chance with you. You *do* like him, don't you?"

"Oh, my god, of course I do. I'm crazy about him!"

"Well, he's in love with you, too, Anthony."

"Why would he think he doesn't have a chance with me? We spent the whole day together yesterday, and it was fantastic. You ought to see him in full leather gear, by the way. He's so beautiful!"

"I'm sure he is," Peter chuckled. "But something is going on. Maybe he's waiting for you to make a move."

"I wanted to all day yesterday, and the night before when we were in the hot tub. I was just afraid it would be too much for him, with all the stress he's under right now."

"I don't know," Peter sighed. "But maybe you should let him know you're interested, because I think he's even more stressed out thinking you don't care about him."

"I'll talk to him," Anthony promised. "I just don't want to scare him away again."

"Just think," Peter said with a smile in his voice. "My little Anthony is finally in love."

Carl and Edna took Jacob out for dinner at the Gibson House, a popular upscale restaurant located in the town of Sterling, about an hour's drive from Green Grove. The friendly hostess seated them at a table overlooking the river and asked them if they

would like to order drinks. Carl ordered a bottle of
Edna's favorite wine, and then turned to Jacob.
"What would you like, Jacob?" he asked.
"I'll have a Miller Lite, please," he told the hostess
with a grin.
Carl and Edna nodded their approval and then
turned to their menus. Jacob took a moment to look
around the elegant dining room. He admired the
pristine white tablecloths and glittering china and
crystal. His eyes opened wide and his mouth
dropped open as he recognized two people sitting
on the far side of the room near the huge fireplace.
"Oh, my god," he said before he could stop himself.
Carl and Edna looked up at him and then turned to
see who he was looking at.
"Oh, my!" Edna exclaimed. "Look, Carl. It's Lance
and Lucas. Isn't that lovely?"
"Yoo hoo!" she called out across the room.
All eyes in the dining room turned to look at her,
but she appeared not to notice.
"Lance, dear! Lucas!" she called. "Over here."
Lance and Lucas frowned at each other for a
moment before walking over to their table.
"Good evening, Carl. Edna, it's nice to see you,"
Lucas said pleasantly. "Jacob."
He looked uneasily over at Lance.
"What a coincidence," Lance said with a careful
smile.
"How nice that you two young men are having
dinner together," Edna said, beaming at them. "I
had a feeling about you two."

Lance blushed.

"Uh, we'll let you get back to your meal," he said.

Edna reached for his hand and gave it a gentle squeeze.

"Lucas is a wonderful man, Lance," she told him in a kind voice. "He's very dear to Carl and me."

Lance blushed an even deeper red as she looked over at Lucas.

"The two of you make a lovely couple," she said. "I think Lance is just right for you, dear."

She released Lance's hand after a final squeeze.

"Now, off you go, boys. Enjoy your evening," she said with a warm smile at both of them.

They nodded and, glancing awkwardly at Jacob, said their goodbyes and returned to their table.

"They make a very nice couple, don't you think, dear?" she said to her husband.

Jacob nodded absently in agreement with Carl as he watched them sit back down across the room.

"You're not upset, seeing them together, I hope," Edna said, looking at him with concern.

"No, of course not," Jacob said honestly. "I hope it works out for them. I just wish I…"

"You have Anthony," Carl reminded him. "Peter told us all about your big day out, and how crazy you two are about each other."

Jacob nodded and smiled in a noncommittal fashion before turning his full attention to his menu.

At noon the next day, Jacob was busily dusting his furniture when he looked up to see Lucas standing outside the front screen door. He pushed the screen open with a friendly smile.

"Come in, Lucas," he said. "Did you enjoy your dinner last night?"

"Yes, it was fine," Lucas told him. "I wanted to talk to you about that."

"About your dinner?" Jacob teased him.

"No," Lucas said uncertainly.

"I'm kidding, Lucas. You want to talk about Lance."

He gestured to the sofa.

"Please, have a seat. Can I get you something to drink?"

"No, I'm fine, thank you," Lucas said, taking a seat on the sofa.

Jacob sat down on the nearby easy chair and waited.

"Jacob, I need to know how you feel about Lance," Lucas blurted out.

Jacob looked at him kindly.

"I like him very much. He's a good friend," he said simply.

"Are you in love with him?" Lucas asked nervously.

"No, of course not. We're just friends."

"But you did fuck?"

Jacob's face turned red.

"Lucas, Lance and I had a few good times together, but now he's just a friend, I promise."

"So you're not in love with him?" Lucas asked again.

"No," Jacob repeated gently. "Are you?"

262

Lucas stood up and paced around the room, looking very distinguished in his expensive suit and tie.

"I think so," he said finally, returning to the sofa and sitting down heavily. He dropped his head into his hands. "And I have no fucking idea what to do about it!"

"Does he feel the same way about you?" Jacob asked.

"I'm not sure," came the muffled reply.

"Well, what do you guys talk about?"

"Oh, everything!" Lucas said, looking up at Jacob. "We talk about everything. We have everything in common, all the same interests. And I know he cares about me."

"But..." Jacob prodded gently.

Lucas stared at him sadly.

"He's married," he finished the thought. "So what the fuck am I supposed to do?"

"Well, I'd say the first thing to do is find out if he loves you, and decide for sure if you love him."

Lucas nodded.

"But after that?"

"If you truly love each other, you'll both find a way to make it work out," Jacob said sagely, not entirely believing his own words as a picture of Anthony flashed through his mind.

"I'm sure of it," he lied. "You need to talk, and be completely honest about everything."

"I don't know," Lucas said, shaking his head.

"Well, I do," Jacob said confidently. "It will work out, but you have to talk. Tell him how you feel."

Lucas stood up with a sigh.

"Thanks, Jacob. I'm sorry to drop all of this on you. I know you're going through a lot of stuff, yourself. What have you heard from the church board?"

"Nothing yet," Jacob told him. "But I'm sure I will."

"We all heard about what you did," Lucas said with a small smile. "You're really something, you know that?"

"No, I'm not," Jacob said with a shake of his head. "Not at all."

"Well, I wish you the best with all that," Lucas said sincerely.

"And I wish you and Lance the best, too. Trust me, it will work out."

That night, Jacob pulled up the Internet and did a search for Indian motorcycles. He looked delightedly at the myriad of pictures of the beautiful bikes. He clicked on a link for leather gear and studied the wide variety of leather clothes and accessories for the avid motorcyclist. Another link at the bottom of one page indicated something about fetish leather for men. Curiously he clicked on it and his eyes opened wide as he looked at the huge array of leather items used as sexual adjuncts. He'd never heard of most of these items, ranging from cock rings to leather vests, and slings to whips. A few of the pictures showed real men wearing leather harnesses, and he found himself becoming instantly aroused. He remembered the feel of the leather outfit he wore the other day, how masculine and sensuous it felt. He pictured Anthony wearing his full leather motorcycle gear, and immediately felt himself growing even harder. Funny that he had never considered leather to be sexy before. But he certainly did now.

Thursday afternoon, Jacob waited eagerly for Anthony to get home from work. As soon as he saw the big Chevy truck pull into the driveway, he hurried out his back door.

"Give me a minute to change," Anthony said, laughing at Jacob's eagerness.

While he went in to change, Jacob found the same jacket and pants he had worn on Tuesday and quickly put them on. He didn't want Anthony to see that he was wearing Anthony's underwear again. It was silly, of course, but it still made him feel closer to the handsome man, knowing that he was wearing an intimate article of his clothing. Now that he was dressed in Anthony's leather clothes as well, he practically swooned at how sexy he felt.

Anthony chose the Harley for today's riding lesson. Once again he went over every detail of the bike, pointing out in particular the differences between it and the Indian that Jacob had ridden before. As usual, Jacob was an excellent student, and it was clear that he wanted to know everything about the shiny motorcycle.

They headed out to Old Church Road as before and began their lesson. Jacob was soon piloting them smoothly up and down the quiet highway. He finally came to a stop in the old grain elevator lot. "You're a pro at this," Anthony exclaimed after they had removed their helmets. "I think you may want to consider getting your motorcycle license."

"How hard is that?" Jacob asked with a frown.

"It's not bad. We can download the manual from the state website. That's the easy part. And then you'll have to do a driving test. It's a little challenging, but you'll breeze through it."

"That would be so cool," Jacob said with a grin. "Can you imagine me having my own motorcycle license?"

"Sure I can," Anthony said with a smile. "You're a natural, Jake."

He wrapped his arms around the younger man from behind as they sat on the back.

"The next thing will be to get your own motorcycle," he said. "Unless you'd like to ride one of mine."

He was careful not to mention Keith's name.

"I don't mind riding yours at all," Jacob said with a happy grin.

"You can ride mine as long as you want to," Anthony told him as he squeezed him tight. "Come on. Drive us home and I'll fix you dinner."

With extreme caution, Jacob drove the few miles back to town, carefully navigating the turns and watching the increased traffic. The Harley came to

an easy stop in Anthony's garage and the two alit.
They carefully put their gear away, but Jacob
hesitated before removing the leather pants.

"You're not getting shy on me now, are you?"
Anthony joked with him.

"No," Jacob said. He stepped out of the pants and
put them away.

Anthony gave a low whistle as he took note of the
underwear Jacob was wearing.

"You know, you still look better in those than I ever
did."

After dinner Jacob sat down on the comfortable
deck settee. Anthony followed a moment later with
two glasses of his favorite Moscato wine.

"Here, I thought I'd class things up a bit," Anthony
teased, handing him a glass. "Try this."

Jacob smiled and took a sip of the sweet wine.

"Hmm, not bad," he said. "I think I still prefer a
beer."

Anthony laughed as he plunked himself down
beside him.

"I do, too, truth be told," he agreed. "But this makes
for a nice change."

Anthony leaned against him as they shared a
companionable silence.

"Lucas came to see me," Jacob said.

"Really? What did he want?"

"He and Lance are a couple now."

"Hmm, I wonder how that's going to work out,"
Anthony said with a frown.

"I told him I thought it would be fine as long as they really loved each other."

"Well, listen to you, telling two men that they should be a couple."

Anthony sat up and put an arm around Jacob.

"You keep surprising me, Jake," he said. "So what about you? Do you think you'll ever fall in love with someone?"

Jacob frowned and sat up straighter. He swallowed hard and looked away as he shook his head a couple of times.

"Really?" Anthony frowned, sitting up as well. "Why not?"

"I don't know, I just don't think so," Jacob said in a small voice.

"Well, I have," Anthony said gently. "I've fallen in love."

"Please, Anthony, I already know, and I'm glad for you. I just don't want to talk about it, if you don't mind."

"Why not?" Anthony asked as he gave him a perplexed look.

"Look, as long as you're happy, I'm happy," Jacob said in a tremulous voice. "Let's just leave it at that."

He stood up and set his glass down.

"I'm not feeling too well; I think I'll go home, if you don't mind."

"Jacob, don't leave," Anthony protested. "I want to talk to you about this!"

The Man Next Door

He stood up, but Jacob was already through the back gate and hurrying to his back door.

CHAPTER TWENTY-ONE

Lance stopped by at lunchtime on Friday. He walked through the open front door and called out for Jacob, who came into the living room from the kitchen.

"Lance, how are you?" he asked with a welcoming smile.

His smile turned to a frown as he saw the stricken look on his face.

"Oh, my god, what's wrong?" he asked, giving the older man a hug. He pulled him over to the sofa and made him sit down.

Lance looked at him through reddened eyes.

"Oh, Jacob," he said, trying to keep his voice steady. "I've lost him!"

"You mean Lucas?" Jacob gasped. "Oh, no! Tell me what happened!"

"We met for dinner last night, and he told me he loved me," Lance said through his tears.

"That's wonderful, Lance," Jacob said gently. "What did you say?"

"I told him that I loved him, too."

"And?" Jacob prodded.

"And he said I had to make a decision. I had to choose him or my marriage."

"So, what did you tell him?" Jacob asked with a sinking feeling that he already knew the answer.

"I told him I wanted to be with him more than anything in the world, but that I couldn't get a divorce."

"I thought so," Jacob said with a sigh. He looked at his friend thoughtfully for several long seconds. "You know what, Lance?" he said at last. "You're a fucking idiot!"

Lance looked up at him with surprise.

"What?"

"You're a fucking idiot!" Jacob repeated, louder this time.

"Jacob –"

"No, I mean it!" Jacob told him. "Here you have a wonderful, beautiful man that you're in love with, and you're lucky enough to have him love you back. What more could you ask for?"

He stood up and paced angrily around the room.

"I would give anything in the world for that! You're acting like a coward! I realize you're afraid. I get that. But why the hell would you stay in a fake marriage when you could be with the man you love forever?"

"But…" Lance began. His words failed him.

"It's time, Lance," Jacob said firmly. "It's time to forget about everyone else and do what you know you should do. Forget about your parents, the church, your friends. You need to make things right with Linda and Lucas. Stop hiding behind an excuse! So what if you lose your job or your fancy house? They're only things; they don't matter!

"Go talk to Linda. For god's sake, get a divorce and let her have her life back. Then you can be with Lucas and be happy for the first time in your life!"

Lance stared at Jacob with his mouth open. Finally he dried his eyes and stood up.

"I'm sorry I can't give you any sympathy, Lance," Jacob said as he followed him to the front door. "You know I love you. I just can't stand seeing you and Lucas break up, just because you think you 'can't' get a divorce. You can do this, Lance."

He grabbed the other man's arm as he tried to leave and pulled him into a fierce hug. Lance hugged him back briefly and then turned and ran to his car.

The call unexpectedly came from Carl, not Pastor Cal, as Jacob thought it would.

"The board wants to meet with you tonight, Jacob," he said in a kind voice.

"What did they decide?" Jacob asked, a little apprehensively.

"I'm not sure," Carl told him. "I put my vote in, and told them all exactly what I thought, but Pastor Cal and Bob, head of the board, will tell everyone tonight. Be there at seven o'clock. And don't worry, Jacob. No matter what happens, you'll be just fine. And all of us are here for you."

"I know, Carl," Jacob told him sincerely. "And I can't tell you how much I love and appreciate all of you."

He ended the call and looked around with a sigh. What he wouldn't give for a motorcycle ride right now. He stepped out onto his back porch and looked over at Anthony's house. The garage was closed up. Aimlessly he walked over to Anthony's back gate and looked around. He opened the gate and walked back to the serenity garden. He stood there for a few minutes before wandering around the path encircling it and admiring the simple elegance of the space. He stepped onto the small bridge and paused to look down at the Buddha statue that sat serenely beside the small stream, facing the house. Just looking at the peaceful, unchanging expression on its face soothed his unsettled nerves just a bit. He checked his watch after standing there for a while. He knew Anthony usually got home from the hospital before four o'clock, and he didn't want to take a chance on running into him. He had avoided seeing him or taking his calls since their last encounter in the hot tub; he had too much to think about right now to deal with his feelings about Anthony.

Surgery ran late that afternoon. Anthony hurried out of the hospital and ran by the grocery store to pick up a few supplies for the party tomorrow night. He had tried to call Jacob a few times but got no answer. Peter had told him about the meeting set for that evening, and he wanted to get home in time to take Jacob to the church, but when he arrived home, Jacob's car was gone and the garage door was standing open.

Edna stood beside Jacob as he faced the board from his position at the foot of the conference table. Pastor Cal once again sat at the head of the long table, wearing the same scowl as before. Bob, the board president, invited him kindly to have a seat. Jacob thanked him but remained standing.

"Jacob," Bob said. "The board has considered your proposal very seriously. We appreciate the fact that you were willing to make an effort to come to a compromise."

He glanced uncomfortably at Pastor Cal for a moment and cleared his throat.

"But the board has discussed it at length and we took a vote. I'm afraid we're back to our original offer. You will apologize to Pastor Cal if you want to keep your job here at the church."

"No," Jacob said simply.

The board members looked at him and each other with surprise, almost as if they didn't understand his response.

"No?" one of the members said.

"No," Jacob repeated evenly. "Not unless the pastor apologizes for lying to the congregation."

"That will never happen, Mr. Porter," Pastor Cal said huffily.

"One thing I've learned since I've been in Green Grove, Mr. Hanson, is to never say never," Jacob replied calmly.

He turned to the board members at large.

"I realize that most of you don't understand my position, so let me explain it very simply. I'm gay, just like all those people that you hate, Pastor Cal." He ignored the surprised stares and gasps.

"But I am not evil, and I'm not a monster, as you would have everyone believe. I didn't choose to be gay, I don't try to recruit children, or sleep with thousands of men. And neither do any of my friends. You believe that garbage because you want to believe it. All the people you warned me against are wonderful, caring, loving, good people. All of them! It is the biggest honor of my life that they call me a friend, and that I can call them my friends – my family.

"I am finally becoming the man that God intended me to be, and I like who I am. And you know what? I found out that God doesn't hate me at all, in spite of what people like you teach. He loves me, just like He always has. The only thing that has changed is that I've stopped hating myself, and that's something you don't want. You want all of us to keep hating ourselves so you can feel justified in hating us, too.

"Well, I finally understand that hate of any kind is not a Christian value, Mr. Hanson. Charlie was right the other night. All we have to do is love God, and each other. It's just that simple. And the sooner we all learn that, the happier we will all be."

He looked around at all of them.

"I'm glad to have gotten to know all of you, and I'm sure I'll see you around. But it won't be in this church. I wish you all God's blessing. Have a good night, gentlemen."

He turned to go.

"Wait, Jacob," a raspy voice called.

Jacob turned back as Charlie stood up slowly from his chair.

"Pastor. Gentlemen," he addressed the assembly in a dignified manner. "Everyone of us in this room could learn something from this young man. Pastor Cal, if you were a smart man, you'd do whatever it takes to keep Jacob here. He's a better man than all of us, and I hope you will all remember his words." He turned to Jacob with a grin.

"Would you mind escorting me to my car?" he said, taking Jacob by the arm. "Come on, Edna! Carl!"

Carl and Edna followed them out through the conference room door without a backward glance.

Jacob hugged Charlie tightly and thanked him for his support as they stood next to his car.

"I'm sorry we won't get to hear your music anymore, Jacob," the elderly gentleman said as he got into the sedan. "But I do hope I get to see you and your friends again. It doesn't mean much to you, I'm sure, but remember that this old man is very proud of you."

"Charlie, that means more to me than I can say," Jacob said sincerely.

With that, Charlie started his ancient, mint condition Buick and drove slowly away.

Carl and Edna insisted that Jacob follow them to Peter and Neil's house. He was too emotionally drained to argue with them, so reluctantly he parked on the street in front of the huge brick house and stepped into the foyer. Peter had called their circle of friends, and they greeted him with loud applause and many hugs. He thanked them all with an embarrassed smile. Somebody passed a glass of white wine into his hand and he took a quick sip as he was swept along into the large living room. Carl and Edna quoted his speech to the assembled party almost word for word, practically bursting with pride as they told the whole story from Jacob's arrival at the meeting until Charlie's departing words to him.

"I'm so proud of you," Myra told him with a big smile. "You stood up for yourself in a very difficult situation. You should be proud of yourself, too."

"That's right," Randall said, shaking his hand enthusiastically. "I would never have had the courage to do that when I was your age. I wish I had."

The praises continued from all of them for some time. Finally he looked around.

"Where's Anthony?" he asked casually.

"Keith was coming in tonight," Neil said. "Anthony wanted to wait for him, but said he'd be over as soon as he could."

"He was very worried about you," Peter added. "He tried to get home in time to take you to the church, but work ran late. He tried to call you, he said. He thought you could use a motorcycle ride."

He winked at Jacob, who looked back at him with a frown before taking a large drink from his wine glass.

The conversation continued for some time, with much laughter and more drinks enjoyed by each of them. Finally Jacob looked at his watch.

"I guess he's not coming," he whispered to Peter.

"Keith must have run late, or something," Peter whispered back. "He really wanted to be here. But don't worry, you'll see him tomorrow."

Jacob tossed and turned that night. He rose early the next morning and looked bleary eyed out his kitchen window in time to see Anthony and Keith drive out on their motorcycles. He stood there at the kitchen sink for a long time, staring blankly out the window. Finally he turned away and walked slowly back to his bedroom. He just wanted to be alone. In spite of his brave words last night, he was feeling a strong measure of rejection from the church, not to mention how deeply his heart ached seeing Anthony and Keith together. After he closed his bedroom curtains and doors, encasing the room in darkness, he crawled onto his bed and curled up under the covers.

He finally climbed out of the bed at noon and sat down wearily at the Clavinova. He closed his eyes and played Debussy's 'The Engulfed Cathedral', one of his favorites from his college days, a slow, poignant piece that always brought tears to his eyes. Today, however, he felt nothing. Today it was just a bunch of notes a stranger had strung together on a piece of paper long ago. The song ended and he sat there listlessly, staring at the keys when a light tap came at the front door. If his blinds had been closed, he probably would have ignored it, but since it was obvious he was at home, he made himself get up and answer the door. He was amazed to see Lucas standing there in the doorway.

"Lucas, come in," he said, rousing himself enough to give his visitor a warm smile.

Lucas stepped into the living room followed closely by Lance.

"Hi, Jacob," Lucas said with a happy smile on his face. "We wanted you to be the first to know."

"Know what?" Jacob asked.

"Linda and I are getting a divorce," Lance said.

"We'd better sit down," Jacob said, pointing to the sofa and chairs. The two men sat together on the sofa, holding hands, and Jacob took a seat in the chair next to them.

"Okay, tell me from the beginning," Jacob said with a smile.

"Well, after I talked to you," Lance said, "I drove around for a little while, and I decided that you were right. The only thing keeping Lucas and me apart was me. And I knew that everything you said was true. None of the things I was clinging to was important. So I went home and sat down with Linda. I told her that I loved her, but it was time to quit pretending. I said we both deserved a life, and then I told her about Lucas, and that I was in love with him."

"Wow!" Jacob said, looking at each of them with astonishment. "I can't believe it."

"I know," Lance said with a happy smile. "I can't believe it myself. But that's not the best part!"

"What?" Jacob asked.

"She said that she loved me, too, and she was only staying in the marriage for me. She knew how important it was to keep up the pretense, so she kept it up for my sake. She had reached the point that she didn't care what her parents or anyone else thought a long time ago, but she wanted me to be happy, so she stayed."

"So she was relieved that you wanted a divorce?" Jacob asked incredulously.

"Not only that," Lucas chimed in as Lance nodded. "She met someone this spring that she's crazy about, so she was happy that Lance and I got together."

"She was ready to move on, but she was sacrificing her own happiness for me," Lance said wonderingly. "Can you believe that?"

"Yes, I think I can," Jacob said with a nod. He had only spoken to Linda a few times, but had been impressed with her kind, gentle, and genuine nature. "So, you two are officially a couple now?" Jacob asked with a warm smile.

"Well, we aren't putting it in the newspaper," Lucas said with a grin.

"But as far as the two of us are concerned, yes," Lance said happily. "We are officially a couple!"

"And your parents?" Jacob asked hesitantly.

"I don't care," Lance said. "For the first time in my life, I can honestly say I don't give a fuck what they think, or what they do. None of that matters anymore. I don't care, because I'm truly happy, Jacob, and it's all thanks to you."

"No," Jacob protested. "That's not true. You were the one who was brave, Lance. And Lucas, you were the one who stood by him. You guys did this together."

"You can say that if you want," Lance said. "But we will always know in our hearts that we have you to thank. You are a wonderful, sweet, beautiful young man, and I will always be grateful to you."

"That makes two of us, Jacob," Lucas agreed as he reached out and grasped Jacob's hand fervently.

"Well," Jacob said, standing up and wiping his eyes, "I'm just so happy for the two of you. Edna was right; you do make a perfect couple."

Lucas and Lance hugged him and headed for the front door. Lance suddenly stopped.

"Oh, my god, Jacob!" he gasped, looking mortified. "I was so wrapped up in my own drama, I forgot to ask you what happened with the church board."

"That's okay, Lance," Jacob said easily. "You've got a lot going on. Let's just say if you need to see me, I'll probably be at work at Larson's, downtown.

"Oh, my god, they fired you?" Lucas exclaimed.

"They went back to the original ultimatum, and I told them again that I couldn't apologize to a pompous ass like Hanson. So we parted ways."

Lance gave him another hug.

"I am so sorry, Jacob!" he said sincerely.

"It's fine, Lance," Jacob told him with a smile. "Just make sure you keep singing. Lucas, this man has one of the most beautiful voices I've ever heard, so don't let him stop. Promise?"

"Of course I won't, Jacob," Lucas said. "And thank you."

"Yes, Jacob," Lance said, giving his hand a squeeze. "Thank you. For everything."

"You'll be at the party tonight next door, won't you?" Lucas asked. "Lance is coming."

"You are?" Jacob gave them a surprised grin. "That's wonderful. Um, yeah, I'll probably see you there."

CHAPTER TWENTY-TWO

Jacob watched his friends gather next door through
his kitchen window. Anthony had knocked on his
door earlier and called his cell phone a few times,
but he had avoided him. He sighed, as he knew that
he could no longer postpone the inevitable. Steeling
himself, he stepped out of the back door and put a
cheerful smile on his face.

There was soft but lively music playing over some
outdoor speakers, and Anthony had put up extra
lights across the backyard, giving the area a festive
atmosphere. Jacob's spirits began to rise as he
entered the backyard. His friends greeted him
warmly, and he spent the evening enjoying their
company while he carefully avoided both Anthony
and Keith. The two of them spent most of their time
at the grill at first, so Jacob kept to the back part of
the serenity garden. He chatted happily with Lucas
and Lance, and was pleased to see both of them
looking happier than he had ever seen either of
them. Myra and Elaine kept his attention for some
time, and when Myra asked to see how all the
pieces he had bought looked in his house, he took
them over to show off his pleasantly inviting home.
Myra was pleased to see the old pieces of furniture
being appreciated and enjoyed. As they walked
back through Anthony's gate, not far from the grill
and serving tables, he heard his name called.
"Hey, Jacob!"

He turned to see Keith coming toward him, and realized that there was no avoiding him this time. "I want to talk to you," Keith said firmly. He took Jacob by the elbow and propelled him through the side door of the garage where the big truck and all three motorcycles were parked.

When he was sure they were alone Keith said, "I wanted to talk about what I said that night at Peter and Neil's. You're never around when I'm here, so…"

"Forget about it," Jacob said without looking at him. He turned to go back to the party.

"Wait!" Keith said. "I'm trying to apologize to you."

"There's no need," Jacob said tersely. "We're not friends. And you said what you honestly thought. So don't apologize."

"Don't be such an asshole," Keith said with a frown.

"Oh, I'm the asshole?" Jacob said loudly, looking him in the eye for the first time. "You laughed at me and mocked me, someone you've never met and knew nothing about, in front of my friends, no less. You made me look and feel like a fool! But you're right; I'm the asshole! Well, now let me tell you what I think of you! You're a rude, inconsiderate, insensitive, obnoxious prick, and I don't know how someone as wonderful as Anthony can have anything to do with you. He's way too good for you!"

"Whoa, calm down, man," Keith said with a grin. "I'm trying to tell you I was completely wrong about you, and I'm sorry. It was a stupid thing to say, and you're right, I was a jerk. You should have heard how all these guys put me in my place, especially that kid, Brandon. He told me off really good."

Jacob looked at him coldly for a few moments.

"I'm glad," he said finally. "Are we done here?"

Keith shrugged.

"Sure, what the hell," he said. "At least I can tell him I gave it a shot."

"You know what?" Jacob said. "You're the asshole! Fuck you!"

He strode angrily out of the garage, followed shortly by Keith, who looked over at Anthony and shrugged. Anthony frowned and walked over to where he was standing.

"What the hell happened?" he said with annoyance. "Didn't you apologize?"

"I tried," Keith told him with a grin. "He told me to fuck off."

"Damn it!" Anthony said. "It's important to me that you two get to be friends."

"He got some of it out of his system," Keith chuckled. "We'll be okay, just give it some time."

Anthony looked over at Jacob who was talking with Brandon and Peter as they sat on the far end of the deck. Brandon was clearly upset at something, but Keith called Anthony back to the grill before he could learn more.

The evening wore on with more music, food,
drinks, and lots of laughter shared among the group
of friends. Jacob laughed until his sides hurt at
Peter's stories of his adventures growing up with his
open minded and fun loving parents. The rest of
them had both hilarious and poignant stories to tell,
and Jacob even persuaded Lance to sing some
karaoke pop songs for them. He looked around and
smiled warmly as he watched Carl sitting with his
arm wrapped affectionately around Edna's waist.
Lucas was sitting close to Lance and was looking
up at him adoringly. Myra and Elaine sat holding
hands, while Peter sat with his head lying on Neil's
shoulder. Brandon and Randall sat beside him,
obviously impressed with Lance's vocal abilities.
Anthony and Keith sat side by side, but Keith was
busy looking at his phone, only looking up
occasionally when Anthony prodded him.
The guy is a child, he thought with exasperation.
Brandon is ten times more mature than he is, so
what the hell does Anthony see in him? I don't get
it at all!
Finally, around midnight, the party wound down
and everyone helped with the clean up. Within
minutes, the backyard was back to normal. As
everyone said good night, Jacob stood in his
driveway next to his gate talking to Lance and
Lucas, praising Lance on his beautiful
performances. He had to admit, he was going to
miss working with him at the church. He also had to
admit that he had had a wonderful time tonight. He

had spent time with his friends, managed to avoid Anthony all together, and even gotten to tell that little prick, Keith, what he thought of him.

Anthony hugged and kissed everyone good night, but kept an eye out for Jacob, who for some reason had avoided him all evening. He stood in his driveway as the last of their friends left, waving goodbye. As he turned he saw Jacob saying his final good night to Lance and Lucas. He strode over and joined them, grabbing hold of Jacob's arm as the other two men walked hand in hand down the drive to Lance's Cadillac. Jacob tried to pull free, but Anthony only tightened his grip.

"What's going on, Jacob?" he said sternly. "Why did you purposely avoid me all night?"

"I…I was busy talking," Jacob sputtered.

"No, I watched you all evening, and you did your best to stay as far away from me as you possibly could. You wouldn't take my calls or answer the door. Now I want to know why?"

"Let go, Anthony," Jacob said, trying to pull away.

"NO, damn it!" Anthony said angrily. "Now come on, you're coming over so we can talk. I haven't even gotten to see you since before your last meeting at the church."

Reluctantly, Jacob allowed himself to be pulled over to Anthony's deck.

"Do you want something to drink?" Anthony asked, pulling two beers from a blue Igloo cooler next to him. Without waiting for an answer, he opened one and handed it to Jacob.

"Where's he at?" Jacob asked sourly as he took the beer from him, referring to Keith.

"He's got to leave early tomorrow, so he went to bed," Anthony told him. "It's just you and me; so come on, let's relax. I'm beat from the ride all day and the party tonight."

He raised the lid of the hot tub, and stripped out of his shorts and tee shirt. He wasn't wearing any underwear tonight, so he stepped naked down into the warm water.

"I really don't think I should," Jacob objected. "Not with Keith here."

"Why not?" Anthony asked with a puzzled expression on his face.

"He probably wouldn't like it," Jacob said, surprised at Anthony's question.

"Why the hell would he care? Now, come on, get in."

With a sigh and a furtive look around him, Jacob stripped down and sat in the bubbling water across from Anthony. Anthony moved over and sat next to him, putting an arm on the back of the hot tub behind him.

"I heard what happened last night," he said. "I'm so sorry I didn't get there. I wanted to be there for you."

"Yeah, well, Keith comes first," Jacob said, taking a drink of his beer as he avoided his gaze. "I understand that."

"No, that's not it; I promised I'd wait for him. He needed to talk about something that he said couldn't wait. It turned out to be nothing, but it was important to him, so what could I do?"

"Can we talk about something other than Keith?" Jacob snapped at him crossly.

"Sure, Jake, what do you want to talk about?" Anthony asked. "Maybe you'll tell me why you've been avoiding me. Why you won't take my calls."

"I just have a lot on my mind."

"I know, and I want to help. But you've got to stop pushing me away."

Tears welled up in Jacob's eyes and he brushed them aside irritably.

"I'm sorry," he said, shaking his head. "It's just that I care about you way more than I should, and sometimes it gets to be too much for me."

"I care about you, too, Jake," Anthony said gently, moving closer to him. "Why is that a problem?"

Jacob shook his head, trying to clear his thoughts. He coughed and cleared his throat.

"So how come Keith is only here on the week ends?" Jacob asked, changing the subject.

"Keith? I thought you didn't want to talk about him, but okay. He lives in Chicago with his folks. He works in surgery at a hospital in the city, Monday through Friday. But he loves to ride, so he comes out here to be with me as often as he can."

"He sure is handsome," Jacob said with a touch of sadness in his voice.

"You said that before," Anthony said with a frown, studying Jacob's face intently. "Wait! Is that what's going on? Do you have the hots for him?"

"No, no, no," Jacob said quickly. "Not at all. So, he still lives with his folks? How old is he?"

"Twenty-one, I think. Why?"

"Wow, he's even younger than I am," Jacob observed thoughtfully.

"You should get to know him better. He's really a great kid. I know he made that rude comment at the party, but he isn't like that, really. He said he tried to apologize to you."

"Yeah, whatever! Well, I suppose I'll get to know him over time. Does he have any plans to move here?"

"No, he's very happy in the city. That's where his friends are. He couldn't live here."

"So, I guess you'll move there, eventually?" Jacob asked, afraid to hear the answer.

Anthony studied him with a frown for several seconds.

"Okay, what's with all the questions about Keith?" he asked, sitting up straighter and turning to face Jacob.

"I'm just curious," Jacob said. "I care about you so much, Anthony, and I just want you to be happy." He stared straight ahead as his tears threatened to fall once again.

"I'm happy right here in Green Grove. Everything I love is here. Why would I want to move to the city?" Anthony said, clearly puzzled.

"Well, how are you two going to be together? Or is it just going to be one of those long distance relationships?"

Anthony stared at him.

"Wait a minute," he said slowly. "Wait a god damned fucking minute. You're surely not thinking that Keith and I are boyfriends, are you?"

"Well, yes, of course," Jacob frowned at him. "Aren't you?"

"Oh, my god, Jake!" Anthony said with a quick laugh. He paused for a minute to consider what Jake was suggesting. "Oh, my god! Now I get it! I think I finally understand what's been going on with you! All this time, you thought... Holy shit!"

He shook his head fondly.

"Jake, Jake, Jake," he said. "Well, there are a couple of problems with him being my boyfriend. First, he's straight."

"He's straight?" Jacob said skeptically. "No, he isn't. You guys are always making out."

"What?" Anthony cried indignantly. "No, we haven't!"

"But I always see you hugging. It seems like that's all you do!"

"Actually, stop and think about that for a minute. Keith is an affectionate guy, but we've never made out, although I guess from your point of view it could appear that way. He always hugs me when he gets here and when he leaves, now that you mention it. But that's it. I promise you, we do not 'make out'!"

Anthony started laughing again.

"What?" Jacob said, thoroughly confused. "I don't..."

"Okay, first of all, like I said, he's straight, and secondly…"

Anthony paused for effect.

"He's my nephew."

This time he couldn't stop his laughter. He grabbed Jacob around the back of his neck and shook him lightly.

"Oh, my god! That is too funny!" he said a few minutes later as his laughter finally subsided.

"So, you're saying he's not your boyfriend?"

"No, of course not," Anthony told him, wiping his eyes.

"And you don't have a boyfriend?" Jacob said, trying desperately to comprehend the situation.

Anthony shook his head, watching Jacob closely.

"When have you ever seen me with a boyfriend? I'm either at work, with clients, with Keith, or with you."

"Are you kidding me?" Jacob asked, totally stunned, and fearful he was misunderstanding what Anthony was telling him. His voice grew louder.

"Are you. Fucking. Kidding me?"

"No, Jake, of course I'm not!" Anthony said gently. Jacob stared at him for a moment, and then suddenly grabbed him and pulled him into a tight hug with tears in his eyes. He sat back and looked at Anthony again.

"Oh, my god! Okay, so you don't have a boyfriend, and Keith is your nephew."

"That's right."

"How the hell do I keep getting everything so wrong?" Jacob cried. "Damn it! I'm the world's biggest idiot!"

Anthony pulled him close and held him tightly. He shook his head silently and then pushed Jacob to arm's length.

"If I was to have a boyfriend, don't you know that it would be you, you idiot? I love you, Jake," he said, his voice full of emotion. "I love you more than anything."

A tear finally trickled from Jacob's left eye.

"You do? Really?" he said breathlessly. "Oh, Anthony! Thank God! Because I love you, too! I can't even tell you how much! I think you're the most wonderful man in the world!"

He leaned forward and kissed Anthony so passionately that he thought his heart would burst with love and joy. Anthony returned the kiss fervently, holding Jacob as tightly as he could. Neither of them wanted it to end, but finally after several minutes, Anthony pushed him away. He stared deeply into his eyes for a moment.

"So, are you sure everything is clear now?" he asked in a very serious tone. "Is there anything else you need to know?"

Jacob looked at him, his eyes shining, and shook his head a few times.

"Then, come to bed with me," Anthony said quietly, standing up and pulling Jacob up with him.

He stood up on the deck, helping Jacob out of the water to stand with him. Their wet naked bodies pressed together as they kissed for a few minutes before they stopped to dry themselves. Then Anthony took his hand and pulled him to the back door.

"What about Keith?" Jacob asked, pulling back slightly.

"I'm sorry, but he can't join us for this," Anthony teased him with a mischievous grin.

"I mean, won't he hear us?"

"Just how loud do you intend to be?" Anthony chuckled.

"I'm serious," Jacob said, grinning at him.

"I hope he does hear. In fact, I hope the whole damn neighborhood hears us!" Anthony said, pulling him through the dark house to the downstairs bedroom. "I want everyone to know how fucking hot my boyfriend is!"

CHAPTER TWENTY-THREE

Jacob lay on the bed watching Anthony light a few candles before climbing on his hands and knees over him until he was staring down at him, just inches from his face. He bent down and kissed him gently, over and over again. Finally, ever so slowly he moved down to tenderly kiss Jacob's trembling neck, his chest, his stomach, until he reached his groin. He took his time enjoying taking Jacob in his mouth and releasing him, then taking him again. He repeated this many times until Jacob gasped.

"Stop!" Jacob said desperately. "I don't want to cum yet."

"Don't worry, Jake, we'll both be cumming more than once tonight, I promise."

Anthony moved back up his body and pressed his weight down on Jacob. They kissed passionately, sometimes with Anthony on top, and sometimes with Jacob on top. Their lovemaking grew more intense until finally, Anthony looked down at him, breathing hard.

"I know you haven't done it before…" he said.

Jacob stared up at him and nodded slightly.

"Yes, I want to," he said quietly. "More than anything."

Anthony looked at him intently, wanting to make sure. He leaned over Jacob and grabbed his supplies from the nightstand.

"Put your legs around my waist, Jake," he instructed gently.

Jacob did as he was told, never taking his eyes from Anthony's handsome face.

"Now just relax," Anthony said as he pressed against him. "I'll go as slow as you want."

Jacob winced and frowned as Anthony very slowly penetrated him.

"Relax, Jake," Anthony whispered. "Relax and take some deep breaths."

Jacob struggled to do as Anthony requested, taking slow deep breaths. Gradually, he became accustomed to having Anthony inside him. They held still for several seconds as Anthony studied his facial expression, making sure he wasn't hurting him. Finally Jacob was able to completely relax and he nodded at Anthony, who very slowly began moving his hips back and forth, in and out of Jacob. After a moment, Jacob reached up and pulled him down, wrapping his arms around him tightly and kissing him deeply.

"Oh, my god, Jake!" Anthony said after a few minutes. His pace quickened and his thrusts became longer and deeper. "Jake!"

"Don't stop, Anthony!" Jacob panted desperately. "Don't ever stop!"

Jacob kissed him again as he matched his speed and rhythm. With a sudden gasp and a spasm that consumed his entire body, Anthony exploded in him before finally collapsing, sweaty and breathless, on top of him. Jacob continued to rock back and forth for a moment before he tensed and gripped Anthony tightly.

"Oh, god!" he cried out as his own orgasm burst out from him. "Oh, Anthony!"

He continued to hold him tightly, unwilling to let him pull out. But finally, Anthony slipped from his body and rolled off of him onto his side. Jacob rolled over and looked at him, placing a hand on his cheek.

"Are you okay?" Anthony asked him. In the back of his mind he was still a little concerned that Jacob wasn't ready for this level of intimacy.

"I'm more than okay," Jacob said with a tender smile. "I have never, ever felt this good in my whole life."

They made love once again before falling asleep with Anthony's arm holding him tightly as they spooned together. A few hours later, Anthony awoke to find Jacob leaning on one arm, staring at him adoringly in the pale, early morning light with an affectionate smile on his face. He smiled back as he stretched sleepily.

"What?" he said with a yawn.

"You are so beautiful, Anthony," Jacob said. "Do you have any idea how handsome you are?"

"About half as handsome as you, I guess," Anthony replied, reaching over and pulling him closer. "How do you feel this morning?"

Jacob considered the question seriously.

"Well, let's see," he said with a frown. "I'm lying in bed next to the most wonderful man in the world, a man that I love more than I've ever loved anybody, after a night of making love to him. I never knew that anything could be this great. So, I'd say I'm good."

He looked over at Anthony to see him grinning back at him.

"I'm serious! I have never felt that kind of love, and joy, that kind of pleasure before. The closest thing to last night is when we are on the motorcycle together. I guess I used to think that pleasure was sinful. But there was nothing evil about last night, Anthony. Last night was about pure love for me, and it was the most beautiful experience I've ever had!"

He grinned shyly at him before laying his head down on Anthony's hairy chest.

"Crazy, huh?"

"Not at all. It felt like that for me, too, Jake," Anthony said, giving him a gentle squeeze as he kissed the top of his head. "I've never felt anything even close to what I felt last night. You are the most incredible man I've ever known."

He pulled Jacob up and kissed him gently.

"I still can't believe you love me," Jacob said as he looked into his eyes. "That I'm lying here in your arms."

"Believe it, because it's absolutely real, Jake," Anthony told him tenderly. They lay in each other's arms, savoring their intimacy until Anthony raised himself up and straddled him. Within seconds, they were both deeply aroused.

"Turn about is fair play," Anthony told him with an arched eyebrow. "Don't you think?"

Later, after Jacob pulled out of Anthony, they collapsed together, sweating, and panting contentedly. Finally, Anthony caught his breath, and slid up until he was leaning against the padded gray headboard.

"You're the first man I ever let do that," he said, looking down at him with a grin.

Jacob stared up at him with a dazed expression on his face, his body limp.

"And if I ever regain the use of my arms and legs, I want to do it again!" Jacob teased him breathlessly. "That was fantastic!"

Anthony laughed before bending down and kissing him.

"Let's talk about the motorcycle," he grinned, "I want you to practice the driving course at the DMV so you can get your license."

"Oh, yeah," Jacob said, sitting up enthusiastically. "And I found a cool website that sells some really hot leather vests and stuff."

"You really like the leather clothes, huh?" Anthony asked with a grin.

"Oh, yeah!" Jacob exclaimed. "There's even some really sexy leather stuff, too. Did you know they make a leather sling, and a really hot harness? I'll show you the website."

"Okay, unless you'd like to see the real thing," Anthony said, winking at him suggestively.

"What are you talking about?" Jacob looked at him with a frown.

"Come on."

Anthony pulled him from the bed and they strode naked, hand in hand through the house, heading to the basement door in the kitchen.

"Hey, guys," Keith said with a wicked grin. He was standing in the kitchen, wearing his full leather gear, making a pot of coffee when they walked in. "Sounded like you two had fun last night."

Jacob frantically covered himself with his hands.

"Please, man, I know what a dick looks like," Keith chuckled. "You don't have to hide it."

"Are you getting ready to head out?" Anthony asked him as he grabbed a couple of cups from a cabinet for Jacob and himself.

"Yeah, I wish I could stay, but it looks like your day is going to be busy anyway," he told his uncle with a wink.

Jacob blushed and Anthony chuckled.

"You're going to show him the basement?" Keith asked with a raised eyebrow. "Already? Are you sure he's ready for that?"

"I think he is," Anthony said with a grin.

Keith shook his head with a grin as he poured some coffee in their cups and then in his travel mug.

"Well, give me a hug," he said. "I gotta hit the road."

Anthony leaned over and hugged him.

"Bye, kid," he said. "Be careful, and tell your folks hello for me."

300

Keith let him go and looked at Jacob. He spread his arms wide.

"So, are you going to hug me, 'Uncle' Jacob?" he said mischievously.

Jacob nodded sheepishly and hugged him. He held him for a moment as he whispered in his ear.

"I'm so sorry I called you an asshole."

"I know," Keith said, hugging him back tightly before releasing him and standing back. "Promise that you'll be good to him, because he loves you a lot. And I'll kick your ass if you hurt him."

"I promise," Jacob said simply.

"Will we see you next week end?" Anthony asked as they walked to the back door. Keith turned and looked at Jacob for a moment. Jacob grinned and gave him a slight nod.

"Yeah," Keith said nonchalantly. "I'll be here."

He walked out the back door and over to the garage. They followed him out onto the deck.

"I want steaks on the grill Friday night," he called back to them.

They watched him climb aboard his Honda Goldwing and put on his matching helmet. With a wave of his hand and a wicked grin, he guided the big bike down the drive and out to the street.

"I think I like him already," Jacob said with a smile as they watched him leave. "Now that I know you're not dating."

Anthony and Jacob poured over the Illinois Rules of the Road booklet after a pleasantly educational and stimulating morning in Anthony's basement playroom. After taking the practice test a few times, Jacob felt fairly confident about his understanding of the rules and guidelines for motorcycles. They donned their leather gear, and then climbed aboard the Harley. They headed for the DMV a few blocks away so that Jacob could practice for the driving test. He was frustrated at first, but became a little more comfortable as he ran the intimidating test course at least a dozen times.

Afterward, they rode over to Peter and Neil's house to tell them about their new relationship status. They found Brandon and Randall there, and the four men enjoying the hot afternoon in the swimming pool.

"Well, it's about time, you little horndogs!" Peter exclaimed with a delighted smile as he looked up at them from the edge of the pool. "I knew it was only a matter of time."

He put a hand to his mouth and whispered loudly, "Just don't show him the basement! You might scare him away."

Anthony laughed at him.

"Too late, I already showed it to him…"

"And I loved it!" Jacob finished the sentence for him with a happy, slightly naughty grin and a cocked eyebrow.

"It's always the quiet ones," Neil joked as he swam up to join his husband.

"Come on, you guys," Brandon called from the far side of the pool. "Get in."

"Thanks, Brandon. We would, but we're going for a ride," Anthony told them. "He's got to practice for his driving test."

"Oh, my god, Jacob, don't let him be a bad influence on you, darling," Peter said with a grin. He turned to his husband. "You know, this is all my fault. I blame myself."

"What's your fault?" Jacob said with a confused smile.

"I put you in that sexy underwear, and now look at you! Wearing leather, drinking, and playing in a sex dungeon! Gurl, you've gone to hell in a hand basket."

"Oh, honey," Jacob said gravely. "You don't even know the half of it! I fuckin' swear, too!"

The group laughed uproariously at these unexpected words from their usually serious friend. Finally Anthony and Jacob agreed to meet them for pizza that evening, said their goodbyes and headed out of town with Jacob in command of the powerful black motorcycle.

Jacob sat down next to Anthony alongside their friends at Ciminello's that evening. Janie, the pretty waitress, took their order with a friendly smile and soon returned with their drinks. He was hungry and tired after a day spent outdoors on the motorcycle, as well as the sleepless and athletic night. They had ridden home and put the bike away, showered, and headed out again in Anthony's big truck to pick up

Peter, Neil, and Brandon. Lance and Lucas had joined them in the parking lot of the restaurant.

"So, Jacob," Lance said, leaning toward him with a knowing smile. "Me and Lucas, and you and Anthony, huh!"

"Yes," Jacob beamed at him. "Me and Anthony. I'm still trying to believe it myself."

"You can believe it, Jake," Anthony said, placing a possessive arm around him. "I am all yours, sweetheart. And even better yet, you are all mine."

CHAPTER TWENTY-FOUR

That night Anthony and Jacob lay sleeping peacefully in Anthony's king size bed, with Anthony's head lying on Jacob's shoulder. As with all new couples, they were finding it almost impossible to keep their hands off of each other. Sometime after one in the morning, Jacob started awake at the sound of a loud banging somewhere outside.

"Jacob!" a voice yelled loudly. "Jacob!"

Warily he climbed out of bed and looked through the blinds.

"Jacob, what is it?" Anthony said sleepily.

"Someone is banging on my front door," Jacob told him quietly. "I can't tell who it is."

"Jacob!" the voice yelled again. "JACOB!"

The two of them quickly slipped on some underwear and together they hurried to Anthony's front door, stepping out onto the stoop so they could see over to Jacob's front porch.

"Brandon?" Jacob called out. "Is that you?"

The teenager looked over in the general direction of Anthony's house. He staggered to the front steps and grabbed for the railing.

"Oh, my god," Jacob exclaimed as they watched the teenager fall the last few steps to land on the front sidewalk. He and Anthony ran over to him.

Anthony looked him over quickly with a nurse's eye.

"He's okay," Anthony said looking up at Jacob. "But he's drunk. Come on, let's get him into the house."

Together they half carried, half dragged the boy over to Anthony's living room and laid him on the sleek gray couch.

"Brandon, what happened?" Jacob asked him as he applied a cool, damp cloth to his forehead. "What are you doing here?"

Brandon looked up at him wanly and without warning grabbed Jacob around his neck and pulled him down to kiss him.

"I love you, Jacob," he said sadly.

Jacob looked up at Anthony with a frown before turning back to the boy.

"I love you, too, Brandon," he said gently. "You're a good friend."

Brandon's eyes filled with tears as he looked up at them. He shook his head.

"That's not what I mean," he said sadly. "I love you. You're all I've got."

"That's not true," Anthony told him kindly. "You've got all of us. We all care about you."

"Today's my eighteenth birthday," Brandon told them as the tears began to trickle down to his ears. "And I told my parents I'm gay."

Anthony and Jacob looked at each other with deep concern in their eyes.

"What happened?" Jacob asked, dreading the answer he expected.

"He kicked me out," Brandon said as the tears flowed harder. "The son of a bitch kicked me out! Said he won't help pay for school as long as I'm like this."

Jacob reached down and hugged him tightly with tears in his own eyes.

"Shh," he whispered. "It's okay, Brandon. It's going to be okay."

As they rocked slowly back and forth, Jacob looked over at Anthony and put his hand to his ear in imitation of a phone. Anthony immediately understood and reached for his cell phone.

Fifteen minutes later, Peter and Neil walked through the front door, followed moments later by Carl and Edna. Edna, Jacob noted with a doting smile, looked as if she had just stepped out of a beauty salon, while Carl looked somewhat disheveled in wrinkled clothes he had obviously grabbed in a hurry. Edna squeezed in next to Brandon and held him in a motherly embrace.

"Darling, tell us what happened," she said in a comforting voice.

Brandon dried his eyes and told them all how he had confronted his father on his poor treatment of Jacob. During their argument, he had let it slip that Jacob, Peter, Neil, Anthony, and the rest had become his good friends, until he finally stood up and told his parents that he himself was gay. His mother had wept, and his father had flown into a rage, ordering him to leave and not come back until he was willing to admit his sin. There would be no assistance with college, and he would not be welcome at home unless he repented. It was at that point that he had jumped in his car and left, planning never to return.

The assembled group grew ever angrier as he relayed his story.

"That bastard!" Anthony said heatedly. "I'd like to wring his neck!"

"So would I!" Neil exclaimed, as Peter nodded in agreement.

"How could any parent treat their child this way?" Edna said, shaking her head sadly.

"We're going to find out," Carl said emphatically. They all turned to look at him, surprised to see him holding his phone to his ear.

"Calvin!" he barked after a moment of waiting. "This is Carl. Did I wake you? Good! I'm here at Anthony Miller's house on Maple. You get your sorry ass over here! NOW!"

Calvin and Mary walked through Anthony's front door and paused just inside as they looked at the unsmiling faces of Brandon and his friends.

"What is this?" Calvin said, scowling at the sight of Anthony and Jacob so scantily clad. "Carl, I don't have anything to say to these people."

"Well, maybe we have something to say to you," Carl told him severely. "So sit down over there. You, too, Mary."

Reluctantly, the two sat down where Carl had pointed.

"I don't know…" Calvin started to say.

"Oh, shut up, Calvin!" Mary cried impatiently.

"Calvin, I just have to know something," Carl said. "What kind of a parent throws his son out of the house on his eighteenth birthday?"

"I did no such thing," Carl protested huffily. "I just told him he couldn't stay there unless he repented of his sin."

"He's no sinner! And what about the sin you're guilty of?" Jacob spoke up swiftly. "The sin of spreading lies and promoting hatred."

"I have told no lies," Calvin sputtered defensively.

"Yes, you have, Dad," Brandon said, struggling to his feet. He held on to Neil's shoulder so that he could stand more steadily. "Gay people are not evil just because we're gay. The same way you're not good just because you call yourself a 'Christian'. You tell people bad things about us because you have convinced yourself that God hates us. But that is not true. I know that God doesn't hate me, but I'm absolutely sure He hates what people like you are doing to me and my friends."

"You've been drinking!" Calvin sputtered.

"Yes, I have, Dad!" Brandon said as his tears started up again. "Because of you, you bastard!" Edna pulled him back onto the sofa beside her. She placed a protective arm around the teenager as she addressed his parents.

"Calvin, Brandon is a wonderful boy. He's honest, he's smart, he's kind. You did a good job raising him," Edna said. "You just have to accept that some people are born gay, just like some people are born with red hair, or dark skin, or blue eyes. It's no different. Mary, can't you see that this is a good boy, and that these are good, moral, loving people?" She gestured to all of them in the room.

"You only say that because you have a gay son," Calvin said grimly.

"Well, so do we, Cal!" Mary said emphatically. "And I love him, no matter what he is. I don't care if he's gay!"

She stood up and looked at all of them.

"Ever since this whole thing came up with Jacob, I've been doing some research. I read the papers Carl and Edna gave to Calvin. And I learned a lot of things, one of which is that people don't choose to be gay."

She looked at her husband pleadingly.

"Brandon didn't choose to be gay any more than you chose to be straight, Cal. It's just who he is. It's who these good people are! How can God condemn them to hell if He made them this way? If it's true that He sends people to hell because of the way He created them in the first place, then I don't want anything to do with Him."

"Mary!" Calvin said, giving her a horrified look.

"I mean it, Cal!" she said firmly.

She looked up at all of them.

"I'm sorry, Brandon, and the rest of you, for the pain that the church has put you through. Jacob, you were right; people believe what they want to believe. It's sad, but it's true. But I want you all to know that I'll do my best to make sure people know the truth. There will be no more sermons on the subject unless it's to teach the facts." She paused to glare at her husband. "And I'm very grateful to all of you for being so kind to my son."

She sat down with tears in her eyes as she finished speaking. Brandon looked at her hopefully for the first time.

"What about it, Calvin?" Carl said gravely. "Do you love your son, or not?"

Calvin looked around at all of them angrily.

"No matter what you all say, homosexuality is a sin according to the Bible."

"So you still think this sweet boy is bound for hell?" Edna asked him, shaking her head. "My, oh my! You worship a very different god than I do, Calvin."

"You didn't answer the question," Jacob reminded him. "Do you love your son, or not?"

"Of course," Calvin said, somewhat reluctantly.

"Well then act like a good parent, damn it!" Jacob snapped. "And for once in your life, try not judging him or the rest of us for a change. I'll just bet you can't stop being a judgmental ass."

Calvin scowled at him.

"I don't need you to tell me how to act."

"Well, you need someone to tell you," Anthony told him sternly, putting his arm around Jacob. "And I can't think of anyone more qualified than this guy right here!"

The next evening, Jacob dialed his parents' phone number. He took a deep breath as he listened to the phone ring several times. Finally, as he expected, the answering machine that sat on a table in their front hall picked up.

"This is Jacob, your gay son in Illinois. Sorry I haven't called since I left Indianapolis, but I just really didn't feel any need to talk to you, any more than you needed to talk to me. I'm sure you've heard about what's happening here, but I promise you, you haven't heard the half of it! I've met some really wonderful people here, and most of them are gay. Some are even Buddhist and atheists! And one is black, too! They're all my friends, and I love them. They truly love me for who I am. Oh, yeah, I almost forgot! I ride a motorcycle now and drink beer.

"Mom, Dad, thank you for sending me here. I'm pretty sure you were just trying to get rid of me, but I want you to know that I will always be grateful to you, because I have met the man of my dreams here.

"You know what, there's no need to call me back, because my real family is right here, and I finally feel truly at home for the first time in my life."

Somewhere in Indianapolis, Jacob's younger brother, James, grinned and silently mouthed the words 'Way to go, Jacob!' while his parents frowned angrily at each other.

On a chilly Sunday morning before Thanksgiving, Jacob and Anthony sat in a pew at Grace Community Church. Next to Anthony were Carl and Edna, Peter and Neil, Lance and Lucas, Randall, and Myra and Elaine. Brandon and his mother sat at the end of the group, next to Jacob. They all looked up expectantly at Pastor Cal as he strode up to the pulpit.

"Good morning, my friends," he said in greeting. "Today we will take our text from the Gospel of Matthew, Chapter twenty-two, verses thirty-seven through thirty-nine."

There was a rustling of paper as several members of the congregation opened their Bibles to the appropriate page.

"The message in these verses is very simple," he said, looking first at Charlie, and then at Jacob. "We can examine the Bible, trying to find deep and hidden meanings in the words that Jesus taught, but I have found through personal experience that it's unnecessary, because when it comes right down to it, everything we need to know is right here in these verses. He told us to love God, and love each other.

"Now, I'll admit, there are a lot of unlovable people in the world. And there are people who are very different from us. Maybe their skin is a different color, or they have strange customs that we don't understand."

He took a deep breath.

"Or maybe they are gay, or from different religions or philosophies. You know what? It doesn't matter who or what people are, we are charged with the task of finding a way to love them. And what is one of the main components of true love? The absence of judgment.

"I'm afraid I've been guilty of the sin of judging people, as most of us are. I said that I loved people with a Christian love, but I see now that it was a false love, because all I was really doing was condemning them without even knowing them.

"It took my son and his friends, as well as an older member of our congregation, to show me that I was wrong. Without even referring to the Bible at all, they have taught me the lesson of true love, the same lesson that you're looking at right now in the book of Matthew. I judged them, this fine group of young people who are sitting with Brandon there this morning, and I tried to get you to judge them, too. And for that, I am truly sorry. Whether I agree with them completely or not makes no difference; I had no right to judge them, or anyone else. And neither do any of you.

"From now on, that will be the focus of this church, as long as I am here. We will do our very best to live up to the simple words that Jesus said, to love God and each other, completely without judgment. It's not going to be easy, but I believe we can do it."

The Man Next Door

As he paused to look at his congregation, Brandon
stood up and began to clap his hands together.
Almost immediately he was joined by his mother,
and soon after by the rest of his friends. All across
the auditorium, people began to stand and applaud
until almost everyone was standing. Pastor Cal
smiled at Charlie, who stood near the pulpit in the
front row, giving him the thumbs up sign, before
turning to smile and wink at Jacob. Jacob raised his
hands above his head as he continued to clap,
nodding and grinning at him. When the noise had
subsided and everyone had resumed his or her seats,
Pastor Cal spoke again.

"Believe it or not, that's all I have to say," he told
the crowd. A smattering of laughter spread across
the room. "Now, I believe that Lance and Jacob
have a song for us."

Lance stepped up to the microphone as Jacob slid
onto the piano bench.

"This song isn't exactly a hymn, or even a Christian
song," Lance told the congregation. "But I think it
should be, because it kind of says it all. I hope
you'll listen to the words and take them to heart."

Jacob gave him the introduction and he began to
sing Andrew Lloyd Webber's beautiful song, 'Love
Changes Everything'.

"'Love, love changes everything, hands and faces,
earth and sky'," Lance sang in his warm baritone
voice.

"'Love, love changes everything, how you live, and how you die'," he continued. "'Nothing in the world will ever be the same!'"

"'All the rules we make, are broken'," Lance sang, looking first at his ex-wife, who smiled warmly at him and nodded, and then lovingly at Lucas, who smiled at him with tears in his eyes. "'Love will never, never let you be the same!'"

He and Jacob ended the climactic final note with a flourish, and the congregation rose to its collective feet with loud applause!

EPILOGUE

Anthony's backyard was a flurry of activity on this sunny June afternoon, with people bustling about carrying flowers or food or linens. Approximately fifty chairs were arranged in several semi-circular rows on the backside of the serenity garden. They faced toward a wooden podium, surrounded by red and yellow flowers, which stood near the back fence facing the house. A rose petal strewn path ran between them from the end of the small walk bridge to the lectern, and potted red rose bushes lined the ends of each row of chairs, filling the air with their heady scent. Guests were beginning to arrive, and Neil and Lucas, both dressed in stylish summer suits, met them at the gate and escorted them to the seating area. Soft instrumental music was playing over a sound system as the guests took their seats.

Sue, a tall, auburn haired woman in her forties smiled at Anthony and Jacob as they stood nervously in the kitchen near the back door.
"Are you ready, guys?" she asked, frowning as she straightened Jacob's bowtie. "It's just about time. You both look so handsome in your tuxedos."
They looked at her with anxious smiles and nodded.
"Where are the best men?" she asked.
"We're coming," Peter called as he and Brandon entered the room. They both wore black tuxedos, like the grooms, but wore black ties and

317

cummerbunds instead of the deep red that Anthony and Jacob wore.

"Where are Keith and James?" Sue asked.

"I'm not sure," Peter told her.

He turned back and yelled," Keith! James! Get your cute butts out here!"

"You'd better go get a seat, honey," Brandon said to Kurt, his boyfriend of the last seven months. Kurt gave him a quick kiss before heading out the back door.

"Peter, Brandon, we'll do just like we rehearsed," Sue told them. "I'll go first, then you follow. Keith and James will follow you."

She turned to Anthony and Jacob.

"You two will follow once Lance starts singing, 'All I Ask of You'. Anthony first, then Jacob."

"Wait, I get to kiss the bride," a voice called out. They all turned to see Keith come into the room, followed closely by Jacob's brother, James. They were also wearing black tuxedos. James looked very like his older brother but without the glasses, and he was shorter and stockier than Jacob. Keith hugged his uncle first, squeezing him as tightly as he could. "You're one lucky son of a bitch," he whispered in his ear. "He is one hell of a guy."

He turned to Jacob who smiled at him warmly.

"I'm sure glad you came along, Jacob," he said sincerely. "You make him happier than I've ever seen him. I hope you know how much he loves you."

His voice broke and he hugged him tightly.

"I love you, Keith," Jacob said emotionally. "We both do."

James hugged both grooms next.

"I'm so proud of you, Jacob," he said. "This is an amazing life you've made for yourself. Anthony is very blessed to have you."

"And don't I know it!" Anthony exclaimed as he put an arm around Jacob.

"I'm the one who's blessed. And I'm so glad you're part of our lives, James," Jacob told him earnestly as Anthony nodded in agreement.

"So am I," James exclaimed with a smile.

Myra opened the door and poked her head through the opening.

"It's time, Sue," she said. "Carl and Edna are waiting outside."

She looked at Jacob and Anthony standing hand in hand.

"Oh, my god, you two look so beautiful," she exclaimed with a hand to her chest. "Even you, Anthony! You aren't gross and disgusting like you usually are!"

"I love you, you bitch!" he said with an affectionate smile.

Myra looked as though she wanted to give him a smart retort, but she was too overcome with emotion. Instead she waved a hand at him and closed the door.

The seven of them walked down the deck steps and waited until the prelude song began. Then Sue, followed by Brandon, and then Peter, walked slowly across the footbridge to stand near the podium and microphone. Keith and James came next, standing at last beside Peter and Brandon. Carl and Edna hugged Anthony and Jacob and then waited for their cue. As Lance began his beautiful rendition of the moving Andrew Lloyd Webber song, Edna took Anthony's arm and the two of them walked slowly up the aisle. When they reached the front, she kissed him on the cheek and then stood next to Peter. They turned and looked back, as did the assembled guests. A moment later, Carl and Jacob followed, arm in arm.

Jacob looked up to where Anthony was standing with Edna and Peter on the left, and smiled. He and Carl passed through a sea of smiling faces, and Jacob took note of as many as he could. Mary, Brandon's mother, smiled tearfully and held a handkerchief to her nose as he passed. He saw Myra and Elaine, holding hands and blowing kisses to him. Lucas, Neil, Kurt, Charlie from the church, as well as a number of other congregants, smiled and waved to him. Anthony's cousin Mike gave him a thumbs up as he passed. Randall and his new friend Steven smiled and nodded encouragingly at him. When they arrived at the front, Carl kissed him on the cheek and then moved to stand beside Brandon. Lance finished his song and winked at Jacob before turning to sit beside Lucas.

"Friends," Sue said with a big smile. "I'm so happy to welcome you today to the wedding of Anthony and Jacob. Thank you for being here and helping these two wonderful men celebrate this happy occasion."

Jacob remembered very little of the remainder of the ceremony. He listened to Sue speak, and said the words that she told him to say. One thing he would always recall, however, was the kiss after Sue pronounced them husbands, as well as the enthusiastic reaction of their friends.

There was a lot of dancing, music, laughter, alcohol and delicious food in the backyard as the evening progressed. Jacob looked up from where he was sitting on the deck with surprise to see Pastor Cal walking toward him through the crowd.

"I didn't think you were coming, Cal," he said dryly.

"Brandon and Kurt made me promise I'd make an appearance," Calvin said gruffly. "And Mary threatened me with physical violence. Anyway, I'm sorry I didn't make it to the ceremony, but I'm here. I'm still not completely sure about this whole marriage thing, Jacob. It's going to take some getting used to."

He looked around before shaking Jacob's hand. "But anyway, congratulations. Anthony is a good man."

"It's about time, Dad," Brandon said, putting an arm around his dad's shoulders. "Better late than never."

"Yes, I'm here like I promised," Cal said as his face softened into a grin. "Where are your mom and Kurt?"

Jacob chuckled as he watched them walk away. Cal had come a long way since last summer, he thought happily.

"How are you doing?" Lance asked as he and Lucas walked up to him, holding plates filled with a variety of delicious foods.

"I'm great," Jacob told them with a smile. "You know, two more weeks and we'll be doing all of this again for you two."

"I can't wait," Lucas said, giving Lance a quick kiss.

Jacob looked at them affectionately. He was extremely gratified to see the two of them so happy. Lance's parents had given him a hard time after the divorce as expected, but surprisingly had allowed him to keep his job. Jacob couldn't help but think it had something to do with the fact that Lance's investment office was the highest grossing office they owned. Lance had moved into Lucas's lovely home last fall after he and Linda had said their amicable goodbyes, allowing her to happily pursue her own new relationship.

Peter and Neil sat with Charlie and a few of Anthony's motorcycle buddies, talking and laughing cheerfully. What a pair they were, Jacob thought fondly. So happy together, so comfortable with who they were. They had become role models to him, Brandon, and Kurt. Even Calvin had taken a

liking to them. How he treasured them! And dear
Charlie, with his warm and gentle nature, had come
to treat Anthony and him like grandsons.
Surprisingly he had become a huge motorcycle fan
and enjoyed going for rides behind Anthony or
himself.
He looked over at Brandon and Kurt, holding hands
as they sat and laughed with Mary and Cal. They
were such an adorable couple, he thought. As he
watched, Kurt doubled over with laughter, clapping
Cal on the back as they all laughed happily with
him. Kurt and Brandon had met last December at
the U of I, and Kurt had won Mary and Cal over
completely. Jacob had to give him a lot of the credit
for Cal's ever growing tolerance and acceptance.
Anthony's brother and sister-in-law, Thomas and
Rachel, appeared to be having an enjoyable
conversation with Carl and Edna. He smiled
adoringly at their small group. Carl and Edna had
become like parents to him, and he loved them with
all of his heart. And Thomas and Rachel had
instantly welcomed him like a brother the first time
he met them. He had quickly come to love them
dearly.
Myra, Elaine, Randall, and Steven seemed to be
hitting it off as they sat together having an animated
conversation. Jacob smiled as he remembered all
the love and support the four of them had shown
him.
Keith sat with James and a group of young men and
women from the church, regaling them with stories

about his motorcycle adventures, no doubt. He thought back to last summer when he had mistaken Keith for Anthony's boyfriend. It seemed so ridiculous now; how could he have been so stupid? Since then, Keith spent many weekends with Anthony and him, and they had had so much fun together, taking lots of day and weekend motorcycle trips. Sometimes Jacob rode with Anthony, and sometimes he rode the Indian so that each of them had their own bike. Keith had proven himself to be a true friend, and Jacob had come to adore the brash young man and his wicked sense of humor.

James had shown up on their doorstep soon after Jacob had left the message on their parent's answering machine, and had declared his intentions to never go back to the stifling and confining atmosphere of their parent's home. Jacob had welcomed him with open arms and had given him the spare bedroom, telling him to stay as long as he liked. Since Jacob spent almost all of his time at Anthony's house, it had just seemed natural to have James more or less take over Jacob's house. He had found a very good job at the Green Grove Community Hospital as assistant Human Resources director, and just recently had begun dating a pretty young woman named Betsy, who also worked at the small hospital. He still kept in touch with their disapproving parents, but had steadfastly avoided going to any church.

Jacob frowned as he looked around for Anthony. He walked through the crowd, smiling and greeting everyone warmly, thanking them for coming and shaking their hands. Finally he stepped out of the gate onto the driveway and looked around, but still saw no sign of Anthony. He walked back into the backyard and through the crowd one more time, starting to become concerned.

A sudden hush from the assembled guests made him turn around. The crowd parted to reveal Anthony standing at the gate, still wearing his tuxedo. He smiled and beckoned to him with a single finger. Puzzled, Jacob walked past the mysteriously smiling guests until he stood next to his new husband.

"I have something for you, Jake," he said. "A wedding present."

Jacob still felt a thrill go up and down his spine whenever Anthony called him 'Jake'. No one else in the world called him that except for Anthony, and that's how Jacob wanted it.

"What did you do?" he asked him with a frown.

Anthony took his hand and kissed it before stepping aside. Jacob looked past him and gasped at the sight of a brand new ivory and blue Indian Roadmaster sitting in the driveway.

"Oh, my god!" Jacob exclaimed. "Oh, my god! Anthony, you bought me a new Indian?"

Anthony hugged him before opening the gate so Jacob could walk up to the new motorcycle.

Together they walked slowly around the elegant bike, which glittered and gleamed in the lights over the deck and backyard.

"Do you like it?" Anthony asked him gently.
"Oh, my god!" Jacob said, hardly able to believe what he was seeing. "I love it! It's the most beautiful bike I've ever seen!"

As the crowd cheered, Jacob buried his face in Anthony's broad shoulder, unable to contain his tears of joy. He wrapped his arms around him and Anthony held him tightly, pleased with the success of the surprise that he and Keith had planned for months.

Finally, Jacob looked up and smiled happily at their many friends. How different his life was, he thought. It was remarkable, really, that just a year ago he had arrived here, scared of his own shadow, lonely, sad, and knowing only a very select group of people from his church. He had been a self-hating, boring young man who never even once considered thinking for himself, and he had resigned himself to a solitary, loveless life.

Now look at him! Here he was standing in his husband's loving arms, being cheered by a widely varied group of friends who even now crowded around the two of them offering shouts of congratulations and admiration.

And all of this had happened because of the man next door, who had come over to help him move furniture that very first day, and had refused to be scared away by his rather extreme emotional and spiritual baggage. He had seen something in Jacob, something that no one else had known was there. Even he himself had not seen his potential. But

Anthony had, thank God! He looked up at Anthony
with his eyes shining, and kissed him while the
crowd cheered.
"I love you, Jake, more than anything in the world!"
Anthony whispered emotionally in his ear after their
kiss ended.
"I love you, too, Anthony," Jacob whispered back.
"More than I can ever say!"

He sighed contentedly in his husband's arms,
basking in the knowledge that he was truly and
utterly a happy man.

THE END

ACKNOWLEDGEMENTS

Thank you to my dear friend Dave and my husband
Eric for their interest, input, and support for this
book. And thank you to all the people who have
been part of my own personal spiritual journey,
including those that made it more difficult.
Naturally, all the characters here are fictitious, even
though they will always be very real to me.
This book is dedicated to my husband, Eric.

Made in the USA
Columbia, SC
30 January 2019